D0912364

THE DEFENDER

SKHARR DEATHEATER™ SERIES BOOK 03

MICHAEL ANDERLE

DISRUPTIVE IMAGINATION™

LMBPN Publishing
PMB 196, 2540 South Maryland Pkwy
Las Vegas, NV 89109

First US edition, December 2020
Version 1.01, January 2021
ebook ISBN: 978-1-64971-372-8
Paperback ISBN: 978-1-64971-373-5

THE DEFENDER

THE DEFENDER TEAM

Thanks to our JIT Team:
Rachel Beckford
Dorothy Lloyd
Kelly O'Donnell
Diane L. Smith
John Ashmore
Jackey Hankard-Brodie
Jeff Goode
James Caplan
Wendy L Bonell
Peter Manis
Angel LaVey
Jeff Eaton
Paul Westman

If I've missed anyone, please let me know!

Editor
SkyHunter Editing Team

To Family, Friends and
Those Who Love
To Read.
May We All Enjoy Grace
To Live The Life We Are
Called.

— ***Michael***

CHAPTER ONE

O f all the filthy bastards in the empire, it had to come down to the one who was the most capable.

He slid on the rings he had earned over the years during all the various positions he'd held in the empire. Not many remembered a time when he wasn't rushing about, making sure that everything didn't fall to pieces. Those who did were those who remembered the chaos that reigned while Emperor Rivar was on a conquering spree.

Yes, the people had reveled in every victory and in the lavish parades he'd arranged when he returned victorious with another series of colonies to add to his glorious empire. He even liked to take those kings, lords, and leaders who had been brought to their knees in front of the Senate to remind them of exactly what would happen if they attempted any kind of insurrection.

But few remembered how costly all those wars had been.

He scowled at himself in the mirror as he studied the lines that had steadily multiplied over the years and the gray streaks in the long black curls that had once been his pride and joy. Unlike those who were content to forget, he recalled the looks in the eyes of the conquered peoples who had been taxed into starvation to pay for those wars. In his mind's eye, he could still see the battlefields littered with the bodies of youths who had no other choice but to fight to reclaim some semblance of freedom.

Those had been the days when he decided he would put an end to Rivar's warring ways. The man who was impossible to defeat on the battlefield had other vices and appetites that decades of enjoyment had only made more voracious—and which he knew he could play on.

Distraction had been easy but keeping the other colonies from erupting into war like they had in the past was more difficult. A marriage of alliance solved that. But the emperor hadn't been happy with a single woman.

He'd had a small harem when that marriage had been arranged but the new Empress had conditions, the kind that forced him to send his concubines away.

"Viceroy Reyvan?"

He startled and looked at the reflection of a young servant girl who stood behind him. "Yes?"

"The ceremony is about to begin."

"Thank you, Elena. I will be there shortly."

She bowed and slipped behind the curtains that led to the servant's entrance to his room, moving delicately. Long gone were the days when he wore a sword at his side. All he had was a dagger, and that had to be hidden since the emperor did not allow anyone to be armed in his presence. Even the guards needed to be at least twenty paces away from him at all times.

Besides, he could no longer ride a horse beyond the odd short distance, and even that was a trial. So much time spent on horseback in his youth had led to pain in his back, one that meant regular visits to the emperor's mages to bring him relief from it. They worked well but in the end, there were certain limits to magic. Despite having lived at least twenty years longer than most humans would have, he was starting to see the end of the line.

That reality made him worried about what would happen to the empire once he was no longer there. Certain elements had been put in place, of course. Rivar's legitimate son—birthed by his wife—was raised to be as incompetent as his father had become over the years. This meant that the death of Rivar would only lead to many, many more years of similar work to that already undertaken by those who cared for the empire's well-being, even once he had passed.

Reyvan shook his head. It had been the perfect plan and it was truly a great pity that his own actions had been his undoing.

He entered the throne room and one of his helpers handed him his cane. It looked a little like a scepter and bore his family's seal. While he carried it, however, he was not allowed within the same twenty paces that the armed guards had to respect.

Still, it helped him to walk, especially on the bad days.

A young man already stood in the throne room, waiting for the emperor to arrive. The viceroy wished he could say that the boy wasn't his sovereign's bastard, but the appearance was too distinctive. Rivar was at least sixty years his senior, but due to the power of magic, he recalled what the man had looked like when he was still young and vital.

He was the spitting image of the youth who waited there now.

A spell was not needed to tell him that this lad was one of the hundreds of bastards who had sprung from the old emperor's loins, but it was still required for the ceremony, just to be sure.

"You don't have to do this, lad," he whispered as he approached. "You can continue the life of luxury your father provided for you no matter whether he openly accepts you as his heir or not. Some old witch's incantation will do nothing to change your life for the better but could make it more difficult."

Tall and statuesque, the young man certainly looked impressive. His long black hair rolled over his shoulders and his muscles coiled under the robes that had been provided for him for the ceremony. Reyvan had already seen his fighting abilities in person. He was the only three-time champion in the Imperial Arena, a feat completed before he was even old enough to have a beard growing from his chin. Of course, this was in the Emperor's Tournament, which was the knightly counterpart to the actual combat-based Emperor's Championship. The young man had therefore excelled at the courtly version but had no real fighting experience where he might have to face more than one blood-thirsty and aggressive opponent. That record had stood had stood for almost eight hundred years before a dwarf named Yaragrim had taken the prize and held it for almost a decade.

"It is my destiny," the boy whispered and nodded firmly. "Proclaimed by the gods and confirmed by all the signs. I must partake in the tests. It is my birthright."

"Old rituals and laws hold no place in a modern world, boy," the viceroy snapped. "You must see that. Your presence will only disrupt the peace that has lasted decades."

"Then the peace will be disrupted. It is the will of the gods."

He took a deep breath and calmed the quick, shallow beats of his heart. Too many had told him it would be the death of him as a result of his love for red meat and wine. A year before, he would have accepted the end with open arms. Old age did not suit him well.

"How many will die because you can't live in peace?"

The boy turned to him and opened his mouth to reply, but no answer seemed forthcoming. He merely shrugged before he turned to face the throne again.

"It is my destiny," he repeated. "It is my birthright. The gods have willed it."

Someone had whispered those words in his ear—and enough times that he had begun to believe them.

Reyvan shook his head, but any further conversation was cut short when trumpets blared to draw their attention to the throne. Rivar himself would make an appearance for the ceremony, which would only make it that much more official.

A herald took his place at a podium as two young, petite women with curly black hair helped lead the man to his throne.

The emperor had a particular preference and that would always be provided to him from all corners of the empire. It made no difference that he had difficulty walking and all his hair had turned white and had even begun to fall out in patches.

He was almost two hundred years old at this point, and there was a limit to what magic could do. The viceroy had made sure that he would never live that long. He refused to live until his teeth began to fall out with his hair and he could only move with the help of young, nubile women.

Even the man's eyes were starting to cloud over and the cataracts became more difficult for his mages to heal.

The emperor groaned softly and finally settled on the throne and relaxed against it. Once he was comfortable, he nodded slightly to the herald.

"The Test of E'Kruleth Damari will begin now," the official announced as he straightened and spoke loudly enough for all those in attendance in the throne room to hear. "A determination through spellwork to ascertain the lineage of the contender for the throne. The contender, Lord Tryam Voldana, will step forward."

The guards parted to allow the boy inside the ring. Reyvan had a feeling that the youth did not need any weapon to kill the picture of frailty that was Emperor Rivar.

A lock of the emperor's white hair was cut and brought by the young women to those presiding over the ceremony. Tryam was told to remove his shirt, which he did to reveal dozens of battle scars that marred his pale, marble-like skin. A lock of his hair was taken as well, and the mages placed it inside a silver chalice and chanted over it slowly as the emperor's hair was added.

Silence reigned while they continued their spell until suddenly, fire surged from the goblet and burned with an intensity too bright to look at. Neither mage seemed perturbed and they continued the chant until the flames gradually subsided. As Reyvan studied the blaze, he could see that the flames had turned purple as they slowly died.

Once it was completely out, the mages both looked at the herald and nodded.

"The contender, Lord Tryam Voldana, has passed the Test of E'Kruleth Damari and is truly the blood of Emperor Rivar," the man stated firmly. "The Test of O'Kruleth Demari begins. He must prove himself worthy of this royal lineage."

The mages poured the ashes from the chalice into their hands and blackened them as they approached Tryam, one to stand in front of him and the second behind. The first placed his hands on the boy's chest and the other on his back. Reyvan could hear and smell skin sizzle and burn, but the candidate showed no sign that the pain affected him. When they drew back, four hand marks had been branded onto his skin.

"May the gods watch over him on the Stygian Path."

Tryam was handed his shirt and he put it on, although he slid it carefully over the places where the brands were still tender. Reyvan stepped away and out of the throne room and moved down one of the many hallways. He ran his fingers through his beard to tame the knots that had appeared.

Another man approached him. He was in the garb of one of the imperial guards, although the sign of the eagle on his breastplate marked him as the lord commander of the Elite warriors charged with the emperor's protection.

"There was never any doubt, was there?"

The viceroy raised an eyebrow as the man removed his helm to reveal a face almost as grizzled as his, although he was considerably less afflicted with ailments. Reyvan had always envied him that.

"You saw the boy, Espin. Say what you want about the old man, but his seed is strong and all his bastards have his very distinctive features."

The other man nodded and moved closer so their whispers wouldn't be heard.

"The die is cast. There is nothing we can do except see if the boy is worthy or not."

"He isn't. Some...ancient law written by savages has no bearing on that fact. But you are wrong in one regard. Cathos remains the heir until Tryam returns without the marks on his skin. There is much that could happen to him between now and that time. He will be afforded an escort of your guards to assist and protect him in completing the test. Should they fail in their task, it would be a tragedy indeed, would it not? They would be forced to fall on their swords to avoid the shame of it, but there is no reason that their families should suffer for it, wouldn't you agree?"

The lord commander nodded but his face remained expressionless. "A true tragedy. Plays would be written depicting it and acted on every stage in the empire."

"An intact empire would indeed mourn it."

———

"Attack!"

Skharr rushed forward and tightened his hold on the comfortable grip of the practice sword in his hands. He slashed toward where Sera stood, waiting for him.

The guild captain carried her sword—a familiar sight with its ivory handle—but the blade was covered by a sheath that she claimed would have no impact on her ability to fight him. And so far, she had been correct.

He swung hard from the left and watched as she swayed slightly to avoid it without so much as lifting her blade to block his. He pulled himself back, kept his balance, and reversed the strike in the hope that he might catch her unprepared.

This time, her high guard did alter and she lifted his blade up and over her head. Her movements were fluid and precise, and he was only able to follow some of them as her sword swept in behind him. She hooked it behind the knee of his supporting leg and upset his balance.

In the same movement, she pivoted in place and raised her sword again to slap him across the forehead. It wasn't a hard blow, but with his balance already compromised, he fell back and was unable to catch himself before he landed on the hard earth and created a large puff of dust with the impact.

Once the cloud dispersed with the wind, he registered that she stood over him with the blade a hairsbreadth from his throat.

Instead of delivering the killing blow, however, she drew the sword back and offered him her hand.

"How did I beat you?" she asked.

Skharr brushed the bright yellow dust that had collected on his clothes. "By being freakishly fast? Is that what those blade-masters teach you?"

Sera shook her head. "No. You are freakishly fast—for your size, at least. But you've fought for too long with a hammer or an ax in your hand and so needed to put your power behind every strike with an unbalanced weapon. Swords are balanced, delicate, and precise. A child could handle an arming sword fine."

She was not wrong. The longsword he had collected from the tower and the one he'd taken from the blademaster were exquisite, but his lack of skill with them meant he'd chosen somewhat reluctantly to sell them to raise funds for the weapon the dwarves were forging. He'd replaced it with a much simpler but nevertheless well-forged blade, but still preferred to use a practice sword during his training. She had insisted that she would not be in any real danger.

"What would you recommend, then?" he asked, hefted the wooden sword, and studied the edge carefully.

"Efficiency," she stated simply, swung her sword over her head in a high guard, and swept the blade down on either side in bold motions. "When you swing from your shoulder, it will be a more powerful blow and in some instances, it is necessary with an unbalanced weapon. But with the sword, the lack of weight at the end will reduce the effectiveness of the power you're committing and slow your strike at the same time. And, more importantly, it will tell any experienced fighter what you are doing in time for them to react. It is why you were only able to defeat those blade-masters you faced through desperate means—the kind they would not expect from someone even if they could read your movements and anticipate them. They expected some kind of trap and found something simple and yet effective at the same time."

Skharr nodded as she demonstrated with simple, slow movements, all while maintaining her balance and a high guard.

He imitated her carefully. Her actions were a little strange and his muscles resisted the challenge to break out of their learned reflexes, but over the past week or so of training with a sword, they had grown more familiar.

"Some people aren't built for perfecting the art of blade mastery," Sera pointed out. "I would say, having watched you swing an ax and a hammer, that you are too used to relying on your natural strength and speed to overwhelm any enemy who is unfortunate enough to come within your striking distance. Or your skill with that bow of yours or other throwing weapons, should they remain far enough away. That has allowed you to survive thus far, but time is the undefeated champion and every man, woman, and child will succumb to it, and so will you. You can delay it, of course, by perfecting your technique before then."

It was frustrating. Slow, precise movements were not what he wanted to do when he had a weapon in hand. Still, he wanted to master the sword or at least be able to anticipate the movements and tactics of those who had. He had barely survived his past two encounters with blademasters and he wanted to be better prepared for the third.

He came to a halt as a low horn sounded in the camp and he frowned as he registered the sun beating down despite it only being a couple of hours after sunrise.

"It will be a scorcher today," Sera noted as she hooked her sword onto her belt. "If there is anything I enjoy about being out in the open like this, it's that we can see those who want to harm us for miles."

She was not wrong. They had moved at an almost frenetic pace to stay ahead of the group that had followed them for the past few days. Already, dust rose in the east to tell them their pursuers were on the move.

"They'll catch us today," Skharr noted as they returned to their camp, which the others had dismantled in preparation for the march ahead. "We'll need to be in an advantageous position when they do."

"It's a little difficult to maneuver a caravan of merchants into an advantageous position."

"They have not overtaken us during our nightly stops, although they could have." He handed her the practice sword, lifted his, and slung it over his back along with the quiver of arrows. His war bow was already strung and strapped on Horse's back, ready for when he needed it.

"What does that tell you?"

"That they are lightly armed and armored and use their speed above all else to overtake and overcome their quarry. They are not interested in an even fight. If we can inflict casualties on them before they feel comfortable to engage us, they will elect to not attack but rather to preserve their numbers and find a less aggressive quarry."

"How do you know that?"

"The western clans can be fairly predictable. Each clan's numbers must be tightly controlled and that precludes senseless engagements, especially this close to the desert."

"If you were leading their party, what would you do?"

Skharr studied their surroundings and pointed in the direction they planned to travel. "They'll try to force us inside that ravine, corner us there, and attack from above with arrows and javelins. Once our warriors are dead, they will descend to finish off the rest."

"Is that what your clan would have done?"

"No. The Clan lives in the mountains." He raised his finger to point farther west into the range that rose in the distance. "They prey on those who travel the passes and paths. We would not pursue anyone but would wait for them to come to us, then rain arrows on them from the rocks above. All warriors were taught to climb them in all conditions from a young age."

"Which explains your skill with the bow, I suppose."

"When you learn to shoot at something a hundred yards below you with wind, rain, sleet, and snow everywhere and while hanging from a precarious rock, you tend to develop those skills, yes."

She laughed. "Well, I hope those same skills will be able to keep us from being decimated in a similar fashion. I would hold you personally responsible."

"That might kill you all. I intend to live a long and happy life after this."

"And I intend to haunt every waking and sleeping moment of it if I die out here in this fucking desert."

"Good company is never something to be sad about."

"Believe me, I wouldn't be good company."

CHAPTER TWO

I t was an amazing bow, a simple truth that brought immense
satisfaction.

Skharr looked at the weapon in his hands. The weight had an
interesting feel to it. He recalled the same sensation when he'd
hefted a particularly thick gold coin and it was certainly pleasing.
The wood had been stressed while still a growing tree and had
been fortified by a bull's horns and sinew, with the string made
from horsehair.

This was a traditional bow, the kind that only a few clans in
the west knew how to make. The BarrakhanHead were famed for
their archery skills and also for their ability to craft the weapons,
as they were one of the few clans that lived in a wooded area. He
had doubted their skills in the past but had come to appreciate
them after Throk AnvilForged presented him with the weapon as
a gift.

Of course, he had made the dwarf more than enough money
and owed him more coin while they continued to work on an ax
he had ordered from them. In the meantime, however, he was
learning to use the sword they had sold him to replace the
other one.

But the bow remained his passion, and Throk insisted that he had no part in the making of the bow itself, only in the arrowheads.

It reached almost to his chest—which was taller than some men—and the draw weight on it was heavier than the weapon he'd had before. This required a little adjustment on his part but as he studied the style and craftsmanship, he knew he was already falling in love with it.

"Have you led soldiers in the past?"

The barbarian looked up from the weapon at the men and women Sera expected him to lead into battle. The motley group of Theros mercenaries had been in combat before, although he doubted that they had ever dealt with folk like the clansmen.

Otherwise, they would have been a good deal more nervous about it. The cloud of dust was approaching quickly.

"Aye," he answered finally. "In another life. A life I thought I'd left behind."

"Do you not like doing it?"

"It means that folk depend on me not to make stupid decisions that will kill them, and I don't appreciate the pressure. I left and started a farm to avoid it, but it would appear that others want to throw their lives in my hands anyway, so I'll need to put myself in the position once again."

The other mercenaries laughed like they thought he was joking.

Which was for the best, he decided. He hadn't meant to say any of that aloud.

"What do you plan to do when they come within range?" another asked.

"You're all archers. We will inflict as many casualties on them as possible before they attack. With any luck, it will drive them away to find easier prey."

"How likely is that?"

Skharr scowled and motioned for them to remain hunkered

among the rock outcroppings they had found for cover. "It will depend on how desperate they are. If they are starving and haven't found any targets to strike at for a few months, they won't mind losing a few of their own."

"How many are there?"

He raised an eyebrow at the woman who'd asked. "Do I look like Gerova? Do I fly in the sky, pull the sun with my wings, and watch over the whole world? How in all the stinking hells would I be able to tell?"

"You are supposed to know everything these clans do. Is that not why Sera told us to follow your instructions?"

The barbarian tried to not roll his eyes. The mercenaries had begun to get on his nerves. He had hoped to move off on his own but the guild captain had insisted that he take a few troops with him, no doubt wanting to avoid something like what had happened the last time. And it had seemed like a good idea at the time, but it was difficult to focus on what he felt with their incessant talk to constantly distract him.

Horses made an impact when they were being ridden across the hard ground and in the absence of being able to see them, he could use that to sense an approximate number for the enemy in pursuit.

He closed his eyes and traced his fingers over the bowstring as he recalled the old words of an old instructor.

The weapon was pressed against one of the rocks, which vibrated faintly with the thundering of at least three dozen horses. This extended to the bowstring, which was easier to feel.

"There are over thirty of them," Skharr said after a few moments of silence from the group. "Fewer than forty."

"How do we have a chance against that many? There are only twenty of us and they are on horseback."

It was a good question. The barbarian eased closer to the rocks. He did not want to be seen but it was good to see that they had not altered their course to pursue the party of warriors that had broken away from the group. They continued on their course toward Citar, although he assumed the raiders would want to intercept the caravan before it crept under the shadow of those particular walls.

"They'll ride past us," he told his team. "When in range, you'll all rain arrows on them and force them to either break their pursuit to deal with us or divide their forces."

Sera would be able to handle the force if it split in fear of an attack from behind, although he truly did hope that the attackers would simply break away.

He doubted it, though. They had been in pursuit for days, and from the looks of their horses as they moved within sight, they had pushed themselves harder than necessary. There were certain elements about them that he could call desperation, and if that were the case, it would be a tough fight. Even the lesser clans knew how to fight when in dire circumstances.

They rode hard, determined to catch their quarry before they could reach the ravine. If they escaped the trap, the fight would be over. Even with only twenty fighters in Sera's party, the others would still offer sufficient resistance to leave them without the numbers to take their loot away if they survived the battle.

Clans that could not farm their own food relied on their horses and their fighters. If they lost too many of either, the clan would starve or simply cease to exist when they were absorbed into another either by their choice or because they were forced into it.

He raised his bow and fitted one of the arrows to it. The projectiles were a little longer than his arm and dwarves had forged the arrowheads. The bodkin points would as easily come out as they went in. Skharr hunted with his bow as much as he used it in combat, and the smaller, slimmer arrowheads would be best to cut through the light armor the raiders wore.

The group was still riding past as they pushed toward the caravan, and he could see Sera draw the mercenaries still with her to circle to the back. All were on horseback, ready to engage the group behind them. They were desperately outnumbered and yet stood their ground as they drew their weapons.

"Fire with me," the barbarian ordered, and the men who were with him drew arrows from their quivers and nocked them to their bows. While he had never seen these men in action, that wasn't the point. He needed to distract the attackers.

A few of the raiders heard and realized they were riding within range of those who would attack them from behind. They tried to draw the attention of the others in their party and alert them to the impending attack.

He drew back on his bow and the muscles in his back strained against the powerful resistance. A satisfying feeling surged when he overcame it and pulled the arrow back with no hint of trembling in his arms. He looked down and watched a few of the horses thunder toward them.

The arrow flew before he could start his exhale. It was a familiar sight and one he enjoyed with every shot fired with the new weapon.

The first man to see them was knocked off his saddle when the arrow punched into his chest. The horse panicked, kicked, and sprinted away, dragging the rider with him when his feet caught in the stirrups.

Two other riders were felled by the next arrows loosed, and the horse of a third was caught in the flank. The arrow didn't kill it but did panic the beast and it galloped away from the group. Its rider was able to regain control quickly and pulled it around.

"Give the godsbedammed sod-sucking bastards another taste of your little pricks!" he bellowed.

"They may be small," one of the men quipped, "but they fuck like a goblin does a well-greased ass—to death."

"And you would know that how?" another asked to a ripple of laughter.

Skharr drew another arrow while the raiders below tried

hastily to decide what they should do. When they realized that the archers were preparing for another volley, that decision was made in an instant and the entire group swung to attack them.

It had always been a possibility but it had been the one he dreaded the most. It was the most likely to result in casualties on their side.

"We need to move!" one of the mercenaries cried.

"Hold your fucking ground or I'll shoot your ugly chicken-feathered ass myself." The barbarian snarled and nocked his arrow. There was a sense of panic in the six he had brought with him but instinct told him they feared him more than they did a faceless group of raiders. That hopefully meant they would stay close to him out of fear of being the targets of his arrows.

A raider fell from his horse as the enemy continued to approach, and the defenders focused on their chosen targets. Skharr was already pulling an arrow from his quiver when he heard the other bows sing—all six of them, so no one had chosen to run yet.

Another had fallen when he turned his gaze to the men who had already reached the stone outcroppings they had positioned themselves on. The others had raised the shields they had hung on their saddles.

The decision to abandon their horses was taken equally quickly, and they huddled beneath their round shields in expec-tation of more arrows. Skharr fired his, but it hammered into the solid wooden defense. They had moved too close too quickly and already expected the projectiles.

"Find your targets," he snapped as he lowered his bow. "Choose them carefully. And if any of you shoot me, I'll be pissed right the fuck off."

"What will you do?"

"Give you the targets."

The barbarian dropped his bow and quiver as he drew his sword from his scabbard. He could hear more horses approaching, heavier than the ponies the raiders were riding, which meant Sera was doing as she had told him she would. She had most likely left a few of her men with the caravan and now brought the rest to help him.

They would use their shields to fend off the attacks from above. He no longer had to worry about them shooting at him from their horses, but he did need to worry about those who had begun to climb.

His mercenaries continued to shoot as he jumped down and kept his balance carefully on the rocks. It reminded him of a game he had played as a child, one he had always won. Climbing rocks had always been fun to him.

He dropped in front of one of the raiders, who immediately paused and studied the size of the man in front of him.

"Come, little dust rat." Skharr growled a challenge and grasped the familiar hilt of his new sword. "Come and die."

The raider carried a saber and a shield but his armor was light and meant for someone fighting on horseback. He had likely left his bow and javelins, as it was quite a chore to climb with them in hand.

As his adversary slashed the saber at his shoulder, the warrior moved to the side. He selected his target below what the man's shield protected and grinned as the sharp edge of the blade sliced through his target's clothes and light armor to inflict a gash on his leg. Rather than kill him, he stepped closer and kicked him hard enough to hurl him off the rocks and into his comrades.

Arrows whistled around him, and it seemed the men had taken his warning as an indication that he wanted to choose which attackers he wanted to deal with and to do it alone. He would have to take a moment to speak to them when this was all over, but for the moment, he didn't mind dealing with the marauders who scaled the rocks without waiting for support.

Another tried to pull himself to where Skharr stood and was kicked down quickly, but two others reached the top almost as soon as he fell. They also carried sabers and were ready for a fight.

The warrior jumped back as both swung their weapons at him and tried to reach his head and chest. When his back foot landed, he immediately pushed forward. His blade arced in a clean motion and one raider's head fell away and blood poured from where it had been severed at the neck.

Maybe Sera had been right. Not much force had been needed for that.

The other man paused and grasped his shield a little tighter as arrows sang over their heads. Skharr grinned at the moment of hesitation and flicked the blood from his sword. One of his other swords seemed to almost clean itself, but Sera had taught him how to twist his wrist to clean the blade enough to continue to use it.

Sera's horses were almost there. They would have reinforcements soon but it would not be in time. He needed to keep them clear of his men above to allow them to shoot unhindered. That was his part to play.

"Come to me, my children," he whispered. The raider grinned and rushed forward.

"My lord?"

He snapped his head toward the voice. The movement was fast enough to catch the attention of his horse, who trotted nervously in place and looked around for any sign of danger.

Warhorses were bred and trained to be as attentive to their riders as possible, to listen to their every command, and to be ready to act on a moment's notice. It had saved his life more than once, but it also meant that one needed to be equally as attentive to the horse as it was to the rider.

A moment of distraction had made him fail his mount in that

fashion, and he patted it gently on the neck and hushed it softly to calm it.

"Should we continue, Lord Tryam?"

He looked up as he continued to pat his horse reassuringly.

The desert had never been his favorite place to be, although he doubted that it appealed to very many. The sun was too abrasive and the sand only made it more uncomfortable. He loved his home—the river lands—above almost anything else. It had provided him with a small thicket next to the river where he played at killing imaginary monsters and saving imaginary maidens who fell desperately in love with him.

His mother had never wanted that for him, but there were certain expectations for the son of the emperor, even the bastards.

Those had brought him into this desert, where the dust kicked up by every passing gust of wind made him scowl. He glared at the sun.

It was a pointless gesture and would ultimately serve no purpose, but he still felt better for it.

"Are they expecting us inside?" Tryam asked as he studied the walls of the city.

They appeared to be golden in the sunlight, which made it difficult to judge their sheer size from a distance. Up close, however, they were quite impressive, and the fact that the city was built around a famous oasis in the middle of this desert made it that much more desirable as a target.

Water was worth more than gold in these parts.

"The city guards have been alerted," his companion confirmed and shielded his eyes from the glare of the sun. "And the queen of Citar has been told to await your arrival, but no others have been alerted. You instructed that no parades should slow you on the Stygian Path."

He nodded and patted his horse's neck a few times before he

nudged it with his boot to push it forward a few steps toward the gate.

A dozen men armed and armored with the imperial seal would draw attention, and more would be paid to the man who boasted no such fineries. But as long as no one knew who he was, he would be safe.

"Do we have accommodations in the city?"

"Yes, my lord. Accommodations have been offered by the queen herself, although if you have a mind to house yourself elsewhere, I can send guards to clear an inn for your arrival."

"There is no need for that." Tryam shook his head as they passed into the blessed shade under the gates. He noticed that more and more people now watched the group enter. "I am sure the queen will be more than welcoming."

"Of course, my lord."

He nudged his horse to the front of the line when the streets around them narrowed. Most lords and ladies preferred to be surrounded by their guards, but he hated that they had been provided in the first place—as though to ease his way.

The center of the streets appeared to always be cleared for horses to come through, and those who broke the unspoken rule jumped quickly out of the way the moment they heard hooves on the cobbles. Numerous foul looks were cast at the newcomers, however.

The people did not know him. He carried no house banners and there was no sign of his nobility. Tryam hated that those who met him thought they knew him better because they knew his father when the fact was that he had only met the man for the first time two weeks before during the ceremony.

Although met was not quite the word he was looking for as no words had been exchanged between the two.

The crowds drew in a little tighter and slowed his procession to a walk as they pushed deeper into the city and toward the oasis around which the queen's palace was built. It was said to be a beautiful place. One needed to see it to believe it, they said.

"Alms, sir?" a voice squeaked to his left. "Alms for the orphans?"

He turned toward a small boy—or maybe a girl, he was not sure. His or her dark curly hair had been cut short—likely to avoid lice—and their clothes were beyond ragged.

Without hesitation, he reached into his coin purse, leaned over his saddle, and poured three silver coins into the small hand.

"Thank you, sir," the child whispered, and their eyes widened when they realized the small fortune they held. "Thank you indeed, sir!"

Tryam avoided meeting the orphan's gaze. The gratitude made him uncomfortable and he nudged his steel-gray stallion forward into the city before any more of it could be offered.

All that had kept him from being one of the orphans on the streets of Citar was one man's preference for lean young women with curly black hair. He disliked being reminded of it.

CHAPTER THREE

The idiot bastard was fighting them himself yet again.

True, the situation he had chosen was the best one possible. He held the high ground, likely the kind he was the most comfortable with. None of those who remained below attempted to engage him as their attention was fixed solely on the six she had sent with Skharr to distract the group.

Others, however, continued to climb and to fight toward him. Sera could see that he said something to those who approached him that appeared to drive them to attack him blindly so they all but threw themselves at his sword.

He demonstrated some of the instructions she had given him but was still a little stiff around the hips. It didn't surprise her, as he was a man more comfortable to attack with all his prodigious strength, not hold back and ebb and flow as the fight demanded.

Nevertheless, he had certainly made progress. She would have to congratulate him on that as well as his willingness to use the skills she had taught him in active combat. Any other fighter would revert to what they knew best until they were certain of their mastery.

The guard captain jumped lightly from her horse, drew her

sword, and advanced on the men who attempted to find a way up the rock outcroppings to where Skharr had positioned her men. At least they had the good sense to not shoot at her and their comrades.

A little under thirty of the marauders were left, although the bodies had begun to pile up. More would come, however. She wondered what Skharr was saying that was sufficient to distract them from the defenders who had come to join the combat.

She stepped behind the closest one, dragged her blade across his neck, and nodded when the head came free from the body before she let both fall.

A flick of the blade to clean it of blood was a residual reflex from her training.

The other raiders had now registered her presence. They reacted far quicker than she had anticipated. While she had hoped to kill at least a couple of them before they realized she was among them, it wasn't a critical factor.

Sera swayed to the side and waited for the saber to flash before she flicked her blade at the back of the man's leg and sliced upward to cut into his hamstrings.

There was no time to finish him, and the rest of her mercenaries pushed in behind. The raiders turned on them, and a few fell with shafts protruding from their backs when those of her mercenaries who were on the rocks loosed more arrows.

A woman among the marauders dove at her with a scream and thrust a spear toward her chest.

The guard captain deflected the blade and tried to find an opening with her sword, but all she could strike was the shield.

It meant another one she had to leave behind for others to deal with. Motion was all she could do to keep herself alive in the melee that ensued. A few of her blows found flesh and blood coated her weapon, but all she could do was distract, poke, slash, and avoid and keep herself in the fight.

A few of the raiders struck at their comrades in their attempts to reach her, and Sera let her mind drift. Her body did what it had been trained to do without interference from her mind. She hummed a tune her mother had often played for her, one of the few memories she had of the woman.

It was odd how the song always came to her in moments of violence.

———

The clash was horrifying to witness and yet somehow beautiful.

His hold on the shield tightened, and he watched for any arrows launched from the rocks above. The archers were not particularly skilled but they did not need to be, not at this range and with their height advantage.

If it were not for two of them, the group would likely already be dead, and he and the others he had trained and taught in the arts of combat—some of them since they had been children— would be looting the caravan with sheer abandon. Food was not the only necessity, of course. Those who spent their lives with the clan were capable of growing their own food and sustaining themselves.

But combat was needed. Trained fighters were the most valued commodity in the desert, those who could take and hold what was needed for survival.

But two adversaries stood in the way. One of them appeared to be the more obvious threat. A giant stood head and shoulders above any of his men and wielded a longsword with no fussy ornamentation but which seemed honed for precision. He was a powerful man but one who knew how to balance on the rocks like he had lived on them since he was a child. His interference prevented the men of the clan from reaching the archers at the top.

But a second had immediately drawn his attention as soon as the other fighters from the caravan arrived to help. The slim woman wore her armor comfortably and carried a long saber with an ivory hilt which she used to great effect.

The giant fought with fury and spewed venom from his lips that appeared to enrage his fighters. He took full advantage of it, but the woman could not be more different. Everything about her was calm and grace. Fluid movements and impeccable foot-work all made her appear to be an easy target until she moved on and left his fighters choking on their blood.

As their captain, watching his men die in the duet between the two was horrifying. But as a man who admired fighting prowess above all else, it was beautiful to watch the duality of the fighters.

He kept his shield up, studied the woman, then turned to look at the man. A curious thought touched him. He wasn't sure which one he preferred to fight.

She answered that question for him when she glided past two of his raiders, left them to the weapons of those mercenaries who followed her, and stepped closer to him. Her gaze seemed fixed somewhere else, and she hummed a tune he did not recognize.

As if without conscious thought, she moved easily and swung her blade at his head. He moved back, avoided the strike, and raised his shield to block a second while he thrust his sword forward to try to catch her stronger arm. Her weapon turned, diverted his blade expertly, and twisted around it until her saber snaked to his hand, aimed at his fingers.

He released his weapon immediately but still felt the incision along his knuckles. Despite this, he reached back for the dagger he carried on his belt.

The woman continued her blade's movement and it swung relentlessly as he tried to block it with his shield. It appeared to almost have a life of its own and swiped viciously as she pivoted in place to open a painful wound in the back of his leg.

All his power seemed to drain from him in the same moment

and she had already stepped behind him with the sword pressed against his neck.

She stopped short of killing him and her eyes suddenly regained focus as she stared at what her sword was touching.

Of course, he knew what she saw. The brand had been left there years before. It had long since healed but the scar remained, plainly visible.

"Tell your raiders to lower their weapons," she said, spoke firmly, and left no lack of clarity as to what would happen if he did not comply. "Surrender, and they will not die at our hands."

His fighters would not give up, not if he did not order it. They would be more than willing to die to the man and not a single one would think of his or her survival.

Yet it was his duty to them to keep them alive. His decisions had led them deep into the desert, dangerously close to civilized territory and far away from their clan, their homes, and their families. At no point had they questioned his orders or contemplated returning home with what spoils they had already acquired.

"Lower your weapons!" he shouted loudly enough for them all to hear.

Discipline was required. They were savage fighters by design, but they stopped fighting immediately when he gave the order, and it was soon followed by the sound of their weapons clattering on the hard earth.

The silence that followed was broken almost immediately.

"Bollocks to that," said a deep, unfamiliar voice.

It was followed by a surprised yelp, and he turned as one of his fighters was kicked from the rocks and landed hard in a flurry of dust.

His annoyance was quickly quelled when he heard the woman groan and rub her back, which was likely bruised from the fall. She was still alive, however.

"Was that necessary?" the woman with her blade to his neck

asked the massive warrior.

"No, not particularly."

"Then why did you do it?"

"I wasn't done fighting yet."

She looked exasperated. "I told him that none of his people would die at our hands if they lowered their weapons."

"Has she died?"

It was a valid argument, although he could not have known that the fighter would not land on her head or break her neck.

"I'm sure he doesn't appreciate that kind of technicality."

The pressure of the sword on his neck indicated that she was talking to him now.

"No," the captain admitted.

"See? Now behave, or I'll climb up there and kick you off too for good measure. Now, what is your name?"

Another nudge indicated that the last question was directed at him.

"Xaro," he replied and looked directly into her eyes. "Xaro SandWinder."

"Well then, Xaro SandWinder, the pettiness of Skharr Death-Eater aside, I accept your surrender and that of your men."

Xaro looked at the man on the rocks and suddenly realized that he recognized his build. "A DeathEater. I should have known."

"I guess you have heard of each other?" the woman asked.

The giant shrugged and dropped lightly from his post on the rocks as the archers started to descend as well. "SandWinders are one of the desert clans. They settle at various oases but never spend too much time around one for fear it will dry out. Aside from a handful of squabbles over the years, they never had much interaction with the DeathEaters."

"You send your young off to fight the wars of others," Xaro said accusingly and shook his head.

"And you let yours die hunting traders and pilgrims on the

desert roads," Skharr replied. "We all have our ways to cull the weak from the ranks."

The SandWinder leader looked around and noted that those of his men who had survived were allowed down from the rocks, relieved of their weapons and all else that they might use, and finally had their hands bound behind their backs with ropes.

There were only seven survivors, himself included, but there would be time to consider the deaths of the others later. For the moment, his only concern was the survival of those who yet lived.

"Do we have time to loot the dead, Captain Ferat?" one of the mercenaries asked.

"Do it quickly," she replied. "We need to catch up with the caravan before nightfall. Skharr, how fast can you run?"

"Not as fast as you on horseback."

"Then I suggest you take one of the ponies with you. Your horse ran away from the comfortable life I set him up with, but he's still with the caravan and he'll miss you if you don't return with us. I know he'll blame me for that too."

"He doesn't blame you for subjecting him to the nagging of your mares. Well, he only blames you for not warning him about it beforehand."

Captain Ferat smirked. "Well, I don't take any of that blame for myself."

The giant shrugged and sheathed his longsword carefully before he circled to the ponies. He didn't appear to be looking to loot them. Instead, he seemed determined to round them up carefully, not wanting any of them to run off into the desert, and spoke softly to calm them as he gathered them in.

"Your man speaks to horses," Xaro noted as he submitted his hands to be bound like the others.

"He does tend to do that, although I assumed it was common among the western clans," she answered and raised an eyebrow.

"Not among my clansmen." He scowled at the ropes and tested

their tightness. "Maybe it is common among DeathEaters. They are known to be quite mad."

The palace was unlike anything he had seen or imagined.

Towers rose into the sky like daggers tipped with gold to overlook the city. He had seen them from a distance but could not understand how they could have been part of the same building, as spread out as they were.

It felt impossible, despite the fact that he stood and stared at them. They were made from marble and so, it seemed, was the outside of the palace, with not a single mark of a chisel over the entire structure.

"I've seen towns smaller than that," Tryam whispered as he studied it and noted men looking down from where they patrolled the tops of the towers.

"Aye," one of the guards muttered. "I've visited three times already and I still can't believe what my eyes tell me. I asked some of the guards and they said magic was used to carve it. From what they told me, the palace was one of the first dungeons to be conquered some five hundred years ago. The Ancients built it and made everything look like it had been designed by the gods themselves."

He raised an eyebrow, unable to think of the amount of work that would have gone into building it, even if magic was involved. It could not drag all the marble slabs from the quarries, after all.

Guards already waited for the group and raised their hands to bring the horses to a halt before they moved through the gates. All the young man could think of as they approached was how difficult it would be to take the city.

He had participated in a handful of sieges on both sides, and he could imagine that trying to take this city would be a nightmare. The outer walls were already enough of a hurdle, but as they continued, the inner keep of the city was designed to create a kill zone for any who might approach. If a handful of mages was placed on the towers, they could rain fire on any attackers stupid enough to attack the gates openly.

Emperor Rivar had taken the city himself, of course, but he had never breached the outer walls. Instead, the siege had lasted almost two years and starved the population inside to the point where the queen at the time had conceded to an offer that would see her people fed one way or the other.

It had been single combat. If her champion won, three hundred wagons of food would be provided for the city. If Rivar's champion won, the wagons would be provided but the gates would be opened and the city surrendered.

He had elected to be his own champion and grievously wounded his opponent but left him alive. It was perhaps an unorthodox way to take the city but it had worked, and the queen remained to rule under his command. Mostly, he left the city of Citar to themselves, although Tryam had heard that certain taxes were levied every year and the queen's troops had to be ready to fight with the empire if called.

These were all the stories he had heard from his mother while in supposed exile from the palace, and he could not think of an odder way to learn about his father. There were a few men he considered closer to the position, those who had taught him to fight, ride, and all the other skills that had kept him alive for the entirety of his adult life.

The guards finally appeared to confer and cleared the path for the contending prince and his retinue.

"The queen wishes to see you in her throne room immediately," one of them stated and extended his hand to take the horse's reins.

It snorted, startled, and backed up as if to prepare for a fight.

"I'll guide him, if you don't mind," Tryam told him quietly and nudged his mount forward to follow the guard.

CHAPTER FOUR

H e wouldn't have said it was possible but the palace was
even more impressive inside. Tryam would have said
without qualms that it was even more beautiful than the one his
father called home.

Horses were allowed into the hallowed halls, and he wasn't
sure how so much light came in through the marble walls and the
ceilings that appeared to be made of gold from the outside. From
within, however, he could see the sky through them, although
not quite as glaringly bright as it had been outside.

Curious and a little awed, he studied his surroundings.
Folk appeared to wander through the halls in reverent
silence. A few paused to inspect a handful of statues that
were spread out to flank the pathway leading directly to the
center of the palace, likely where the official rooms were
situated.

The doors were drawn open and Tryam continued into the
actual throne room on his horse, followed by his entourage. It
appeared to be the crowning jewel for the rest of the palace.
Massive trees towered high and provided the throne with shade,
although the path leading to it was still comprised of the same

pale white marble that the structure as a whole appeared to be made of.

A small river circled the throne like a moat. Although a bridge spanned it, he did not feel comfortable riding over it. Instead, he brought his horse to a halt and dismounted.

"Stay here," he said quietly and patted his mount's neck before he walked over the bridge. He gestured for his guards to remain with the beast as he approached the throne.

It was elevated three steps above the pathway, and two more guards waited in front of him with their halberds lowered in an X that would prevent him from advancing up the steps.

The queen was seated on the throne and waited for him to approach. She was tall with a stately look about her. Her skin was darkened by the sun, and her long black hair was wound in an elegant bun held in place by the crown she wore. The silver and gold diadem was inset here and there with bright sapphires.

"I welcome you to my home," the woman declared, stood graciously, and gestured to the palace with her hands. "Lord Tryam Voldana, prince and contender for the imperial throne. May you find any comforts required on your path here."

He nodded, unsure of how to respond to that kind of welcome. He hadn't spent much of his life around nobility or royalty, but there were certain expectations from those who held status. Learning all of them had been a challenge, and he certainly felt a little out of his element.

The best lesson he ever learned was from one of his trainers early on in his life, who had told him that those who kept their mouths shut could never be mistaken for fools.

And it did appear to be the best situation as the queen began to descend the steps. She glanced at her council, who waited at the base of the throne.

"We are finished with all the formalities, yes?" she asked and looked from one to the other. "No more bowing and scraping required?"

Each man nodded, although they watched the visitor out of the corners of their eyes and tried to find any sign that the youth had been offended by the queen's words.

There was no objection from him, of course, and she waved the guards out of her way and advanced on him. She was no small woman, yet she looked up at him with a judgmental stare.

"You are a large bastard, aren't you?" she asked and raised an eyebrow as he met her cold green eyes. "No pun intended, of course. Your father does have a way about him that would spread to all his children. I imagine even the women would have broad shoulders and a square jaw."

"I've...never met any of my half-brothers or sisters," Tryam admitted.

"Well, I suppose that makes sense. Come, walk with me. The gardens are something that must be seen by all visiting dignitaries, and I suppose you classify as such. Follow me. We'll leave the escorts behind for this, yes?"

He doubted that she would take no for an answer at this point so simply shrugged and followed her out of the throne room and through a few hallways until the doors opened for them again.

It looked like a small forest was growing inside. Hundreds of trees clumped around the same water that had been in the moat around the throne, although it appeared to be a real river this time.

Amazingly, he could hear insects buzzing and birds chirping, and animals prowled the area. Even a handful of monkeys studied them as they entered the gardens.

"The magic here is quite...interesting," she noted. "It's one of the few places where it was meant to encourage life and growth. Pilgrims come and visit every year, hoping to enjoy some of the benefits that seem to fill the air. You would think, for instance, that the animals were brought in to live here, yes?"

If Tryam were to tell the truth, he'd had not thought about

what might go into sustaining something like this. Silence was once again his ally.

"No," she continued, undeterred by his lack of response. "When my ancestors took control, it was quite similar to what you see now. The city was created as one of the most prolific water sources in this damned desert, and the rest is history— right up until your father appeared, starved my grandmother into submission, and forced us under the empire's benevolent rule. I have been in power for ten years since my mother abdicated when I was only twenty years of age, and I can understand why."

He nodded slowly but once again made no answer as she continued to lead him through the garden. It proved interesting as he realized that the marble paths continued through this area as well, although slightly elevated, and he felt as though he was above everything and looking down.

The queen paused, looked at him, and shook her head gently. "I apologize. There aren't too many people who would listen to my frustrations in this, of course. If the truth be told, things could have gone far worse for us after your father left us in his wake, although I suppose that had more to do with how he could not afford to fight insurrection after insurrection."

"I can't deny that," Tryam answered and prompted the woman to continue speaking.

"I also assume he enjoyed the victories more than having to rule over the cities he conquered. Warriors like him rarely think too far ahead—although in this case, I cannot blame him. We have mountains to the west, swamplands in the south, and only a short strip of malleable land to the east where most of our food comes from. The quarries and mines in the mountains do allow us some type of export. I suppose we should enjoy that, although the clans in the west and the desert all around us are more than a nuisance."

"How do you mean?"

"Most bandits and raiders would avoid engaging the profes-

sional soldiers and guards who patrol our lands, but the clans…
Well, they appear to enjoy the conflict. They will actively engage
any of my men on patrol and in some cases, break away from any
villages or caravans they were attacking to fight the guards. They
lose most of those encounters, of course, but they are quick to
retreat and so avoid too much loss of life. In the cases when they
win, they secure better weapons and armor for their next fight."

He nodded and felt a little disappointed that he and his guards
had not run into any of the roving clans that might have tested
their strength. Perhaps he would have better luck when he left.

"But it's the swamps I would be more worried about," he noted
and folded his arms. "In my experience, the necromancers always
prefer to do their nasty work in the swamps, although I can't for
the life of me find out why."

"I assume because so many things die there, but I would never
claim to know what drives the mind of a mage who delves into
that type of nonsense. Any caught doing so is clapped in restric-
tion chains and sent to work in the mines, although I do reserve a
couple for public humiliation and execution. The people have
come to expect that from the criminals my guards apprehend,
although it is mostly reserved for those raiders who are captured.
Not many of them are, of course, but those few we do manage to
take alive need to be displayed as a warning against such things."

"Am I to understand that this is how you treat all those who
would defy the law here?"

"Well, I'll treat you and your men with some restraint. A lifetime in the mines would set you right, wouldn't you agree?"

She smirked and he could tell that she had made an attempt at
humor, although he knew it would change if he ever tried to
commit any crimes in her city.

"Your warning is noted, Your Grace."

"While we are in private, I would insist that you call me Reya,
which is my given name. Too many bootlickers try to garner my
favor by using all the right words and all the right bows and

formalities, and it honestly makes me a little sick. I almost long for the days when I rode out to fight raiders with my Equites."

"Almost?"

"Never let it be said that remaining in the palace does not have its many, many benefits, despite how much you hear me complain. I took an arrow to my shoulder that has begun to ache severely every day, even with the help of a handful of mages."

"I hear you might have problems with your back in later years as well if you spend too much time on horseback. It seems to be a curse for tall riders."

She nodded. "Well then, I suppose we'll have to find you and your men a place to remain for the night. That could take a few hours, however, and if you have a mind to explore the city before word starts to spread of your origins, I advise that you do so as quickly as possible. And take as few guards with you as you can."

He had a feeling that this was her show of being welcoming to him and as she began to move away, he could only hope that her first impression had been a good one.

"How high do you think those walls are?"

Skharr peered over his shoulder at one of the mercenaries who rode behind him, then returned his attention to the walls the man had mentioned. He shielded his eyes against the glare as the sun reflected off them.

"Too fucking high if you're trying to get your sneaky ass over them," he responded with a grin and noticed that a moat extended around the walls, although it was almost impossible to see until they moved closer. Instead of water, spikes and pitch were laid out in wait for those who might approach before a flaming arrow engulfed them all in fire.

"Were you one of those who tried?"

"That was…almost a hundred years ago, now," Sera pointed

out and pushed her mount closer as she heard the conversation. "I assume Skharr is not that elderly."

He shook his head although he could tell that she was hoping for the actual number, and he laughed.

Horse appeared to notice it as well and snorted.

The barbarian scowled. "You're one to talk. You left a life of comfort and all the apples you could eat to come into the fucking desert, only to complain about it."

Most of the mercenaries were used to his behavior around Horse at this point, although he assumed a few couldn't understand how the beast had appeared in their camp two days after leaving Verenvan.

The gates were still open and more than a handful of caravans wound through them as the sun began its steady descent toward the eastern horizon.

Their group was quickly waved past the barrier, however, and a few gazes were cast at their prisoners.

"Where are you taking them?" one of the guards asked, stepped in front of Sera's horse, and brought it to a halt as the rest of the caravan continued past her.

"I'll surrender them to the justice of my guild," she snapped immediately and maintained a tight hold on the reins. "That is my right as they are my prisoners."

"Our queen offers a reward on these dung-sucking bastards." The man growled his distaste. "Three silvers for every head offered to our chopping block and a gold piece for any marked with their brands."

"And I'm sure my guildmaster will take advantage of that." She nudged her horse forward a step and forced the guard to take a step back. "Until then, however, I would ask that you move out of our way. We've had a long day and the heat of this godsbe-dammed place has made it longer. Unless you wish to take my prisoners by force, you should leave me to proceed with my caravan."

Skharr sometimes forgot that the woman commanded troops and that she possessed a certain arrogance that came from her heritage. This was sensed by those around her, especially when she wanted it to be.

The guard glared at her but after a few moments of thought, he stepped aside. She clicked her tongue and gestured for the whole line to continue rather than stop to wait for her.

"What will you do, Skharr?" the guild captain asked as they began to traverse the narrow streets of the city. "I assume you'll not want to be with me to complete all the tedious paperwork required for a person in my position?"

"You know me too well. What will you do with the ponies?"

"I'll sell them to the guild's stables. They try to keep horses for their messengers and they'll want those used to the desert above all. In these parts, at least. All my men will receive a cut from what profits we make, of course. But I don't think you'll be too interested. Will you donate your share to the others? It will help them to like you a little better after you threatened to kill them."

"Did they tell you that?"

"Oh, yes. They said you would...uh, shoot them yourself if they tried to run."

"In fairness, I was only half-serious."

"Will you be a generous man, then?"

Skharr tilted his head thoughtfully. "That depends on how much coin is in my share. Will you let me know?"

"Of course. Where will I find you?"

The barbarian looked around the street and patted Horse on the forehead when the beast nudged him in the back. "I don't know the city very well, but I assume you'll find me drowning my sorrows at the nearest inn or tavern."

"What sorrows do you have to drown?"

"The kind that are unusually good swimmers. I'll send you a message if I don't see you come morning."

She nodded and rejoined the mercenaries and prisoners to

continue deeper into the city. He remained where he was for a few moments longer, took a deep breath, and shook his head.

Horse butted him again.

"Yes, I know," he retorted. "It's time for us to find somewhere cool in his hellish place or failing that, enough drinks to take that care away."

More than a few stares lingered on him, although he knew it had less to do with the oddity of a man talking to his horse and more because they recognized his origins.

While he had changed a few things about his appearance over the years, those who lived in this area would be able to identify him as a man from the clans almost immediately.

Given that others of his kind were a problem for civilized folk in this part of the world, they would not easily forgive him for it.

Thankfully, he did not need them to. He chuckled, patted Horse's neck, and strode purposefully down the road.

CHAPTER FIVE

A small courtyard outside was admittedly unusual, but Skharr knew a tavern when he saw one, even in these parts.

The sign outside was the most telling indicator, of course, but all such establishments—or those that wanted customers, anyway —had large common rooms, fires burning at all times, and a roomy stable for their customers to leave their horses and come in without having to worry about the safety of their possessions.

Horse followed him into the courtyard and it seemed that the hostility the locals had toward a man from the clans vanished instantly. A young man approached in a rush, wearing what looked like a servant's uniform.

"Good evening, my lord," he called with a polite smile on his face. "How can I help you?"

Skharr looked at the sky. The sun was out of sight behind the walls but there was still enough light out to make him think it wasn't quite evening yet.

Maybe the desert folk thought it was, even if there was still light in the sky, although it felt like the kind of thing he should have discovered earlier.

"Horse will need stable," he responded and patted the horse in question. "Fresh hay, fresh water. Apples, if possible." He tossed the boy a silver coin and let him catch it before he clicked his tongue at Horse. "No problems," he stated in a warning growl.

"There will not be, good sir. Should I bring your possessions to your room?"

"Not talking to you. And yes. To the room of Skharr DeathEater."

He patted Horse on the neck again to reinforce his words and the stallion allowed the young man to lead him into the stables. A couple of stable hands waited within and already began to remove some of the weight from his back as they took him toward a stall away from the door. Skharr approached the inn with real interest.

A few tables had been set up outside the building and these enabled the patrons to enjoy the comfort of shade and the cooler temperature. The barbarian noted the furniture that was used and frowned as he leaned forward to study it a little more closely.

It was constructed far better than any inn furniture he had seen before. The tables were bolted to the ground with steel braces. The chairs stood freely, but they had the same braces, which seemed intended to prevent them from breaking. He assumed an innkeeper would only pay for that type of furniture if he had lost too much money replacing those that broke too easily and too often.

This was the kind of tavern Skharr was the most likely to feel comfortable in. He smiled and nodded as other horses approached the inn and he stepped inside. It was possible for him to think of how the night could end if not with his fist breaking someone's bones, but there was an odd part of him that wished for it.

While there had been violence aplenty for the day already, he'd had a quiet few weeks leading up to the fight with the raiders and something in him wanted a little more before the day was through.

It had been something of a chore to persuade his retinue to only have two guards accompany him into the city, but it was worth it in the end. He discovered that the narrow streets were a little easier to navigate if he didn't have the Emperor's Elite trailing his every step and it certainly attracted less attention.

"Are you sure, my lord?"

Tryam ignored the question, stepped from the saddle, and made sure his sword was settled at his hip. All markings that would have distinguished them as imperial men had been removed before they left the palace and each was only allowed a sword and no armor. He knew the men neither understood nor liked it, but he did not intend to parade his name and origins through the city.

"My lord!" a young man shouted as he hurried forward to take the reins. "How may I help you this evening?"

"A stable for the horses while we remain," he told the young ostler and noticed that the stable hands seemed to have some difficulty managing a sturdy, older steel-gray stallion at the door. "We shan't remain long."

"Of course, my lord."

The guards moved with the horses to check that they were stabled correctly—and likely to ensure that the skittish warhorses did not cause any trouble to the staff. It was a wise choice and one of them moved to the stable hands. A few shouted words were exchanged but the horse appeared completely unperturbed by it all and simply looked around and shifted lazily to the side.

As the newcomer reached toward the reins, the horse moved, took a step forward, and rammed his head into his face.

It looked like such a gentle action, but even those were powerful when performed by a beast that weighed over a thousand pounds. The man lost his footing and sprawled awkwardly, and a shocked expression settled on his face.

The stallion whinnied and shook its mane before it continued to walk lazily into the stables.

"Son of a...nit-infested fucking one-legged whore!"

He pushed to his feet and reached for his sword.

"Stop what you are doing!" Tryam snapped and rolled his eyes. "Unless you truly wish to demand satisfaction from and duel a horse for your honor."

The man stopped as ordered, considered what he was doing, and released his weapon slowly.

"There's a good lad," the contender muttered. "Now stop mucking about and let's all drink like we mean it."

His companions both scowled at him but said nothing as they moved toward the inn. A few customers seated outside darted a curious glance at them but quickly turned their attention to the food and drink in front of them. It seemed like his kind of place —one that wouldn't ask any questions and would help him gain a finer feel for the city before it was closed off to him.

Not that anyone would restrict his actual movements, but many there disliked the emperor and would make any time he spent in the city nightmarish if they learned who he was.

Or, rather, who his father was.

The inn was a spacious room and its construction seemed designed to resist both the heat that would come during the day and the icy breeze that would filter in once the sun was gone.

Fires roared while meat cooked on the spit and large pots with soups simmered slowly. The ovens were likely in the back and the whole area smelled of bread. It was a mouthwatering aroma, the kind that overwhelmed any that might be a little fouler.

All types of people were seated inside and few cared to look up from their drinks at the newcomers. A young woman was singing in the corner while she played an instrument like a lute but with a narrower body and a longer neck and only six strings. The sound was thick, and her soft voice quickly enraptured those who were listening.

One man in particular caught Tryam's attention—one he'd caught a glimpse of as they drew close to the tavern, which possibly meant he was a new arrival as well. The stranger was taller than most, with broad shoulders and arms thicker than most men's legs. His hair was fairly long and was tied back with a simple leather band. A hint of a beard appeared on his face, but what drew his attention were his bright green eyes.

It was a little difficult to ignore them as he felt like they were digging thoroughly into the back of his head to ferret out every secret thought he would have liked to keep hidden.

Before he could react, the man appeared to lose interest. He turned to the innkeeper, and Tryam felt like he had been slightly insulted. With a sheepish smile, he shook his head and turned to one of his guards.

"Get us some drinks," he ordered. "Something cold if they have it. I'll get the next round and we shall continue in that way."

The Elite nodded and proceeded to where the massive bulk of a man had stood but had already moved away, likely to find a corner to enjoy a drink on his own. Or perhaps he had friends waiting for him. He did not look like a local—he was too large and his skin was a little lighter—but surprisingly, that did not make him stand out much. Many who traveled through the city were not locals.

Still curious, Tryam continued to inspect his surroundings. One of the guards found them a table and the other soon brought large mugs of something frothy. They did not wait for him but tapped their mugs together and took long gulps of the brew.

It appeared to be refreshing, and the contender shook his head and turned his attention to the food that was being prepared. It was odd how the only people who desired a change in food types were those who could afford it. Anyone who couldn't enjoyed the same fare as their counterparts across the world—some kind of bread, meat, and a bowl of something warm to fill the body and the soul.

He had enjoyed food like that many times and under various circumstances. Soldiers were forced to eat almost anything they could get their hands on and sometimes, that went to extremes. Folk in peacetime tended to forget that the rules changed in times of war.

A sound made him turn almost before he realized what was happening. The low grunt was accompanied by feet scraping across the floor to approach him from behind, but the person came to a sudden halt.

Tryam's gaze locked with that of a young man not old enough to grow a beard yet. The skin stretched over his bones indicated a familiar kind of desperation—the kind he was only too familiar with.

The youngster looked surprised and perhaps even shocked. His expression changed to one of disappointment when both their gazes drifted to the man's hand.

Held an inch away from Tryam's stomach was a wide dagger three inches long—more than enough to bury itself in him, cut him, and open him for the world to see. It would have gone into his back but something had stopped it.

He flicked his gaze away from the weapon.

A large hand attached to a large body held the would-be assassin by the wrist to prevent the dagger from finding its target. The contender stared into the eyes of the giant he had noticed earlier.

"You are surprisingly calm for a man who was almost killed," his rescuer rumbled and bones ground on bones as the large hand squeezed the wrist tighter until the assassin released the knife and uttered a pained scream.

"This is not the first time someone has tried to kill me," Tryam admitted. "It is the first time they've tried to stab me in the back, however."

"I wish I could say you'll get used to it."

The warrior smirked and pushed the assassin aside with sufficient force to make him stumble across the room.

"You are surprisingly calm for a man who stopped another from being murdered."

The massive shoulders raised in a casual shrug. "It's not the first time."

Tryam glanced toward his guards, who approached quickly and he could see the conclusion that they were already coming to. An attempt had been made on the prince's life and the giant was the assassin.

It was an idiotic assumption. A man that large would not need a knife to kill him, especially in these close quarters. Besides, the weapon was already on the ground.

"Step away!" one of his men shouted, although he did not specify to whom the order was directed. They began to draw their swords in an effort to have them in hand before they reached the stranger. It was not how he wanted them to react, but it was a curious thing to watch.

The man moved almost impossibly quickly. He was not armed with any weapons, not even a dagger strapped to his hip, but the contender had a feeling he had no need for weapons if he truly had a mind to unleash violence.

With no warning, he lashed his hand out to catch the closest man across the jaw with a backhand.

It was forceful enough to spin him powerfully into a nearby wall.

Tryam thought it interesting that the innkeeper paid no mind to the fight that had begun in his place of business. He merely looked at the group and shook his head, rolled his eyes, and returned to the work of cleaning the mugs that were not in use.

"While they resolve their disagreement," the young prince said as he looked at the would-be assassin and gestured at the melee, "why don't you tell me why you tried to kill me?"

"I wanted your coin purse," the boy whispered.

"No, I do not believe that. Dozens of people here are better dressed than I am and likely carrying more coin than I do. You ignored them all and if it weren't for the intervention of that hulking mass of humanity, your blade would be buried in my back."

At the mention of the dagger, the assassin looked to where it had fallen and his eyes narrowed speculatively.

"Don't you try it," Tryam warned.

The warning was not heeded and his assailant scrambled forward and snatched the weapon up. Instead of trying to make another attempt on his quarry's life, however, he dragged the blade across his own neck.

"Oh...bloody hell," the innkeeper protested and finally took notice. "Did you even try to stop him? I'll have to clean all that blood up myself, you know!"

"I doubt it."

They both looked at the giant, who grasped one of the guards by his collar, lifted him, and drove his head into the floor with a powerful thud.

"How do you mean?" the young prince asked with a glance of distaste at the dead man in front of him whose blood still pooled red around him.

"Well, you do have a few servants on hand who will clean the blood up and remove the body for you." The warrior retrieved his coin pouch, drew a gold coin from it, and handed it to the innkeeper. "If you have any problems with the city guard, you can tell them this one tried to murder one of your patrons. I am sure that they will understand."

The proprietor took the coin and shouted something to a couple of the servants in a local dialect that neither of his two patrons could understand. His staff immediately began to clean the mess.

"I believe I owe you my life, giant stranger." The boy offered his hand to the barbarian. "What is your name?"

"Skharr DeathEater," he replied. "And you owe me your life in more ways than you imagine. It is curious, is it not, that your men failed to act until they saw me approach you, yes?"

"Curious," Tryam agreed.

"Although they saw the assassin even before I did and made no move to protect you. Similarly curious."

The contender looked at the two men on the ground and a sense of realization swept over him as he studied both while they pushed slowly to their feet.

"If you have a mind to ask anyone about who wants you dead, I would suggest asking them," Skharr noted, collected a mug from the counter, and took a sip.

"Or I could pay you to ask them for me," Tryam suggested quickly. "You appear to know your way around such dreary matters."

"Can you afford me?"

"I might. More importantly, I will be more than capable of affording you once I am finished with the Stygian Path."

The warrior paused, studied him more carefully, and shrugged in an offhand way. "I suggest we discover who wants you dead before we charge into any dungeons. And that is rather cheap. You pay for my drinks and we can discuss you and your life and who wants to see you dead."

The prince grinned and nodded. "That is cheap."

"And more than worthwhile."

CHAPTER SIX

There had been no sign of the newly confirmed prince the night before. He'd taken that as evidence that everything had happened precisely as it had been intended to and slept as peacefully as he could have wished to.

Ingold watched as the sun began to rise over the city walls. The populace could be heard going about their business with the traditional bustle and noise that came from having so many people living their lives in so small an area.

And there was still no sign of the prince.

He had gone to bed expecting the guards who had escorted him to return with the good news, but as the cock crows woke him and there was still no sign of the guards or their man, he realized he would have to assume that something had gone wrong. There was no outcry through the city yet about one of the emperor's sons having been murdered, but there was also no sign of an outcry over an attempted murder either. He wasn't sure which would be the most likely to catch the attention of the citizens.

It wasn't like the boy's father was overly popular there, of course, but some people would still attempt to make a scene that would hopefully endear them to the ruler. Nobles and the like were strange when it came to foolish responses like that.

Having no news had begun to grate on his nerves, and he ignored the offers of a morning meal from the yawning serving staff.

"Up, you lazy maggots!" he roared as he entered the room where the other guards were sleeping. All were in the same room situated outside the chamber that had been reserved for the prince. They were supposed to guard him with their lives, after all.

To their credit, they scrambled from their pallets as soon as they heard his voice and reached for their weapons, A few had drawn them in seconds and were ready for a fight.

They were the emperor's Elites, and he expected nothing less.

"All is well, captain?"

"No," Ingold snapped, poured himself some water, and drank it quickly. "We had no word from the prince all night and we'll need to search for him and find what happened to him."

"Isn't no news the ideal situation?" one of the guards asked, even though he had already begun to pull his armor on.

"Not likely. There should have been word—something, at least. No word is starting to make me nervous and we will have to make sure that the prince is...safe."

The men did not exchange looks as they continued to prepare themselves. They knew what their work there was, and their time spent in the emperor's palace told them that even in this city, the walls were likely to have ears. There was no point in saying aloud what they already knew.

Spending the night in something that resembled civilization was certainly a boon, but Skharr was in the mood for something else entirely as they strode to the Guild Hall. It had been a long night, and the boy he had run into at the inn the night before had been tight-lipped about why someone would want to kill him, no matter how well-plied he was with alcohol.

All he said was that he wanted a man like the barbarian at his side on the Stygian Path, and no more was said after all the drinks the young man could buy were swilled.

Whatever else could be said about him, he could certainly hold his liquor—although the look of him the next morning said he wasn't quite as used to drinking so much in one night.

"Why can't we simply…wait a little while?"

The warrior scowled and patted him roughly on the shoulder. "An assassin willing to kill himself before divulging information is not the kind to work alone. He knew where to find you, so I would say there are many who would be able to fill his role. It is best to stay on the move and given that we have business to attend to this morning, it would fulfill two purposes."

Tryam groaned softly, rubbed his temples, and turned instinctively away from the bright morning sun that was already baking down on them.

"I understand the danger I am in—"

"Although you still have not explained why they would want to spill your guts."

"Folk want to stick their blades in nobles all the time."

"So you said last night."

The boy seemed determined to keep his lips sealed about the reason, although Skharr felt that pressing him to share was more for his peace of mind. Too much of his time in the past had been spent extricating himself from political situations he had stumbled into and that could have been avoided if he'd simply minded his own business.

It had also netted him more than his fair share of coin and other rewards, but in the end, not all of it was worth it.

Horse was waiting for him at the inn, but he did not want to find himself in a combat situation again without some weapons.

His sword hung from his back and would likely not be drawn unless he engaged in an actual fight, but a dagger was hidden behind his hip in case something short and nasty was needed. The narrow streets of the city were enough to make him worried, as anyone with a crossbow could look at them from above and fire almost before anyone could do anything.

Fortunately, the Guild Hall rose in front of them before too long and with it, a slight lifting of the concern he had felt over the young man's safety.

Not entirely, of course. The assassin who had died the night before by his own hand had been desperate, and desperate men made stupid decisions.

"Stay close to me," Skharr warned in a rough tone.

"Why?"

"Because I can't be your meat shield if you're not close and I'll be tempted to kill you myself if I have to pursue you in order to keep you alive again."

Tryam nodded and studied their surroundings with some interest. "Noted. Although if you kill me yourself you won't be paid."

"It'll be worth it."

The young man laughed and shook his head as they stepped out of the blazing sunlight and into the shade of the hall. It was not quite as impressive as it's contemporary at Verenvan, which was considerably larger and with the elaborate detail that certainly set an enviable precedent. Citar's Guild Hall was a large, sturdy structure in its own right, but nothing set it apart from the rest of the city.

Groups of mercenaries were gathered around the building to talk, accept contracts, and discuss business amongst themselves. The sight of two more fighters drew no attention as they stepped inside.

"I think they make these with the intention of it being cooler inside than outside," Skharr muttered when he felt the sudden change in temperature around him. "In all the other places I've been, they have to spell the building to do that."

"Why do you think they didn't spell this one?"

He shrugged. "I doubt they would be able or willing to spell every single building in the city, much less maintain the magic."

One person appeared to notice their arrival almost immediately, but it was a familiar face, thankfully enough.

Sera waved at them and told the man who was in front of her to stop talking for a few moments until the other two men approached.

"Well, it's good to see you alive and somewhat intact," she said once they were in earshot. "Although I didn't expect you to find yourself a stray this soon."

"I'm not a stray," Tryam grumbled.

She nodded, although she did not look convinced. "What is the story behind this one?"

"I have not heard it all yet, but it would appear that he is in need of someone who knows his way around dungeons, and I happen to be in the business for exactly that kind of adventure."

That did catch his companion by surprise and he glanced at Skharr, who laughed.

"What do you mean by that?" the boy asked.

"Did you not think it odd that I would agree to follow you into a dungeon on this quest of yours without so much as a pause?"

Tryam nodded and seemed to be surprised that it had somehow gone over his head.

"He's not the brightest fellow, this one," Sera noted.

"That's not quite right. He's clever enough. But an attempt was made on his life last night and he spent most of the night drinking his worries away, so he is not at his sharpest today."

She shrugged. "So I suppose you will not join us on our return trip to Verenvan?"

Skharr shook his head. "I'll escort our noble here and try to keep him alive."

"It's for the best." The guild captain scowled. "The city guard is far more interested in raiders here than they generally are and they are making a fuss with the guild about keeping prisoners, so I'll be required to stay here until the situation is resolved. It should result in some gold coming our way on top of what you are already owed."

"If I don't return before then, you can share whatever is owed to me with the rest of the peloton," Skharr said and squeezed her shoulder. "If not, I'll have to buy their affections another way—with a few rounds of drinks, perhaps."

The woman smirked. "That would be what they spend it on anyway. Be safe. I'd hate to have to mourn your death, barbarian."

He nodded, although he could make no promises and she knew it. Heading into a dungeon of his own free will certainly negated any attempt to be safe.

He gestured to a hovering guildmaster, who listened to the terms they had agreed to and began to prepare the contract.

"Are you and she lovers?" Tryam asked as the warrior began to look through a few scrolls from the desk while the guildmaster worked.

"No," he replied.

"Is she open, then, to becoming intimate with others?"

He looked up from the contract that was being drawn up and shrugged evasively. "Possibly. I doubt it, though."

"Why? Is she a princess saving herself for a real prince to save her from a life of mercenary work?"

"She could be a princess, although I am not sure how the whole situation would work. But no. I suggest against it because if you piss her off, I'll have to save your life from her and I have no intention of fighting someone as skilled as Captain Sera Ferat.

55

She has been training me, and I would not look forward to testing myself against her when her intentions were to kill me."

Tryam's eyebrows raised, a hint of surprise that indicated that he knew who Sera was, at least by name.

"Fair enough."

"Now, sign here..." Skharr indicated a line on the contract scroll that he and the guildmaster had discussed, and the other man handed Tryam a quill. "And I will see you to wherever you came from to collect your things."

"We'll need to return to the Queen's palace," the young man answered and scribbled his name as indicated. The ink turned from black to red and the guildmaster took the scroll and sealed it with wax. "And if you truly do fear that my guards plan to have me killed, you should know there are twenty of them—minus the two you manhandled last night—and they will likely not be pleased that I am no longer interested in their services."

It certainly seemed like the kind of establishment Tryam would frequent.

Ingold had heard much about the boy. He was an impressive fighter by all accounts, but his skills were limited to the more courtly form of swordsmanship but a few character traits were a little too common for an emperor in the making.

Which was why certain people were invested in making sure he did not survive the trial. Most of those wanted to arrange that he died before he even started it, although it seemed far easier to simply let the dungeon do the deed—as it surely would.

So many died every year trying to explore dungeons. He had never understood why they even tried it at all. He assumed some were desperate enough and others were arrogant enough to want to prove themselves against famed monsters.

But one needed to live to reap the benefits, and so few did that it felt like it was not worth it.

Still, Tryam was in a situation where he had to prove himself that way, and it seemed the common boy needed to drink a path through the city's inns and taverns to keep himself steady on the task. Then again, they had come to a very sudden halt at a place called the Golden Oasis so perhaps a path wasn't necessarily correct.

He could tell they had come and not left due to their horses still being in the stables.

"How can I help you gentlemen?" the innkeeper asked and dried his hands quickly as he approached the group. "We'll not have enough room at a table for all of you, but we might bring two together if you wish it."

"We are not here to partake of your meals," Ingold responded sharply. "You have three horses in your stables that belong to members of our party. We need to reunite with them before we can continue with our business. If you could tell us where they are, we shall be on our way."

"I'm not sure how inns work where you come from," the man muttered, "but it is not the practice here to openly share the details of those under my roof, no matter who wishes to find them. If your comrades wish to find you, they will do so on their terms."

Ingold narrowed his eyes. He'd had a feeling that folk would be difficult in this city but had hoped otherwise.

"I come from the imperial city and where I come from, the sight of the emperor's eagle on a man's breastplate means that those who are being questioned, talk. Those who do not know better incur the wrath of the emperor."

"Well, if the emperor's wrath is incurred, he knows where to find me," the innkeeper replied. "Until then, I'll need you to leave —unless you've changed your mind about partaking of my food."

A couple of his men reached for their weapons, likely with the intention to intimidate the man into providing the information they sought.

He could also hear the sounds of the others in the common room with them. Their sovereign was not a popular man in these parts, and more than a few of the patrons appeared to be noblemen who bore their personal sigils in some form or another.

The guards' aggressive movements prompted them to ready their weapons as well.

Quickly, he raised his hand to stop his men from escalating the situation. He had more to do with his life than find himself entangled in a brawl.

"Should our comrades appear again, let them know that Captain Ingold came asking for them." He motioned with his hand again to be sure the men knew he was telling them to move away and step outside before things got worse.

"I'll do what I can," the innkeeper replied and looked unruffled by the whole affair as he returned to cleaning dishes.

CHAPTER SEVEN

Tryam noticed the same look on Skharr's face that he had no doubt worn when he approached the palace for the first time.

It was as if he stared at something that his mind told him was impossible, and there was some confusion as to whether what he saw was real or not.

"Magic," the giant decided suddenly with a firm nod. "Only magic could have built this. Common architects would not be able to make something quite so…clean."

Clean? That was an interesting description of it but also accurate. There were no signs of chisels or any other tool on the outside of the palace, which made it look almost like it had grown from the sands of the desert with no human intervention.

"It is most certainly magic. You know, the queen told me this was one of the first dungeons to be conquered, and the fact that it appeared to draw water from the ground was enough to entice people to live in its proximity."

Skharr nodded but still looked as if his mind could not accept the evidence of his eyes. "It sounds accurate. I've seen a place like this in the past, although on a far lesser scale. It too looked like something that simply sprouted from the ground one day."

At this astute observation, Tryam wondered how it all came to be. He knew a few elements of magic. A couple of his caretakers had been mages and had thought that he might have some talent for it—although they rapidly lost interest once it became clear that he didn't.

"Once, I saw a mage chanting on a beach," he whispered. "The sand formed into a solid castle and after a few seconds, it had turned to glass. A full castle, completely functional in every way but in glass and smaller than a person's bed. It took him days, and he said that he would not be able to gather that much power for another year but it was worth it. He sold the castle to a collector for enough gold to buy an actual castle."

"You'd think they would find something better to spend their coin on."

Tryam chuckled and decided he liked the way the giant thought. He wasn't dull-witted by any means, and he had an odd intelligence about him. At the same time, he still managed to view the world in simple terms—his terms—and saw no reason to view it otherwise.

He would want to talk to him once he was emperor and perhaps find a way to make the man a part of his empire and give him some kind of position.

It seemed unlikely, however. Everything about Skharr—from his name to his attitude—resisted living under the restraints of civilization for long. He was a member of one of the clans. Even Tryam had heard of the DeathEaters, an unusual group that somehow produced some of the greatest warriors ever seen, who would appear in moments of brilliance in battles and wars, only to disappear at the end.

The sound of horses arriving at the palace with them was enough to catch his attention and he lowered his hand to his sword as he looked around. The horses that approached were familiar, the same kind of warhorses he rode himself although of different breeds.

The emperor demanded only the best for his men, and the breeders who produced mounts for his armies were paid well for their efforts in rearing some of the finest stallions in the world.

Ingold dismounted from his horse immediately, while all the others remained in the saddle, fully armored and looking like they were ready for a battle.

"My prince," the man shouted as he drew closer. "You must stand clear of the barbarian. He means you harm and has already inflicted it on the two men who were guarding you."

Tryam narrowed his eyes, looked at Skharr, and finally laughed. "Well, if he did mean me harm, he's rather unsuccessful at it since all the harm he's done to me has been a woeful headache."

"In my defense, you did all that damage to yourself," the barbarian answered. "I didn't pry your mouth open and pour the golden spirits down your throat, after all. Did you call him a prince?"

Frustrated, the young contender closed his eyes and shook his head. He didn't want to deal with that at all and he certainly didn't intend to do so now.

"My prince, please," Ingold insisted and gestured to Tryam. "Move away from the barbarian. Allow us to deal with him."

"I suppose eighteen of you would be what is required to do so," he conceded. "But from what I saw last night of the two you sent with me, I feel I am safer close to him than apart."

"What makes you say that?"

A woman's voice interrupted the tense situation with a tone of levity. A group of guards followed her as well, but she stepped ahead of the men who were supposed to keep her safe.

The gesture spoke clearly of a woman who was more used to leading than following—a true queen.

She wore her crown and the same long, flowing robes she had

worn the day before, although he suspected these were new.

"Your Grace." Tryam bowed his head politely.

She had no objections to him calling her by her title in public like this, and she stopped in front of Skharr almost immediately. His people and hers were natural enemies, it seemed, and she sensed it almost as soon as she saw him.

"Answer the question, Lord Tryam," she said while she studied his companion carefully. "Why would you feel safer in the presence of this…surly creature than your guards?"

"Because the men who were supposed to protect me last night were in league with an assassin who attempted to take my life," he told her. "The surly creature was there to intercept a dagger meant for my back, and after they were interrogated, they admitted that they were there to make sure the assassin did not fail and that he did not survive the attempt on my life either."

"I trust that you turned the guilty party over to the proper authorities?" the queen asked and continued to glare at Skharr, who seemed more than a little amused.

"I would have, but he slit his own throat before I could. Which was why I was forced to question my guards once it was noted that they had watched the man while he made his attempt but only rose to my aid when it was clear that he had failed. The two were turned over to the city guard once my friend here had finished dragging the truth from them."

She studied the barbarian carefully but a sudden smile settled her face as she turned her gaze to Ingold.

"What have you to say about these accusations, Captain?"

He shook his head. "My men were all loyal to the emperor and I would vouch for every single one of them. They would not have turned on their charge as he says they did—not in a hundred years and not for all the coin in the world."

"Well then, it would appear that one of you is lying." She shook her head. "Honestly, if it were only the barbarian, I would take your word over his as I admittedly have a bias against his kind. But with the word of the prince, I find you are not as trust-worthy as you might appear."

"Why does everyone keep calling him the prince?" Skharr asked and glanced expectantly at them.

"I'll…explain it later." Tryam rubbed his temples.

"You'll explain it if you want me to know what I'm protecting you against."

The queen turned to the contender. "This man protects you?"

"Under a guild contract."

She turned to the barbarian. "You would protect a son of the emperor?"

"I didn't know he was the son of the emperor but yes, I would."

"Why?"

He shrugged. "I'm bored and there was a fight. The assassin all but shouted his intent and I decided it was my time to intervene. When the prince enticed me with the promise of gold and more fights to come… Well, how could I resist?"

"A violent fellow to the last." The queen's sneer was almost mocking but not quite. "But you did spare me the trouble of having to explain to the emperor why his son was slain in my city and that does endear me to you somewhat."

The other guards had dismounted from their horses and the queen's escort looked like they anticipated a fight.

Tryam reached for the sword at his side almost unconsciously.

"Your accusations are not appreciated," Ingold snapped and shook his head. "Every man under my command has proven himself worthy of the trust your father places in him a hundred times over and I will not see them so disrespected."

"It's not their competence or courage I take issue with," the young man pointed out calmly. "It's the fact that they stood shoulder-to-shoulder with two men who would see me dead, which begs the question—are you all so incompetent that you did not see the betrayal by two of your group, or were you party to it? Either way, I fear I would lose my life if I were to trust you again, Captain Ingold."

"Enough!"

Ingold was no small man and he moved his hand to draw his sword quickly with a soft hiss. He had been made a captain of the Emperor's Elites for a reason, and the young man knew he would have to fight him. Even if he wasn't guilty of trying to assassinate a prince, he would have to defend his honor against the accusation.

He grasped his sword and drew it halfway out of the scabbard before he realized that Skharr was already in motion.

Once again, it seemed impossible that a man so large could move so quickly. He made no effort to retrieve the sword that hung on his back but advanced on Ingold unarmed.

The captain almost didn't realize that he was being attacked from the side and when he did, his opponent had already closed the distance.

At that range, he had no need for a weapon and simply stepped close, pushed Ingold's sword to the side, and swung his closed fist across his jaw.

No second blow was needed. The guard was no slouch and many of those who had taught Tryam had been trained by the very same man. He was a legend.

But even a legend was only human, and a human was vulnerable to a ham-sized fist that collided with his jaw at tremendous speed. He staggered and fell, still conscious but certainly not in any position to fight.

A stunned silence descended over the group as they tried to come to terms with what had happened.

"Did you see him move?" Reya whispered to Tryam.

He tilted his head. "Some. Not all."

She nodded.

The guards were the first to react and a united cry issued

from their ranks as they drew their swords in a single motion, advanced to where Ingold had fallen, and immediately surrounded him to protect him.

Once they were sure their captain was still alive, they all turned to Skharr, who had loosed the sword from his shoulder and drawn it from its scabbard.

He was ready to face them all, and Tryam decided that he wasn't sure if the barbarian couldn't simply kill them all if he wanted to.

"Stop this at once!" The queen stepped between the warrior and the Elites. She carried no weapon of her own but her guards did, and they rushed forward to her side, ready to defend her if they were needed. "Now, if you want to turn on and kill each other, I encourage you to do it outside Citar's walls. There, you can gorge on as much violence as your little hearts and cocks desire, but while you are in my city, you will live by my laws of peace!"

Her voice rang through the silent courtyard in front of the palace and instantly demanded the attention of all present.

"The prince has the right to name his defenders as he pleases," she stated coldly and looked at Skharr with a scowl but turned her gaze back to the guards. "If he finds you no longer acceptable as guards, you will return to the emperor, whom you serve, and you will not enter my palace without his approval. And if you continue to disturb the peace in my city, you will be punished as my laws dictate. Now, choose."

The guards all exchanged glances and after a few seconds, they made their decision, picked Ingold up, and returned to their horses.

The queen's guards watched like hawks to ensure that they caused no further trouble, and the ruler turned and moved to where Tryam realized that he still had his hand on his sword.

"Come on, then. Let us go into the palace," she whispered and smirked. "And out of this fucking godsbedamned heat."

CHAPTER EIGHT

The sun had vanished.

He wasn't sure how it was possible, but the sky was dark and it felt as if it had been dark forever—like even the concept of a sun in the sky was nothing more than a distant memory that dissipated rapidly. It was, he thought with a sense of panic, like he had already begun to forget what it looked like to have a sun hanging over them.

But there was another source of light and although it was dim, they could at least see what was happening. Fires burned all around them. A battle raged and the stench of blood and human death filled the air, even beyond the reek of the smoke that obscured his view.

It was the smoke that covered the sun, he realized. He could think of no other logical deduction.

The sword felt heavy in his hand like he had spent the day wielding it and other weapons. His eyes stung from the acrid smoke and every inch of his body begged for rest.

The steel blade was black with blood. He looked around in an attempt to locate the threat that made his heart thunder painfully in his chest.

A man stood near him, a massive human with every inch of him covered in blood and gore. He wore no armor, only a leather belt around his waist, and his hands grasped a battle-ax. Despite his size and intimidating appearance, he was not the threat.

"Do you intend to simply stand around, like a godsbedammed pissant?" Skharr asked, twirled his ax in his hand, and turned his attention to something that approached them from a nearby burning building.

Tryam looked at the sword he held, but his arms were ridiculously heavy and sluggish, which made it difficult to move at all.

"Stand around, then," the giant rumbled and raised his weapon to strike at the monster.

The creature moved fast. Scales covered its skin and it was even taller than Skharr. Talons jutted from its fingers and a long tail whipped around to try to sever the barbarian's head.

It attacked but jumped back to avoid the swing of the ax. The sharp talons raked viciously to open a broad wound across the giant's chest. He roared with pain but continued his assault but each time he swiped the ax in a wide sweep in an attempt to strike the creature, it had already moved away. After a few variations of this maneuver, it leaned back on its powerful legs and lunged forward to snap its fangs around his neck.

A sickening crack followed and his head came away, while blood poured from the enormous wound. Skharr released his ax and fell to his knees. His head was still attached, but barely, and hung over his shoulder.

"Oh…fuck." Tryam gasped and tried to raise his weapon as the creature's slitted gaze flicked to look at him.

His sword arm moved but not quickly enough. The monster rushed forward with its talons fully extended and fangs bared as they lashed toward him.

The darkness overtook him, and the knife-like teeth sank into his neck and razor-sharp claws raked his chest.

A light appeared and seemed to call him and draw him to it.

Breathing was suddenly possible. He flailed blindly for the monster that had chewed on his neck but it was no longer there. The light was all around him now and with it, some semblance of warmth—a little too much warmth for comfort but not hot enough to be the fires burning in the buildings.

His eyes opened and he clutched something that felt like sheets as he looked cautiously around him.

Silk sheets, he realized with a trace of bemusement. Tryam shook his head to clear the last remnants of sleep and focused on his surroundings. The walls and floor were marble streaked with silver and gold and tall pillars supported the ceiling. Long red drapes blocked the windows to impede the sunlight that would stream through after sunrise.

He pushed to his feet from where he had fallen from the bed, still a little confused, and tried to regain his equilibrium.

Nothing seemed out of place. His weapons were neatly stowed to one side with no indication that they had been used or even drawn in a fight. The pristine chamber showed no sign of the fires, the smoke, and the lizard-like monster.

With a heartfelt sigh, he sat on the bed and felt his neck tentatively where the fangs had shredded the flesh to render him little more than mincemeat.

It had been a painful experience despite the fact that he knew it wasn't real, and even the memory of it traced a chill along his spine. Even now, in wakefulness, it was difficult to put it from his mind.

"Godsbedammed life-sucking nightmares," he whispered and took a deep breath as he looked up when someone knocked on the door.

Tryam stood again and moved quickly to yank it open. It annoyed him that the man who filled the doorway—quite literally—still made his mouth run dry.

"Are you all right?" Skharr asked and peered around the room.

"Why…why wouldn't I be?"

"Because you look more tired than when you went to bed. And you're sweating enough to fill a river."

The contender looked at his bare chest and realized that he was right. "The heat gets under the skin here."

"It's not the only thing that gets under the skin, I regret to say. Magic seeps through every room here and it tends to inspire dreams."

He shook his head and tried to dislodge the image of the slitted eyes that had settled on him after the beast had killed the giant.

The unsettling thought almost brought a shudder but he managed to resist it.

"Are you ready to go, then?" he asked when he noticed that Skharr was already half-dressed in his gambeson and trousers, although he still seemed to be in the process of preparing himself.

"More ready than you are," his new bodyguard pointed out as he tightened his belt. "Some food is coming for the morning meal. If you'd rather hang about and sleep for a few more hours, I wouldn't hold it against you."

Tryam shook his head. "I'm afraid the dreams would follow me. It's best to get on with the day."

The warrior nodded, stepped out of the way, and gestured at the doorway. Two servants had set a table for them in the antichamber where they could enjoy a meal, and the morning heat began to make itself felt despite the magic the queen had referred to. The prince preferred the chill when night fell, but he would have to settle for the mediated temperature inside the palace.

A little stiff, he settled on one of the pillowed seats and inspected the small feast that had been brought for them, as well as a selection of drinks and tisanes.

The women poured some of the brews into tiny ceramic cups that were thin enough to be almost transparent, with depictions of tiny blue flowers on them.

"A herb tisane to help improve the energy for the day," one explained and handed both of them a cup.

Skharr looked curious and dubious at the same time but followed suit when Tryam took a sip. It was soft, sweet, and refreshing despite being served warm, thanks to the mint that infused the flavor.

Sure enough, he did feel a little more energetic, even after only one sip.

"Enjoy your meal, sirs." The servant bowed and motioned for the other servants to follow.

"Hold," the barbarian growled as he leaned over one of the dishes that had been laid out for him. "I think you'll need to take this fish away. It's gone bad."

"No, it hasn't," Tryam answered, picked one of the strips up, and tossed it into his mouth. He smiled as the flavor filled his senses. "That is fasa, a traditional pickled and fermented fish. While it does take getting used to—as I imagine one would need to with the cheese that turns blue—it is quite tasty. The recipe originated with the traders who needed a way to preserve the fish during the long trip to Citar."

"Why would the nobles eat preserved foods?" Skharr asked and sat as far away from the dish as possible. "I thought that was generally reserved for the lower classes."

"Over time, I suppose, as more people develop a taste for it, more folk start to eat it no matter what their station. My mother used to make it for me. As a child, I hated it, but I grew to like it."

"Your mother was Citarii?"

The young prince nodded as he served himself a generous helping and Skharr did the same. "She grew up here but she never returned after she was brought to my father."

"Your father, the emperor."

He responded with another nod as he popped an olive into his mouth and chewed it thoughtfully. "I didn't mean to lie about it, but…this is not the city in which to tell people about that."

"I'd imagine not."

"It doesn't matter. The emperor has certain tastes when it comes to women, and few of them remain in the palace for longer than a week. I suppose that's what the empress demands from him. Either way, those who happen to be with child after their time with him are given a modest title and a few riches with which to raise the bastard. It's no surprise that my father's council wished to know where all the bastards were in the kingdom. I am not the only one who has tried to take an official position in the empire, but all the others failed."

"And now you know why," Skharr muttered from around what looked like a pastry with meat and cheese baked inside. "It would appear there are many who would prefer it that the line of succession remains as it is. You would introduce chaos into their ordered little world."

"Ordered is peaceful," Tryam said softly. "The empire has been at peace for longer than my lifetime. How many would die if I were to become emperor?"

"Peace under tyranny is no peace at all." The barbarian paused and studied his food before he took another bite. "But…I suppose I would say that given how I was raised."

"Your clans aren't those who would fall under the emperor's reign, I take it?"

"Those who lived in this region and had settled in the lowlands did fall—or at least aligned themselves with the civilizations that marched through. Those that made their living in the mountains, in the deserts, or in the woodlands were considerably more difficult to defeat, of course. Sending an army into the mountains would not be worth the mediocre return even if they were successful, so the smaller, wilder clans are allowed to remain free—for the moment."

The contender smiled and shook his head. "You make yourself out to be a simple creature, but your mind is considerably more intelligent than folk tend to assume."

"Their assumptions are my advantage. And in the end, I am a simple creature. I merely…understand certain things."

Tryam chuckled, but they were interrupted when someone tapped on their door. It was an announcement more than anything else as the young woman circled from behind the curtains that hung in front of the door and stepped inside.

"My lords," she said softly in a practiced, respectful fashion. "The queen has requested the pleasure of your presence as the sun rises. She will expect you to be properly prepared for the occasion as well."

"Both of us?" Skharr asked and tossed a piece of meat in his mouth.

"Why not both of us?" the prince countered.

"Well, I don't see why in all the hells a queen would want to have a word with the bodyguard when she has a prince to talk to."

"She has asked to see both lords who are enjoying the comforts of her home," the servant insisted. "Although it was the prince she insisted on speaking to personally."

"Maybe she merely wants to make sure a barbarian like you won't look for fights," Tryam commented.

"I would suggest taking a bath first," the warrior retorted. "No offense to the prince, but he does smell like he went rolling in pig shit."

"A bath will be prepared for him." The servant bowed and exited the room as quickly as she had arrived.

In minutes, a group swept through the servant's entrance. Two men carried a heavy bronze bath and four women brought buckets of steaming, scented water. One more held sponges and scrubs and other amenities that were required to bathe.

"In his room," Skharr instructed as Tryam rose from his seat, finished with his meal. "The prince requires privacy as he bathes."

The young man nodded. He was relieved as he preferred that but hadn't wanted to have to make a point of it. Perhaps the barbarian had no concept of modesty and it would be impolite to bring it up himself.

He returned to his room, where the bath was being prepared for him, and thanked the servants when they left the chamber quickly and closed the doors behind them.

Despite the temptation to linger, he restricted himself to a hasty scrub—he did not want to keep the queen waiting, after all. His clothes remained where they had been left and he dressed hurriedly but paused before he strapped his sword to his hip.

Common sense insisted that there was no reason to not be careful in the palace. Intrigue and murder felt like they had dogged his heels all his life. Staying in the shadows had kept him safe from it, but as he entered the realm of royalty, there would be no more hiding.

He moved toward the door, pushed it open, and strode out to where Skharr waited for him.

It was unsettling to see the barbarian as prepared for battle as he was. Chain mail over a gambeson covered his chest, with steel pauldrons fitted to his shoulders. It was expert handiwork, every inch of it, from the helm fitted to his skull with a bull's head fitted on the brow to the steel-tipped boots.

He was still collecting his weapons when he saw Tryam staring.

"Are you ready to meet the queen?" the barbarian asked and slid his longsword over his shoulder.

The prince recalled a few other weapons being at the man's disposal when they had retrieved his horse and possessions from the inn, including a massive war bow and a pair of throwing axes, but he only carried the sword and a dagger this time. Perhaps he'd decided he would be able to deal with anything they encountered with the two and anything else would be considered insulting to the queen and her guard.

When he realized he was still staring, he looked away.

"Do you have something on your mind?" his large companion asked.

"A few things. I realized that you are what a barbarian knight would look like, I suppose. Although you would be among the first of your kind to be knighted. Do you think you'll be the first?"

"I doubt it. I've no desire to kneel for hours at a time while old men recite shit over my head."

"That is understandable. I did have to submit to the ceremony, although the recitation of the creed was considerably shorter than I thought it would be. I suppose they have gradually removed the requirements they know knights won't abide by. Still, a barbarian knight does have some appeal to it, wouldn't you agree?"

"Oddly, yes, it does roll off the tongue rather nicely." Skharr grinned and motioned for him to step out with him. They walked purposefully to where one of the staff waited for them to leave and the man led them toward the queen's quarters.

He could understand why they waited without needing to be asked. The palace was a damn maze, and Tryam was surprised that they didn't provide horses to navigate the miles and miles of hallways.

Thankfully, the walk from their quarters was not as long as he feared it would be, and a short while later, the servant gestured wordlessly for them to sit and wait while he entered a room through a side door.

"So," the prince muttered as they complied, "your Captain Ferat said you were knowledgeable with regard to dungeons. I suppose that means you have navigated a few in your adventures."

The warrior nodded, drew his sword from his back, and rested it across his lap. "That's fairly accurate."

"Will you force me to ask you outright to share a few tales about what we might expect?"

Skharr smirked. "I believe you just did. But the stories would be better told by those with…more imagination than I. In the end, all that can be said about those godsbedammed hell-spawned places is that I was glad to escape with my life."

"What about the first one you raided?"

"It wasn't particularly interesting. The dungeon had already been raided successfully and a group had been paid by a local lord to clear the place of anything distasteful. A fair number of creatures remained, but most of the treasures had been taken already.

"The second was a little more interesting. Myself and a group of…eight, if I recall correctly, entered a smaller one on a cliff next to the sea. The damn fortress was built into a rockface that was slowly being eroded. We encountered many more monsters there, including one that was a massive skeletal creature on a throne. It could not move an inch but fired blasts of flame from its eyes until we managed to crush the skull."

"I heard that story." Tryam tucked a few errant strands of hair behind his ear. "The Calos Dungeon, yes? That was cleared almost ten years ago now."

"Ten years sounds about right. I then avoided jobs that led us to dungeons after that until recently when I was handed a contract to clear one near the mountains in the north. A Lich inside attempted to raise a demon but lacked a body to house it in. He had to wait…well, the gods know how long until someone strolled in for him to use."

"How did you kill him?" A noblewoman with dark skin, long black hair, gray eyes, and a voluptuous figure hidden under silk robes asked the question.

The prince looked around and noticed that a few others had been attracted by the conversation.

Skharr shrugged casually. "Liches commit their life forces to a non-decaying body and thus enable themselves to live forever—or at least while the phylactery they store their life source in remains undamaged. It was a matter of letting him beat me until I found it and destroyed it."

"But what happened to the demon he summoned?" a lord asked.

"I…well, a group of thieves followed me and waited outside, hoping to slit my throat when I exited the dungeon. I led them in again and let them summon the demon, while I barely escaped." He lowered one of his pauldrons to reveal a bright red scar over his back that looked like it had only recently healed. "From what I was able to tell, summoning it without a Lich there to control it brought the whole mountain down. The demon is currently buried at the bottom of it, mostly powerless in a human body."

Tryam nodded. His own experience had been limited to his role as a squire in the battlefields and knightly tournaments in the arena, all of which had some rules that mostly prohibited certain forms of magic. Fighting in a dungeon would call for another set of skills entirely.

"Was that the most recent?" the prince asked.

"No. The…the last one was Ivehnshaw Tower."

"Oh…I heard there were three survivors this last time in. I suppose you were one of them?"

"Myself, a dwarf, and another mercenary. Almost three hundred went into the tower with us, and…well most of them died."

"Did you lose your memory of it?" the first noblewoman asked and leaned a little closer. "Like the others, I mean, or do you have tales of what you saw inside?"

Tryam thought that he could see a hint of annoyance in the barbarian's face as he shrugged non-committally.

"There were trials that needed to be passed," Skharr said finally. "Some required escaping impossible numbers of monsters and others killed us if we fell asleep in the wrong place. The worst, of course, were those that required us to cull our numbers. If I were to guess, those who claimed to forget simply did not want to discuss the murder of their fellow mercenaries on the whim of a dungeon."

That certainly sounded like something he would want to forget if he ever experienced it, although Tryam doubted that it would be something he would have to engage in on the Stygian Path. He had been sent with a group of guards, and those likely would not be required to kill each other.

"Well," the noblewoman said as she stood from her seat across from Skharr, "if you ever have a mind to share more of those stories—preferably at night—you will find a generous payment in exchange."

"How generous?" the barbarian asked.

"That is always negotiable."

The woman moved away, knowing both men watched her as she did so, and the prince shook his head.

"Does that happen often?" he asked, still studying the noble-woman as she glided down the hall with a few servants rushing behind her.

"More often than you might think," his companion answered. "Mostly with nobility, however."

Tryam nodded and leaned back in his seat. "If I had known that dungeon stories were what made women excited, I would have started this a great deal earlier."

The side door opened and the servant stepped out and bowed politely. "Her Majesty, Queen Reya'Ipare, will see you now. Please follow me."

Things had not gone their way. Ingold was unsure of what they would do next, and he could tell that his indecision was telling on his men.

They had barely been able to collect their belongings before they were removed from the palace. Finding a place to house all eighteen had proven to be impossible, which left them with no other option but to pitch their tents outside the walls.

It was an uncomfortable situation, of course, and he knew their morale was drooping.

"We should have killed the godsbedammed brat right there," one of the men stated and took a bite of a strip of dried beef. "Gutted the snot-nosed pretender in front of the queen. Or better, fucking killed him on the journey here."

"You're a godsbedammed maggot-brained fucking idiot," another interjected. "The point of having him murdered here was so there would be people to blame if those who are backing the brat want to lash out. The political idealists with carrots up their fucking asses are the kind that want him on the throne, and we needed to make sure their ire was turned on the rulers of this fucking city when their little pet was slaughtered."

The other Elites either nodded in agreement or shook their heads, and Ingold sighed when the group started to argue the benefits and disadvantages of killing the prince before they were removed from the palace.

"Enough," he ordered finally, his tone impatient. "You're all half-brained idiots, and I cannot believe that I must explain it to you."

They fell silent and turned to look at him.

"You act as though we've failed in our mission, but have you forgotten where your allegiance lies?" He stood and fixed the group with a scowl. "Even if our first attempt failed, our allegiance to the empire does not falter. The contender is still alive and still on his quest. We will follow him to the Path and kill him on the way. Failing that, he will either die in the dungeon or we will kill him once he returns. Now, stop arguing like children and think about how we can succeed in that."

His group exchanged glances and nodded slowly. They were still soldiers of the empire, the best of the best, and he knew that all it would take was a nudge from him to return them to the discipline that put them leagues above the rest.

CHAPTER NINE

They had been brought to what must surely be the queen's personal quarters, and a steady stream of serving staff moved in and out to prepare refreshments while others cleaned. It appeared that they were not the queen's first meeting for the day, as a few groups of nobles now emerged from the room hidden behind heavy drapes.

Before the two companions could approach, one of the guards stepped in front of the giant.

"I cannot allow you before the queen so armed, barbarian," the man told him gruffly.

"I am armed as well," Tryam pointed out and tapped his sword.

"You are royalty and I cannot disarm you, just as I cannot disarm my queen. Your guard must turn his weapons over or wait here for your return."

Skharr shrugged. "I'll wait here. Guards are allowed to partake in the refreshments, yes?"

The man had no answer to that, and the prince simply smiled as he continued despite the irritation of having to step around the nobility who almost didn't notice his presence.

A servant drew the drapes back for him to walk through and revealed an office, with the queen seated behind a massive mahogany desk. Hundreds of sheaves of paper and scrolls were spread on the surface and a couple of servants constantly arranged them so she could read through each one and sign it.

The chamber was enormous, with collections of seats in various positions and even a few on a balcony shielded by umbrellas and a handful of growing trees.

Tryam cleared his throat, and one of the servants leaned closer to whisper in the queen's ear.

She looked up, a hint of surprise on her face as she stood from her desk.

"Make sure those papers are delivered to every captain of the city guard before nightfall," she said and one of the young women bowed deeply and collected one of the piles as the royal came around the desk to greet him. "My apologies. We've had issues with prisoners being brought into the city and not turned over to the city guard, so some alterations need to be made. The guilds in this city are most useful but a little too independent for my tastes."

Tryam merely nodded as she motioned for him to follow her to the seats on the balcony.

Surprisingly, a light breeze drifted across the open space that kept it cool despite the blazing sun.

"Now," she said and gestured for him to sit as she did the same. "I feel we need to talk about what happened yesterday. I'll need the details, of course, to ensure that there are no misunderstandings. Would you like a drink?"

He doubted that she would have put her busy day on pause simply to confirm something that she already knew, but he was more than willing to play along.

"As you know, I took two of my guards with me into the city for some exploration. We entered an inn, the name of which escapes me at the moment. I was there for only a few minutes when an assassin tried to stab me in the back and he was stopped by Skharr."

"Yes, I remember the giant of a barbarian. Why did he not come in with you?"

"Your guards said he would not be allowed in your presence while armed, and he elected to wait for me outside."

Reya nodded slowly and sipped from her goblet. "Well, so much the better. I would feel uncomfortable talking about him in his presence. He saved your life, then?"

"And the guards attacked him for it. He handled them effortlessly—"

"Both of them?"

"Yes."

"On his own."

"I think he genuinely enjoyed the opportunity."

She nodded, impressed. "I see. And you questioned the guards—"

"He did but I was present for it. They admitted that they were given the task of ending my life, although they refused to say who had given them the order before we turned them over to your city guard."

"Well then, it would appear that you have placed your trust in the barbarian. It is a little odd to hear myself say this but in the end, there must be a few exceptions to the rule."

Tryam shrugged casually. "And in the end, he could prove more than useful."

"He did deal handily with two of the Emperor's Elites. I would have paid to watch that."

"Well yes, of course. But he also has some experience with dungeons—two of them quite recently from the sound of it."

"That would be rather useful on the Stygian Path. Are there any I might have heard of or merely the smaller ones on the edges of the continent?"

"One of them was the Tower of Ivehnshaw. He was one of the three most recent survivors of that particular dungeon."

"Oh. He would be the Barbarian of Theros, then. I have heard of him. In that case, yes, he would most definitely be of use to you. A few have tried to make a name for themselves through the years and none have returned, even from dungeons not quite as famed as the tower. Still, I suppose it is not that surprising."

Tryam narrowed his eyes and selected a grape from a cluster that had been placed nearby. "How do you mean?"

"I would wager that so many know about the Tower because of the survivors, who claim there is more coin to be gained."

"I suppose that makes sense," he muttered. "In the end, however, escaping the dungeon with my life is not what the trial is about. I've heard it dozens of times and I still cannot recite the name of the test from memory."

"E'Kruleth Damari," Reya reminded him. "It is an elvish dialect since your father claims that his line runs to the high elves who originally inhabited his lands. If I remember correctly, it means 'The Recovery of that Which is Lost.'"

"There is so much lost in those dungeons," he pointed out dryly. "I don't suppose you would know if it means anything specific?"

She shook her head. "Honestly, imperial traditions are something of a mystery to me. I would suggest that it might have something to do with the fact that your father might invent these so-called traditions as needed."

He narrowed his eyes, although a small smile touched his lips despite his best intentions. "Are you telling me these long-standing traditions of the proud empire are not, in fact, long-standing?"

"I can't speak for the traditions of a foreign country." She smirked, removed her crown, and placed it on a nearby cushion and allowed one of the servants to take it. With a small sigh, she freed her hair and let the curls tumble over her shoulders. "But yes, that is precisely what I am saying."

The contender laughed. "Well, I suppose that is in keeping with everything I know about the man."

"What do you know about him?"

"Mostly the rumors." Tryam shook his head. "He was a legendary fighter in his prime, which is long past. These days, he spends all his days being waited on hand, foot, and…in other places by the beautiful women collected from the empire's provinces for precisely that purpose. I don't know if he is capable of creating any more heirs, but in the end, I don't think any would care if he was. Too many vultures are circling in wait for the moment when he finally passes away. Most of them already have their minds set on who they want on the throne and what they want that person to do for them."

"I suppose that is the same whenever there is a position of power that needs to be filled. I remember how many pressed for my mother to abdicate, hoping that I would give them something for trying to push me onto the throne. In the end, when they don't get what they want, they feel betrayed and lash out."

"How do they lash out?"

"You've already experienced the most openly aggressive type of attack. A dagger in the back does tell you definitively that you are not wanted."

"How many attempts have you survived?"

She tilted her head and stared at the tree that shaded them from the sun. "I lost count after the tenth. In the end, it benefits you to be on good terms with those who are guarding you. They react faster and put more effort into keeping you alive."

Tryam sighed. "I still have not been named heir. First, I have to find something in the dungeon that will remove these marks from my chest to confirm that I have passed the test."

She shrugged with apparent unconcern. "Even so, it cannot hurt to be prepared for success, yes?"

"In the event of success, I will consider that there will be others who want to take my life before I return to the capital. Hells, when I think about it, many might want to kill me before I even leave the city if they believe I'll survive the dungeon."

The queen drew a deep breath and sipped her drink again. "Well, I could give you authorization to leave the city before the gates are open. There are a few egress ports my guards can lead you to. It would give you a head start on any who might mean you harm."

It was an interesting offer, and Tryam nodded slowly. "Well… that would be appreciated. But I must wonder what you hope to gain from me with all this support?"

"I would simply say it would be in my best interest to be on good terms with the man who might be emperor over my kingdom in the future. And I would hope that you remember those who helped you."

"So, you do have ulterior motives."

"More than a few, but we should discuss those when you return from the dungeon—alive and well, and with a few tales of your own."

The young prince pushed from his seat and smiled as she did the same. "If I felt optimistic about my chances, I would say this could be the beginning of a very interesting friendship."

She mirrored his smile as he extended his hand and she took it warmly with both of hers. "I would be happy to consider you my friend, Tryam. And you should know that I do hope you succeed. While I cannot extend aid that might be construed as acting against the interests of the emperor—or might cast your final success into debate with accusations of cheating—I assure you that the empire would be so much better under your rule."

"There are those who suspect I would bring an end to the peace that has been maintained over the decades."

"I doubt it. You are a soldier or have been in the past. You, above all others, would know about the horrors of war and would avoid engaging in it on a whim. Too many view it with the rose-colored pince-nez of glory and honor and all the other words used to euphemize it. In the end, you have the potential to be better than your father, unlike your brother who is being groomed for the position now. Even if he does not send his armies, he will send his assassins."

"It is all I hope for. And thank you again for all your help. It will not be forgotten."

"Is she truly helping you?"

Tryam nodded.

"Out of the kindness of her heart?"

"I doubt it. She has her motives, but… Well, I feel as though she honestly wants what is best for her people and in the end, if I were emperor, they would be my people as well, yes?"

Skharr nodded and nibbled the smoked ribs that had been provided to them as their midday meal. "Well, I suppose so but as emperor, you would have to consider that all the people are yours."

After a few moments of inspecting a steaming plate of something that smelled of herbs, the young contender finally laughed. While he knew it would taste amazing, he wasn't quite ready to test for himself,. "I just realized that I don't know anything about ruling an empire. What in all the hells do I know about what that would require?"

The barbarian had a rib in his mouth, and he bit into the meat and pulled it off the bone before he answered. "Well, here is your first lesson—let others do most of the work for you. You'll not have much of a problem with people doubting your capabilities if you can blame all your failures on others."

Tryam laughed. "Is that how you would run an empire?"

"I would be a terrible emperor. I would want nothing to do with any of the work."

"But you just said—"

"I said most of the work. There is much that can take place as publicly as possible, and you need to make sure folk see you doing those things."

"But make sure the people see me performing some of the actions and let others do most of the work."

"They are the ones who know how to run an empire. For instance, you would not interfere with the queen here and how she rules her people."

"They would be my people as well, yes?" Tryam asked.

"Well, yes, but you would be a distant ruler, not one the people know much of at all. You would be who she turns to when she has troubles but you would let her rule uninterrupted since she knows how to rule this city. You will learn a great deal but in the end, you will have to trust the members of your counsel to help you."

"Would you accept if I offered you an appointment on my council?"

Skharr shook his head vehemently. "I would be terrible at that as well."

"Why?"

"I would still turn all the work over to others. You would be better off letting the others have the honor of serving you directly."

"But what would you do with your life?"

"Fuck noblewomen. Fight monsters. End up with a dagger in my back. Oh, no…wait, that last one would be you, wouldn't it?"

The prince laughed and threw his spoon across the table at his companion, who ducked under it.

As the laughter subsided, his mind wandered to the matter of what he was attempting. Until now, he'd simply been a man with a minor title and a father who couldn't have cared less about him until he was finally confirmed to be his child.

There was much to consider with regard to how he had come thus far, but he would be better off if he put those thoughts aside. He still needed to succeed.

"I'll need your help on the Stygian Path," Tryam said finally and toyed with the food in front of him. "I can fight. I've fought since I was a child, but there are things that no training in the world can prepare a man for. I'll feel better about my chances knowing you are at my side."

"Of course," Skharr muttered, his focus seemingly still on the ribs. "I always assumed you wanted my protection for the dungeon as well."

"I did not want to assume. I think some guards might escort me to the dungeon and wait outside, assuming I would have to perform the task on my own. I think that is what the Elites were to do."

"If they did not kill you before you arrived," the barbarian pointed out. "I could wait outside if you wanted me to. The glory would belong to you and only you."

"I'd prefer to share the glory and survive, thank you."

"You'll need proper weapons and armor as well if you plan to walk away with all your limbs intact."

"I do have armor. And weapons."

"Not enough. And you'll need something a great deal more effective against monsters that allows you to keep your distance while still killing the everlasting fucking dungeon-crawlers."

"I cannot shoot a bow."

"A spear, then. Very little training is needed—if you're not fighting men with shields, at least. There will be a good selection for you to choose from. You won't need to pay a princely sum but the city's blacksmiths will have good armor, and you'll find what you need and for a decent price. You'll also want to talk to a mage about some charms that will protect you from being torn to pieces by the first magical being you come across."

"I thought barbarians like you didn't believe much in magic."

Skharr shook his head. "And yet, in the end, when you find yourself against monsters that have no such qualms, you will want to have something to fight back with."

"I understand that." Tryam retrieved his spoon, wiped it on his sleeve, and took another mouthful of his food before tapped the utensil thoughtfully on the table. "Do you have any suggestions of where we could find such helpful items?"

"Given that I haven't been in this city long, only one comes to mind."

"The Guild Hall?"

"Can you think of a better place to buy items to equip mercenaries than where those mercenaries come together? If we cannot find anything there, we might be able to speak to a few people who would be able to point us in the right direction."

"We could ask the guards here. They would know where to buy weapons and armor, yes?"

"As they do not buy their own, perhaps not. But they are fighters so it might be a good place to start."

"Admit it."

Skharr scowled but he finally released a resigned sigh. "You need to hear me say it aloud, don't you?"

The boy laughed. "You cannot deny me your admission. You are so knowledgeable about how the world works and yet you neglected to even consider that the guards of the queen's palace would know the best place to find information on where to look in the city for those items we'll need for a quest into a dungeon. They even knew the best place to find food prepared for a long trip."

He did have a point, and the barbarian raised his hands in surrender. "Very well, you had a good idea and we did save time and coin with that idea. I'll concede that. Now, if you will, consider finding yourself some rest before we start tomorrow."

"We'll leave early," Tryam reminded him. "The queen will permit us to exit the city through the little-used gates unknown to the public before anyone else would be able to follow us."

"I know, which is why I suggest you sleep early and well. For all the purchases from the mages, you'd think they would come up with one where sleep is not required. But no, all they offered was equipment that helps when attacking a Lich-filled dungeon —the kind that would make a man stupid enough to seek riches instead of a bed with the warmth of a woman in it."

The contender nodded at that. "I suppose that should come later. And who knows? Maybe one day, I'll have both riches and a warm bed with a woman in it."

"For now, a cold bed will have to do," Skharr retorted and gestured for him to return to his room. "I'll wake you when the time comes."

CHAPTER TEN

A sickening chill lingered in the air.

Or maybe it simply felt unpleasant because it was early in the morning. He was not against the kind of discipline that required folk to rise before the sun, but he still detested it. He preferred to spend his time awake throughout the night and sleep through most of the morning.

But in the end, his life depended on it. The prince wasn't sure why Skharr had elected to join him in his fight and while he appreciated the man's support, there was no reason for it. He seemed to simply be a barbarian who was bored with his life and entered into any fight he encountered on his journeys.

"Why are you here?" Tryam asked as they rode under the escort of the queen's personal guard.

"Well, because you have eighteen Imperial Elites who desire to murder you and we need to leave the city early to evade them and avoid any trap they might try to set."

"No, I mean you. Folk of your…particular tendencies generally remain on the other side of the mountains and fight in the wars that rage continually beyond the empire's influence."

"What tendencies do you think I have?"

"A bloodlust, for one. You enjoy the heat of battle, combat, and blood rushing over your blade after you've spilled it from some other poor sod. You'll find no shortage of that outside the empire. They'd throw you castles, women, and power or anything else you want if you fight the way you did here."

An odd expression crossed the man's face, visible in the torchlight, and he immediately regretted the question.

"I know I shouldn't pry," he admitted and nudged his horse forward. "Although I suppose there's nothing else to do while we ride to the gate. Or, rather, I ride and you walk. What is the point of having a horse if you won't ride it?"

"You don't ride your brothers."

"The horse…is your brother?"

"Not by blood."

The fact that the barbarian felt the need to clarify that made Tryam smile.

"There are wars I could be fighting," Skharr said finally. "But rules change when we fight wars—rules that cannot be replaced when they are broken. It pulls out the worst in all creatures, and…well, when you fight wars against mages, the worst can be appalling."

The young prince nodded as they approached the gates. The streets were still empty, which made moving through them a great deal easier, and the guards held their formation. They looked around constantly to ensure that there weren't any assassins stationed in the windows above them, who could make a world of difference with a single crossbow bolt.

There were none, fortunately, and they reached the walls without hindrance, where a handful of guards were already waiting. The group leaned against nearby posts and yawned so widely that it seemed their jaws would come unhinged.

"Are these the fuckers?" one of them muttered. "Maybe the giant, but the ponce riding the horse looks like he should be holding fast to his mother's skirts."

"The ponce can hear you," Tryam retorted.

"Oh...sorry, milord."

Skharr smirked. "No, don't apologize. You clearly meant it, and there is no need for pretenses simply because the fucker who put a baby in his mother happened to be a little richer than most other people."

The prince narrowed his eyes. There was no point in forcing a conflict. The men would find themselves in too much trouble as it was, and he didn't need to make anything of it, especially since they wouldn't be there long enough to see it through.

"To the gate," one of the guards instructed and motioned for them to follow him. Tunnels ran through the walls and led underground. This one was large enough for a horse to move through but not a man mounted on a horse. Tryam dismounted and approached on foot.

The guards pushed one of the gates open. It was well-hidden in the wall and positioned in such a way that it would be impossible to access by an attacking army from the outside.

Their horses were allowed out first, followed by the two men.

"Good luck on your quest, Prince Tryam," the captain called as they drew the gate closed again.

He nodded and made sure that the packhorse followed his closely. Skharr studied the barrier as it closed into the wall.

"It disappeared," the barbarian stated with surprise. "It must be magic."

"Or clever engineering. I've seen what clever men can do with their hands and their minds and in the end, some powers out there are not only magical in nature."

His companion nodded and patted his horse on the neck. "Well then, I propose we leave here before whatever lead we may have gained on your would-be assassins evaporates while we chew the fat all fucking day long."

"Are you sure you will be able to keep up with me on foot?"

Tryam asked as they began to move toward the road. "Especially when the sun comes up when you'll no doubt long for some rest."

"I'll tell you what," Skharr responded with a neutral expression. "The moment I feel too tired to walk, I'll mount up on Horse and we'll continue on our merry way."

"On...the horse?"

"Yes, on Horse."

"Why haven't you given your horse a name? All horses are deserving of an honorable, kingly name."

"I have. Horse."

Tryam narrowed his eyes. "You named your horse...Horse?"

"Horse is a kingly name. Any horse is more worthy of a crown than any man I've ever met, which makes Horse kinglier a name than...any, I suppose."

The contender tilted his head and allowed his mount to proceed at a leisurely pace. "Well, I called my horse Yulroy. My mother said that was her father's name, and he was a famed warrior and a hero among her people. She never told me what made him a hero, but I've named all my horses after him—although, I've only had two and they were both stallions."

"What would you call a mare if you had one?"

"What would you?"

"Horse. Genitals don't change the nobility of the beast."

The horse snorted.

"Of course, he might think differently," the giant continued. "He gave up on a life of siring colts and eating apples to join me on this ridiculous path of mine."

"What?"

Skharr patted the stallion and scratched his forehead. "I left him on a farm near Verenvan, where he should have spent his days wandering fields, eating, and fucking, but he escaped and found his way to where we were two days later."

After a few moments, Tryam laughed. "Well, to answer your question, I would name my first mare Kalasha—my mother's name. If there was ever a queen in the world who never got to wear her crown, it was her."

"Kalasha. It's a beautiful name."

"I like to think so."

The warrior patted Horse on the neck again. "Come on then, little one. I'll show you why DeathEaters don't need to ride horses to travel the world."

He broke into a run and the beast trotted behind him. The prince chuckled and nudged his mount into a trot to keep pace with him. He anticipated that his companion would soon slow his pace to enable him to rest somewhat.

It wasn't long before the sun appeared on the horizon and began to climb to blaze on the landscape with unforgiving ferocity. And yet the barbarian continued. Tryam's horse started to sweat and pant under him, and the packhorse fared no better.

Skharr sweated and was breathing hard, but he continued regardless. He did not wear any armor and most of the weight he would have carried was on Horse's back, but he ran like he couldn't feel the heat of the sun or any kind of strain in his limbs.

Finally, when a good few hours had passed, they had little choice but to call a halt.

"We need to rest the horses," Tryam said firmly. "I don't know how it is possible for you to push on in these conditions, but the horses can't continue to move in this heat without a rest. It might kill them."

The barbarian nodded in agreement, leaned on his knees, and sucked in deep breaths before he took the water skin from his pouch and drank thirstily from it. He poured from another skin into a small bucket and held it under Horse's head to allow the beast to drink.

"Honestly," the contender muttered as he dismounted and offered his mount water as well. "Do you have any non-human blood in you? Well, your size would indicate that, of course, but what exactly are you? You are beyond even the extremes of simple mortality."

The giant chuckled and patted Horse gently. "I am a DeathEater. That should explain anything else you might want to know."

"Are you saying that all DeathEaters share your strength and stamina?"

"Most but not all. A few of my kin are a little too lazy, although those inevitably die young and fail to make much of themselves. Or they leave and join merchant caravans and live off the notoriety that other DeathEaters have earned. It is not uncommon, unfortunately, although they would never dare to show their faces among The Clan again. Still, they would be able to make a short living for themselves until someone with skill comes along and tests their purported strength."

"I take it you have done your fair share of testing those who would claim to be strong in your presence?"

Skharr shrugged. "If I did, it would only be when they deserved it. A handful of thieving pilgrims are a favored test of my strength."

Tryam stretched slowly and relaxed a little when some energy returned to his limbs. "Come on, then. We need to keep moving. The maps tell of a small settlement near a well where we can replenish our water supplies. From there, it should be a short march until nightfall, and thereafter, we should be able to leave this fucking desert easily enough."

His companion nodded and rolled his shoulders. "Very well. After you, princeling."

"I think I should have kept my identity hidden from you."

"Aye, but then there would be no trust between us. Do you want to head into a dungeon with a man you cannot fully trust?"

"That's a fair point," Tryam conceded, mounted up again, and clicked his tongue to get the horses moving.

They would continue to test a DeathEater's stamina in the desert.

"Up, you vermin-crusted dung piles, before I burn this whole fucking camp to the ground with you maggot-brained idiots in it!"

His voice rang over their camp and well beyond. It bounced back from the walls nearby as if to emphasize that his mood was more than a little murderous.

The Elites scrambled to their feet and drew their weapons, ready for combat, and Ingold contemplated giving them their wish. It was about time they were yanked from the comfort he had allowed them.

"Come on, then!" he snapped and looked at each one in turn. "Would any of you like to question why your captain is berating you this early in the morning, or will you simply stand and stare at me like your minds have turned to mush?"

"What happened?" one of them asked finally.

"Word has come from the palace," he stated belligerently. "Our quarry escaped us during the night. The prince and his barbarian bodyguard slipped away in the darkness and are gone from the city, which leaves us with fucking godsbedammed nothing. How do you feel about those who thought we would not need to leave someone to watch the gate?"

"It is unlike him to slip away like that," one of the guards muttered. "He has...well, nothing in him that would suggest it. Certainly no sense of the intrigue that follows him."

"I thought the same, but he is not alone now, is he?" Ingold moved past them to retrieve a water skin and poured some into his mouth. "That barbarian has changed everything about what we can expect from him, and we need to account for that in our plans. The pathetic little pup will not make it far, of course, but we are already hours behind. Pack the camp up and be ready to move before the hour is out or I will burn it to the ground—with you in it, as promised."

The men responded immediately, used to such threats. They were not necessarily empty, but their leader knew there would be no need to act on it. Each would do as they were ordered without delay, and they would be ready to start tracking the boy.

It helped that they already knew where he was going, but in the end, losing him for so much as a day could lead to things ending badly for all of them. Failure would not be received well by those who had set them this task.

The roads were far behind them. Some still led to where they were going, of course, but there was no point in following them.

All it would do, Skharr had pointed out, was make it easier for them to be found.

Traveling beyond the known routes made them a little slower but they cut across terrain that was circled by those same roads. It was not too difficult to navigate in the desert, not with the sun and the stars to tell them where they were at all times.

Tryam forced himself not to drink from his water skin too often. They had stopped to refill all of them but even so, in the heat and dry air, it was difficult to not indulge the desire for water too often.

A few sips here and there were all he would allow himself. It appeared to be what Skharr limited himself to as well, and even the warrior's stamina had begun to falter. He had slowed their pace almost to a walk.

Still, the maps said they had made good time. They could afford to let themselves rest a little, especially as night had begun to fall.

Without so much as saying a word, the barbarian brought their little convoy to a halt and after a few moments during which they studied the ground around them, the two companions both opened their packs. The sun was already coloring the sky a bright red instead of blue, which meant they would have to endure the icy evening out in the open.

In all honesty, Tryam was a little surprised that Skharr allowed them to halt. He had suspected that he would make them travel through the night.

He complied without question, however, stepped down from his saddle, and took most of the weight off the packhorse's back so both animals could rest with their feed bags.

The barbarian was not ready to stop, however. He had begun to strap his armor on, as ridiculous as it seemed.

"What are you doing?" Tryam asked and finally broke the silence between them.

"I…well, I have an instructor teaching me how to fight with the sword, and she said I need to train every day. I usually give myself the time in the morning, but as we were a little too busy to do anything earlier, I'll have to train now. Would you like to join me?"

Dumbfounded, the prince stared at him. He couldn't understand how the man could run all day and still have the energy to train—and in full armor, no less.

Still, he was surprisingly reluctant to let himself be outperformed by the warrior. Tryam had spent most of the day in the saddle and spending some time encouraging the blood to flow did have a certain appeal to it.

He put his armor on quickly as he watched Skharr remove the sword from his pack instead of the bow or the axes.

"Why do you need to train, though?" Tryam drew his sword clear and flicked it from side to side to loosen his wrists. "You are something of a veteran yourself, so I'd imagine that the training you would have needed would be in the past."

"I was never much good with the sword," his large companion explained. "I always preferred an ax or failing that, a hammer. I decided it was time to change that and my instructor agreed."

He assumed a high guard and moved slowly through a variety

of striking motions in which the blade sliced powerfully from almost every angle.

The prince recalled the training he had undergone. The eagle guard was a good start and he imitated the motions. His body began to relax a little more with the different activities.

It felt like warming himself up, and he was interested to see that Skharr showed considerably more proficiency with the sword than he had seen in many soldiers.

Then again, most soldiers' training consisted of how to lower their pikes and step on the end.

After a few minutes of these maneuvers, Tryam stopped and rolled his shoulders. "How would you like to spar a little now that we're good and ready for a fight?"

The barbarian nodded, circled, and assumed the same high guard as he had before once he'd fitted his scabbard over the sword to prevent the edge from cutting. The young man did the same and mirrored his pose, realizing for what felt like the first time exactly how massive his sparring partner was.

His opponent moved forward first and his blade arced downward. The prince stepped out of the way and tried to push the blade to the side while he attempted to launch a counterattack on Skharr's exposed flank.

But the giant had already moved and Tryam had only a moment in which to register that his adversary now stood in a slightly angled position before the barbarian's blade slid behind him and hooked into the back of his knee. It broke his balance and thoroughly removed it when the sheathed weapon hammered him in the face.

And what was worse was that he could sense that the man held his strikes in check as well.

The hard landing knocked the breath out of him and he sprawled on his back and scowled when the sword pressed against his neck.

"I thought you said you weren't much good with a sword,"

Tryam muttered and accepted the man's offer to haul him to his feet.

"I wasn't," Skharr admitted. "I did have a little instruction from the best, however."

"Captain Ferat?"

"The very same. She is a blademaster and one of the finest fighters I've ever seen. I am not ashamed to admit that she inflicted more than a few bruises while instructing me."

"I might consider having her for a trainer instead of you."

"That would be recommended but until then, I will have to do."

The young prince raised his sword into the ready position. "You should not sell yourself short. How did you do that—hit me in the back of the leg and the head in the same motion?"

"It is simple but it requires some practice." Skharr swung and let him watch, then stepped to the side as he swept the sword up and tapped the back of Tryam's leg where he had struck harder the last time. From there, he continued the swing for the strike to the head.

"I'll have to remember that," the boy muttered.

"But you have some skill of your own with the sword, yes?" the barbarian asked as they continued to spar. "Some training?"

"Yes, but not quite what you would expect. I joined my father's military when I was fourteen years of age but only as a squire, and I fought with them in a couple of campaigns until I was seventeen. From there, I stepped into the Imperial Arena and fought there for three years, winning the gold every year. I was far more athletic in those days."

"An arena?"

"Yes…" He paused as he moved quickly to avoid a blow to the side of the head, but a thrust caught him in the gut instead. "The exhibition fights and blood sports are the most popular, but I fought only in the Emperor's Tournament not the Championship where you face a single opponent and there are much stricter rules. No killing is one, although wounding is allowed. In the end, my victories had—fuck!'

Skharr laughed as he upended the young contender again. "You'll have to remember that you are fighting with more than only your sword. A swift kick to your opponent's knees will end the fight as surely as a slash to the throat."

"And you chose to kick the legs out from under me," Tryam grumbled. "It's appreciated, although you'll have to teach me that as well."

"Gladly. But you were telling me what happened to you after your third win in the arena."

He pushed to his feet and brushed the dust from his armor. "By my third year of winning the gold—which means the third consecutive year with the most victories over the other aspiring knights—many said I was the true heir to my father's empire."

"I assume they wanted you to remember their calls for your ascension to your father's throne."

"Indeed. A year passed of learning to act the part and the noble arts of persuasion and asskissery."

"Ass…"

"Asskissery."

Skharr nodded. "Well, I've never heard it called that before."

The young prince laughed. "Nobility is more the art of asskissery and defending against those who kiss one's ass more skillfully than you do. I suppose that should I become emperor, I'll have to deal with it a little less. However, a rather large amount of bending over and allowing them to pucker up is required."

"That is a…vivid mental image." The barbarian winced and shook his head. "I believe I'd rather negotiate with steel."

He sighed. "Yes, I have to admit that the taste of ass in the morning is rather awful. The shit one has to suffer through to run a kingdom peacefully does make a ruler understand the temptation of simply killing those who displease you."

His companion paused and sipped from his water skin. "Well, yes, but in the end, you are reminded that as emperor, your subjects far outnumber you."

It was a good point, and Tryam took a moment to drink a little water as well. "Don't think your games fool me at all, barbarian. You may be one of the best at violent ventures and a barbarian by birth, but my eyes tell me you are dangerous in more than one way. I've seen you speak like a clumsy oaf around some, and then like a learned man around others. Your crafty nature has not escaped me, and I've noticed how you see when others react. If I had you as a mentor, I feel my life would be different."

"I agree." Skharr nodded and his gaze shifted to the darkening desert around them. "You would not have decided to try for your father's throne, for one thing. Now, I would pull the scabbard off your sword if I were you."

The contender looked at him in surprise. "Why? Do you honestly think I would want to risk injuring you in training, even if by accident?"

"No, but the other sneak-assed fuckers you will want to injure intentionally are approaching."

CHAPTER ELEVEN

I t felt impossible. This could not be happening to them, not now. He chafed under the need to start moving again, but everything in the city seemed determined to push him toward insanity born of frustration.

The guards had delayed what seemed like the whole city, and he had a feeling that they enjoyed the work.

Ingold drew a deep breath and sensed that his nervous nature had begun to tell on the horses. It had been a mistake to return to the city to procure what they needed for the journey, but none of his group were willing to risk entering the desert without the proper supplies. He would not have allowed his men into battle with empty bellies and dry mouths.

But as he watched the sun begin its descent in the western half of the sky, he could not ignore the fact that they had yet to leave the infernal godsbedammed fucking city.

For some inexplicable reason, the guards delayed those who tried to leave, and it had slowed movement to a crawl when the narrow streets were forced to accommodate the overflow of caravans and convoys that were now stuck.

Somehow, he had allowed his men to be caught in the middle of it.

The heat was more than unbearable and the crush of people who were caught up in the mess the streets had become made this one of the worst situations in his life.

He would have preferred to fight a battle in the deep of winter than to be caught doing nothing in the middle of a city he desperately wanted to leave.

"I don't suppose we would be able to cut and hack a path out of this fucking place," one of his guards grumbled under her breath. "That would clear the streets rather quickly, wouldn't you say?"

"These are all citizens of the empire," another one reminded her. "Do you think the emperor would approve of his Elites cutting down innocent citizens?"

"He would allow it if he knew these people were interfering with imperial business," the first guard noted. "If they kept his Elites from their sworn duty, he would understand and even approve. These people stand in the way of the empire functioning as it should."

"This isn't in the name of the emperor and you know it," her comrade retorted

"Even if the emperor does not know what we are doing, we are doing it for his benefit and for that of the empire. Do you honestly think anyone would mind if we push forcibly through the streets? And it would not even result in too many deaths—or any deaths, for that matter. A few of them would be wounded and the rest would run away from us so quickly that we wouldn't even need to hurt them."

His men had returned to that particular debate numerous times while they inched toward the gate, and Ingold could not bring himself to silence them. He knew they were wrong to even think it and would not act without his orders, but he was also aware that the same thought had run through his mind at almost every minute as they made their infuriatingly slow progress.

Thankfully, they finally moved under the shade of the gate and he realized that the guards were thoroughly searching any who tried to leave the city under their watch. It was a slow, meticulous process, and they went about it with bored precision like they had been doing it all day.

Which, he supposed, they had. There were too many people in this city and a quick culling was usually the best way around that. It had been conquered without many of the population dying during the process. As a result, a large number had survived and the city simply continued to grow.

"What are you holding us up for?" Ingold asked once the guards finally approached them. "We are here on imperial business, and this delay has impeded us from enacting the orders of the emperor himself."

"The emperor himself, yes?" one of the guards asked. "I thought you were the group who camped outside the city because the prince you were sent to guard no longer trusts you to protect him."

The man's comrades snickered, and Ingold scowled when a few of his men grumbled audibly.

He held his hand up to stop them from replying. "As we are no longer required, the emperor orders that we return to the capital. Will you prevent the orders from being carried out?"

The guards exchanged a look, and he finally understood what was afoot. The queen had most likely helped the boy leave the city and was intentionally delaying them. The woman must believe that they intended to pursue him.

She was craftier than he would have given her credit for and it had cost them most of the day. A word from him to the viceroy would see her pay for her actions but for the moment, they needed to play the part of dutiful servants of the empire.

"Unfortunately, there has been a spree of robberies in the city

—rather concerning, you understand," the captain of the guards stated and folded his arms. "The thieves have not been caught, and we are searching all those leaving the city to ensure they are not attempting to escape."

"We, as members of the Emperor's Elite, should not be required to undergo such a search," one of Ingold's guards muttered.

"Unfortunately, there cannot be a show of favoritism, even for those who are...ahem, working under orders from the emperor." The city guards exchanged another look between them. "I am afraid you will have to submit to a search exactly like the rest."

Ingold drew a deep breath before he dismounted from his horse, raised his arms, and shook his head. There was no time for them to fight through these guards, and it would cause too much trouble for the viceroy to explain it and help them. He had in the past, of course. The man had considerable influence over the empire, but there were limits to what he was capable of in the end.

"We will need to search all your men as well." The captain motioned for the group to dismount, and the Elite captain nodded.

He could picture himself slitting the man's throat and it wouldn't be while he slept. One of his idiosyncrasies was that he enjoyed watching the eyes of those he was killing. They would go from utter surprise—like they could not believe that their entire life had led to a single killing stroke—to blank acceptance. Sometimes, it would shift to pain, especially if he had taken them in the stomach so the moment would last longer.

Others simply fell dead or would clutch their wounds and curl into the fetal position.

The guard, he decided as he studied him, would squirm when he felt his guts pouring out. He would know why he was being killed, so there would be no confusion. The man would fully understand what was happening to him and why, and the realization would be the last thought to pass through his mind.

But regrettably, it would not happen today. Perhaps when they were on their own in the desert, where there would be no witnesses to say it wasn't a group of bandits. They infested the desert areas and the mountains as well, which made things difficult for those who lived there.

Even better, these bandits were well-known for actively pursuing patrols that were supposed to find and kill them. It would be perfect.

But for another time, he thought. There would be many opportunities for petty revenge in the future. For the moment, they needed to find the prince and end his life.

And the barbarian, he reminded himself. He doubted that the man would simply take some coin to look the other way and disappear into the mountains with the rest of his people.

And Ingold would enjoy that murder as well. He had a fair amount of retribution he needed to exact from him. He was not the type to forget the kind of injury he'd received. Punching him in front of his Elites would ensure the man a slow, painful end—and many of those would be found in the desert as well.

"You look like you intend to travel through the desert," the guard noted and motioned for the rest of the men to mount. "It is unfortunate that there are too many thieves among us, which is why you must understand why we are searching all who pass through our gates."

"And as you can see, we carry no stolen goods," Ingold stated coldly.

"But how can we know you've not got stolen goods in your things?"

"Are you accusing my men of thievery?"

"There are no accusations being leveled here. We're simply having a discussion, good Captain, guard to guard."

"Guard to guard?" Ingold asked and took a step forward. "We

will be on our way. You can hinder us if you so choose, or you can let us through. Be sure you make the correct choice."

The guard captain raised his hands and a smile played across his features. "Very well, carry on then. Be on your way and travel well. You never know what you will find standing in your way."

He forced a smile and swung onto his horse. Yes, his imagination elaborated as he settled in the saddle. A stab in the gut would do nicely, especially if he filled the wound with honey and left him out for the ants to consume. That would be how he killed the smug whorefucker.

CHAPTER TWELVE

The sun had not fully set and sufficient light remained for them to see the group that approached.

It was difficult to determine precise numbers at this point, but he could tell there were too many to intimidate them into leaving without bloodshed.

Skharr glanced at where Horse stood calmly and continued to eat from his feed bag, while the other two horses pranced nervously. The one the prince had ridden was a warhorse and usually involved in combat and it seemed to look around for some kind of indication that would tell it what to do.

"What are they?" the boy asked as he slid the sheath off his sword.

What, not who, which seemed an odd question. The barbarian peered through the glare of the sun as it reflected off the sand which still made it difficult to gauge their numbers accurately. They were not on horseback so the vibrations in the ground wouldn't tell him how many of them would attack.

While it might be odd, it was a valid question. He had difficulty deciding what they were too. Some looked human, but the others were not. The latter were shorter but too short to be dwarves, yet they were stocky and moved quickly over the open ground.

They were all armed, however. That much was obvious enough, and he wished he had discovered their presence earlier, which would have afforded him the opportunity to thin their ranks somewhat from a distance with his bow. Instead, he had elected to train and converse with the boy.

It wasn't a crisis, of course. They were armed, armored, and ready for a battle.

Ten large humans, he finally counted, but that did not include those with them. Their smaller, stunted comrades wore coverings over their eyes, although their long ears twitched from side to side.

The shielding on their eyes was attached to chains held by the men with them. Even across the distance still between them, Skharr could almost feel the powerful stench that emanated from the smaller creatures.

"What in all the hells are those?" Tryam asked and adjusted his grasp on his sword.

"Goblins," he muttered with a deep scowl.

"Gob— I thought they were myths spread by dwarves."

"Not myths. Very deadly."

"But they're…small."

"So is a werecat and it could still rip your throat out."

"Why are they chained?"

The barbarian paused and studied them as they moved closer and came to a halt when they were some ten paces away. The bindings over the goblins' eyes did not look too firm for the creatures to rip off easily if they wanted to.

"They're not," he realized suddenly. "They're being led by those chains. The ass-fuckers are used to living in caves and they are very unaccustomed to light. They would be able to see at night and would lead the men in turn, but during the day, it would be a little too painful for them to see for long periods at a time."

"Ah. Violent creatures, then?"

"They will try to break your spine and use their fangs to skin you alive. If you're lucky."

The boy nodded and held his weapon a little tighter. His demeanor suggested that he had not moved through dwarven tunnels before, which was not something Skharr would have wished on many people—although some deserved it. The hope was always that the vicious little fuckers would remain in those subterranean passages and fight their mortal enemies, but something had drawn this group out. It was a worrying sight. They bred quickly and could easily become an infestation if they desired to push their tribes out from under the mountains.

Those that approached hesitated, raised their noses and sniffed, and chattered quickly amongst themselves. Their prey was close and they salivated with anticipation as drool dripped from the corners of their mouths.

"I've never heard of raiders needing goblins to find their way in the desert," Skharr shouted. "How can you be sure that they won't turn on you once they're finished with us?"

Either the raiders couldn't understand him or had no intention to answer. Instead, they began to remove the coverings from their diminutive comrades and the abnormally large eyes flicked avid gazes around them. They avoided looking at the setting sun but focused immediately on the men.

"Kill?" one demanded in garbled common. "Kill now?"

"Kill them both," the leader muttered. "Eat their flesh but leave their weapons for us, yes?"

"Yes. Can'ts eats steel."

That was something he didn't know about them. From the condition he had found a couple of their victims in, he could have sworn they at least had nothing against gobbling steel rings with their meals.

All the goblins were released and they banded together and fixed their gazes on the men who were their targets.

"Tactically speaking, do you have any suggestions?" Tryam asked quietly.

"Aye. Keep them at a distance."

That was all he had time to say before the seven beasts dropped to all fours and prowled across the open ground like they tried to decide how they would attack. The group continued to chatter in an unintelligible language before they surged to full speed and attacked with no warning.

They had decided to attack the smaller one who appeared to be the weaker of the two.

Their mistake cost them dearly.

The barbarian grinned, held his sword with both hands, and waited as the creatures tried to skirt him to strike the young prince.

"Take the left," he snapped. He could probably kill all seven of their enemy on his own and his instincts demanded he do so. But he had vaguely promised to teach the boy and there was something to be said for letting him learn a thing or two about dealing with monsters who were not humanoid.

Four of them approached from the right, and Skharr moved into the group that had hoped to circle him.

The first managed to skid to a halt, dug its claws into the sand, and scrabbled to jump away. Two others were not so lucky, and he swung his weapon before they could react. One's head was lopped off in a single stroke and it raised a cloud of dust when it rolled across the ground. Another screeched when his blade circled, severed the hands from the creature, and thus removed its weapons. The warrior arced it into the other two and dark-green blood splashed onto its comrades as they tried to back away.

"Are you stinking piles of hells-turd running so soon?" He snarled, drew a dagger from his belt, and threw it quickly for a killing strike on the one missing its hands to make sure it was out of the fight for good.

The other two turned their backs and attempted to join their comrades who had attacked Tryam, but the barbarian launched in pursuit.

The lack of armor was certainly a boon, and the first goblin fell as he buried his sword into its back and pinned it into the desert dust. He left it there and simply caught its partner by the ears. It didn't weigh very much so wasn't difficult to lift off its feet, but it scratched its claws desperately against him before he drove his gauntleted fist into the back of its neck.

After a loud crack, the creature's body went limp. Its massive eyes rolled into the back of its head, although they remained open. A dwarf had told him that goblins were unable to close their eyes—which he assumed was a painful existence—but it showed every indication that it was dead and he appreciated that at least.

"How do you fare against yours, Tryam?" Skharr asked and circled to pull his sword free.

As far as he could see, things could have gone better. One of the creatures lay dead with its throat slashed, but the remaining two had drawn back and now fought in a safer manner. They attempted to surge in when they saw an opening and retreated quickly when the prince swung his sword to stop them.

"Can't you help me?" the young man shouted without moving his gaze from the two goblins in front of him. He swished his blade a little wildly to prevent them from getting too close.

"I am helping you." Skharr pointed and made sure that none of the humans were advancing on the group yet before he returned his attention to the boy. Aside from the fact that he felt he should give him the opportunity to fight alone, he also wanted to see his skills in action. Entering a dungeon with someone meant trust and for that, he needed to know what Tryam was capable of.

"Helping me?" the prince demanded and scowled although he still didn't look at him.

"I am letting you fight creatures on your own. I hope you understand that you need to improve your skills before we enter a dungeon where you will fight things that are not human. I doubt you've even fought a dwarf in his or her prime."

"There was a handful in the...arena!" The prince darted away as one of the claws raked toward his ankles.

"Well then, you understand the creatures that know how to play to their inferior size and force you to enter their particular style of fighting. Goblins prefer to fight in tighter surroundings where you cannot escape them, and they will rush at you on all fours and bite and scratch you with claws. Out here, their tactics change. Watch how they move away from you and time their attacks and feints, and remember that your comrades can help you. Also remember to help those same comrades when you can."

He demonstrated by sweeping his sword into the leg of the creature closest to him. It hadn't seen him approach, and while the blade did not cut deep, it was enough to make it stumble forward when it readied itself for a diving assault.

Tryam lunged quickly and killed it with a powerful stab through its back before it could regain its feet. As another creature rushed in desperately to attack, he drew his dagger, planted it firmly into its skull, and buried it to the hilt before he shook the dead goblin off.

"I do understand that," the prince retorted when he paused to draw breath and yanked his blade clear. "I've fought in a shield wall before."

"You're not fighting in a shield wall now, boy," he snapped and turned his attention to the group that had watched them eliminate the goblins without so much as a hint of compassion about their deaths. "You'll know how to fight in a melee, and keeping your wits about you will save your life and those of any you fight alongside."

The young contender nodded and cleaned the green blood from his weapon as the group of ten now began to advance on them.

The one closest—who seemed to be the leader of the group—removed the wrappings that had covered her face to reveal features that Skharr could admit he hadn't seen often. Her dark skin had a leathery consistency over high cheekbones, and her narrow eyes were a little sunken to protect them from the blazing sun. Tusks jutted from her bottom lip.

"Orcs," Tryam commented dourly.

"And rather far from home as well," the warrior added. "Which would explain why you aren't riding horses."

"Prefer camels," the orc chieftain grunted.

"I know." He regarded her warily as the others began to circle, and he rested his sword on his shoulder. While the nine kept their face wrappings in place as they came closer, their black eyes indicated that they were all orcs. "I guess that explains the goblins as well. Orcs don't see very well at night."

"Lesser brothers fallen, many more to be found," the chieftain retorted before she hissed and growled a few more words to the group. Seven positioned themselves to fight him, possibly an attempt to isolate him from the prince.

"Now," he told his young companion, "you might feel that they have us outnumbered and that this puts us at an immediate disadvantage, and you would be right to consider that. But you will also find they will need to be more careful and more precise in their strikes for fear of— Well, you'll see."

Skharr stepped forward and moved his sword from resting on his shoulder into a lightning-fast swing to arc it forward and catch one of the orcs across the shoulder. He dragged the blade to deepen the wound and drew himself back as another thrust at him with a spear.

The weapon missed him but his assailant found the belly of one of his comrades who had attempted to press its perceived advantage with a shorter saber. He uttered a whined cry of pain, and before the spear could be drawn out again, the barbarian swung his weapon across the throat of the enemy with the spear, slashed it cleanly, and raised the weapon into a high guard.

Three orcs fell, dead or dying.

"At some other point, I will impress on you the importance of wearing armor in a melee," he commented, his attention fixed on the three who had started to circle Tryam. They glanced at their chieftain, unsure of what to do next.

She snapped another few commands and drew a heavy falchion from her belt as she advanced toward Skharr. The four who remained against him did not so much as hesitate and surged forward immediately, while another two broke away from where they readied themselves to attack their original target and focused on the barbarian instead.

The young prince acted quickly, lashed out with his longsword, and caught the orc in the knee. His opponent lurched into a couple of his comrades and diverted them from their intended assault.

It was only a moment's reprieve, but that was all the warrior needed. He uttered a low growl that built rapidly into a roar as he surged toward the weakened line of orcs. With little difficulty, he evaded those who were still on their feet as the drills Sera had put him through worked their magic. One orc fell away, its throat slashed. With a twist of the wrist, he swiped the blade and a gaping wound appeared on a second enemy's chest before he spun to attack the chieftain from behind the others.

She raised her falchion quickly to block a thrust aimed at her stomach, and Skharr reacted instantly to twirl his blade and catch her fingers.

The chieftain fell back with a roar of pain when two digits were neatly severed and deep lacerations appeared on the other two. Before she could reach for the seax she carried on her back,

Skharr had lunged forward and drove his sword into her exposed chest.

It was a good, quick thrust, the kind Sera had always told him to avoid as a blade could be trapped in an opponent's body. With a firm kick, he dislodged the chieftain from his weapon and turned to focus on those who had regrouped and now prepared for another assault.

Only three were left to try to engage him, and no hint of hesitation or fear showed in their eyes. The warrior stepped away, parried a spear thrust at his stomach, and lowered his shoulder to take a saber slash in the pauldron. He pushed forward and a swift kick upended his attacker before he stamped his boot hard on his skull and swung his blade out. The intention had been to catch one of the orcs in the head, but the blow simply deflected off a pair of tusks instead.

Another of the enemy stabbed viciously, and Skharr grasped the spearhead and uttered a roar as he dragged the orc close enough to drive his sword through his opponent's chest with such force that it pushed the blade far enough to emerge on the other side. He shifted, lifted the impaled raider off his feet, and shoved him into his comrade. His sword remained buried in the first fighter's chest up to the hilt, but the part that protruded punched into the second assailant's stomach with the barbarian's full weight and that of another orc to drive the point home.

Skharr couldn't help a sadistic chuckle as he pushed up from the pile of two he had made and pulled his sword clear of the two large bodies it was buried in.

He turned his attention to Tryam's fight with the last raider. The young man showed good basics. His footwork maintained his balance and although shorter than his opponent, he held him at a distance with defensive thrusts and sweeping strokes aimed at the head.

Both were locked in an interesting stalemate, and the

barbarian took a few moments to make sure the others were dead or to kill those who were wounded but alive.

"Won't you fucking help?" Tryam asked and he sounded desperate.

"When you need it," he responded calmly.

That was enough to distract the sole remaining orc. He turned, realized that all his comrades had already fallen, and a look of shock slid onto his face.

The prince used the opportunity to lunge closer, slashed his blade low behind his adversary's knee, and raised the sword to swipe it across the orc's throat in a familiar motion.

Skharr grinned and cleaned his sword casually as the boy stared at the corpse. After a few seconds, he stumbled away and vomited on the sand with a low, guttural groan.

"Are you all right there, lad?" he asked as he moved closer to him.

"Hard…" The young man shook his head. "It's…difficult to… You could have killed the last one for me, yes?"

"True, but it is good to learn to deal with your opponents on your own."

"Please do not make a habit of it."

"I make no promises, at least not until we find ourselves in a serious fight."

Tryam looked at ten dead orcs and seven dead goblins in something close to disbelief while he cleaned his mouth carefully. "I would hate to see what you consider a serious fight."

"You will."

"I will see a serious fight, or I will hate it when I see it?"

Skharr regarded him with a small grin. "Both, most likely."

CHAPTER THIRTEEN

She would have to ask him how he did it. Surely there was some kind of secret Skharr possessed that enabled him to draw the attention of so many nobles.

Which included herself as well, although Sera was willing to bet there was another reason for all the attention. This one had little to do with anything the man might or might not have done intentionally and more to do with the fact that his size was enough to catch the interest of any who might encounter him.

There would inevitably be those who wanted to know a little more about him.

The guild captain looked at the palace that towered above the city and tried to ignore a sense of discomfort as she studied it. While it was an amazing monument of days gone by, something about it unsettled her as she approached—like she did not belong anywhere near a structure like that.

"Sera Ferat?" one of the guards at the entrance asked.

She nodded and tried to disguise the unease that seeped into her stomach.

"Follow me. The queen awaits you."

It was the end of what had already been a long day. The last thing she had expected was for the queen of the city to send word that her presence was requested for an evening meal. The attraction of decent food without having to pay for it was certainly there, but she doubted that the royal had asked to see her merely for her sparkling personality.

"No one may come before the queen armed," the guard noted as they continued through the hallways, each more impressive than the last.

"If that is the case, I must thank her for her invitation but decline it. I cannot be parted from my weapon."

"I understand that," he muttered, having anticipated the challenge. "I was merely reminding you of the law. Despite this, however, you will be allowed into the queen's presence with your sword as we are willing to make an exception for a blademaster."

"Then why did you—"

"But you must be warned that if you begin to draw your sword, three crossbowmen in hidden windows will immediately shoot you through the heart. Is that understood?"

Sera nodded without comment and let him lead her until they reached what looked like the queen's personal quarters. The door was pushed open and she was allowed entry.

The serving staff had just finished setting out an evening meal that smelled mouthwatering, and the guild captain was suddenly distracted from all thoughts as to the reason why she had been invited. She studied the feast and tried to regain her usual calm watchfulness.

"Dame Sera Ferat, is that correct?" the queen asked. She was a tall, regal woman, with her black curls swept up and held in place by her crown.

The blademaster shook her head, looked around, and tried to see where the crossbowmen were hiding, waiting in readiness to end her life if she made a single wrong movement.

"No. Dame Micah Ferat is my sister. She was made a knight by the Count of Verenvan for the services she provided him. For myself, I am known as Captain Sera Ferat. Or lady, depending on what circles you prefer to run in."

"We'll say Captain Ferat." The queen rose from her seat and smiled as she approached. "I know this might be a little unorthodox, but would you mind terribly if I were able to see your sword? I have never laid eyes on a blademaster's weapon, and it has always been a matter of curiosity for me."

She studied the room warily again. "I was told I would be killed immediately and without hesitation if I were to draw my weapon."

"Oh, that is only my guards being a little overprotective. They know my fighting abilities, but something in them still requires that they act as though they were fathers or brothers with a defenseless woman to protect."

"It has been many years since my men have felt the same way," Sera noted and slowly and carefully drew her sword with her forefinger and thumb only while she remained alert for any bolts aimed at her chest. "Then again, they have seen my fighting skills displayed regularly and know I would beat them senseless if they ever tried to act like I was a defenseless woman."

"I am afraid there aren't too many opportunities for a queen to show her martial prowess." She stepped closer as Sera held the weapon out so she could see it. "May I?"

After only a moment's hesitation, she turned the blade so the queen could take it by the handle, lift it, and inspect it in the glow that still filtered in although the sun was setting.

"It's so light," she whispered as she held it almost reverently and swept it in slow arcs a few times. "And the balance is perfect. I don't think I have ever seen a weapon quite like it. The legends of the blademasters' smiths are true, I suppose."

The woman handed her the sword once she was finished with it, and Sera sheathed it carefully as her royal hostess gestured for them to turn their attention to the food and drinks set out for them.

"Unfortunately, as much as I would enjoy speaking of nothing but our adventures out in the field, I must first address the reason why I wished to speak to you."

It was what she had expected, and the guild captain took her seat and focused her attention on the woman. She waited politely for her to serve herself before she began to pile a generous helping on her plate.

"I am sure you already know why I have asked to speak to you." The queen took a few slices cut from a suckling pig, poured a trickle of gravy over it, and took a mouthful. "I have had folk ask around the city for me, and it was said that you entered the gates in the company of one Skharr DeathEater, a barbarian by birth. Is that true?"

She resisted the urge to roll her eyes as she chewed a mouthful of the heavily spiced food before she answered. "I did, and I've traveled with the man in the past. He has proven himself more than merely a capable warrior and a cunning ally. In case you were wondering, he is trustworthy as well."

"No, I did not wonder about that as you are not the first one to tell me of the man's qualities." The queen spoke while she chewed so her words were a little muffled. "But I did want to hear them from someone who knows the man well. I'll admit to personal curiosity as I spent most of my time fighting barbarians like him and it is interesting to see one who can be relied upon. That aside, there are other reasons."

Sera narrowed her eyes and resisted the urge to ask the woman what those reasons were.

"I am curious as to why that big bastard seems to always attract the interest of nobility wherever he goes." She took another mouthful of the food she had heaped on her plate and the heat of the spices immediately warmed her entire body. "Have you spoken to him? Skharr, I mean?"

"No. I have not exchanged a word with the man, but I spoke to Prince Tryam about why he had chosen to trust the barbarian, and he supported him. He's an impressive specimen, even among the clans. There was something about him that radiated danger like a zooka cat might—immobile yet...he gave me the feeling he was ready to pounce."

That certainly sounded like the man, and Sera paused to consider her words carefully before she spoke. "I don't suppose you've ever seen an avalanche in action?"

The queen nodded. "A few—snow, mud, and rocks as well."

"I've always thought Skharr was something of a human avalanche. He does not attack you so much as...fall on you in a flurry and gives you few opportunities to retaliate before his prodigious strength lands a blow that will end your life."

"You would fear for your life even as a blademaster?"

She tilted her head thoughtfully but nodded slowly. "I've trained with the man, and I would say I have the skill to beat him, but so did the other two blademasters he faced. I would not want to test him if he were in a situation where he is fighting for his life. I'm sorry, did you call him Prince Tryam?"

Her hostess nodded. "I thought you knew. The bastard son of the emperor is making an attempt to solidify his position as heir to the empire when Rivar finally dies."

"Ah. I see."

The less said about that the better, however, and the guild captain focused her attention on the food again without further comment.

It was late, and Sera didn't think she would find any of her men still awake when she returned to the inn. It was one of the cheaper establishments in the city and one of the few that was able to accommodate her whole group. The guild had said that they were more than willing to give them a place to stay for the evening, but she did not want to have to rely on that. Too many relied on the housing they provided.

Surprisingly, a few of her men lingered in the common room, waiting for her as she stepped inside.

A pall fell over the group as she entered and their gazes settled on her.

"Well?" Regor asked after she tried to move to their rooms without engaging them. "How did your meeting with the queen go?"

She took a deep breath and tried to not roll her eyes again. "You don't have to ask. She wanted to know what Skharr was hiding behind his loincloth, exactly like all the other noble-women who see him."

"You know that includes you as well, right?"

With a smirk, she nodded slowly. "But I won't pay him a gold coin. We all know that's the only way he'll join me in the sheets."

"You could hire some for much less in Verenvan," one of the mercenaries muttered but was quickly hushed by the rest.

"What did you tell her?" Regor asked and once again inter-rupted her planned retreat.

"That he's a fighter, not a lover. I assume that is how he acts when bedding a woman, no matter what her position in any kingdom."

The group agreed quickly, and she took the opportunity to slip away and climb the steps as she unhooked her sword from her belt.

"That bastard will be the death of me," she whispered as she slipped into her room and closed the door behind her.

―――――

They had moved away from their original campsite and Skharr hadn't needed to explain why. Large numbers of scavengers roamed in the desert, especially at night, and if they had remained in the area, they would be attacked by any of those that weren't allowed to partake in the feast.

The sun had already set by the time they stopped again, and Tryam shivered with the cold as he lit their campfire. The barbarian worked to prepare a meal for them both and despite the dried food he used, the addition of a handful of spices made the young man's mouth water before he poured the soup into two wooden bowls they had brought on the journey.

As soups went, it was easily the finest the prince had ever tried and even somehow made the waybread served with it more palatable.

"Thank you," Skharr said softly as he took a mouthful of his food.

"What was that?"

The barbarian glared at him. "I said thank you. Did you not hear me the first time?"

"I did but could not understand it. And I don't think you understand it either."

"What is your difficulty? Your quick strike when the orcs attempted to swarm me likely saved my life, and so I thanked you for it."

Tryam laughed and shook his head. "You did kill all but one of them."

"Counting those I killed do not reflect the actual numbers. If they had swarmed me, they could have killed me or left me grievously injured. Your actions prevented that and showed that you have a mind for combat tactics."

"I did not…think, to be honest. I saw an opening and took it."

"That is what I mean." The warrior finished his food and leaned back against his pack as Horse settled behind him. "You take the first watch. Wake me in the middle of the night and I'll take the second."

"Right." He nodded and watched as his companion turned to

find a comfortable position to sleep in. "Wait, wait—how do I know when it's the middle of the night?"

Skharr growled his irritation and turned to point at the clear sky above them. "Do you see those two stars? The brighter ones?"

He narrowed his eyes in concentration and finally saw the two in question. "Yes. Those two next to the very faint one."

"Aye. When the top one moves below the bottom one, it will be the middle of the night."

"Top one moves below the bottom one. Understood. Sleep… sleep well."

The barbarian rumbled something unintelligible, rolled over, and closed his eyes.

CHAPTER FOURTEEN

The stop for the night was short as Ingold was adamant that they could make up for the time they lost while trying to leave the city.

He allowed them only a handful of hours of rest before they were on the move again and followed the semblance of a road as it meandered across the godsbedammed desert.

"Captain?"

He knew his men would pay for the delay, but he would suffer for it as well. They were all tired and irritable, and he heard far more angry grumbling than he had the day before.

While his irritation and frustration were such that he was tempted to add his complaints, he was the captain. As such, he carried the responsibility to ensure that they did their job correctly and that they were all alive at the end.

"Captain?"

His horse snorted and nickered nervously as he yanked the reins to bring it to a sudden halt. He turned to look at the man who had disturbed his thoughts.

"What?"

"You'll want to look at that."

The sun had barely begun to rise, banish the chill of night, and brighten the world enough to see again. In the dawn light, he noticed birds circling in the distance.

"Carrion," he muttered. "Is that what you had to point out to me? It's probably some creature that died of thirst. What interest would we have in it?"

"Or it could be that some bandits found our targets and ended their lives," another of his Elites answered. "Many of them raid in this area. It would be best to check, especially since they likely know they are being followed and will try to avoid the main roads."

As much as Ingold wanted to berate the man, good points had been put forward. The princeling pretender would likely not think to leave the roads on his own but the crafty barbarian would have a mind for it.

"All right." He urged his horse from the road and onto the open sand. "But if we get lost in the desert and run out of food, you'll be the first to be eaten."

The group laughed, which he supposed was a pleasant change from the complaints he'd had to field from the start of their early morning march.

Still, the muttered protests resumed when the heat continued to grow more intense with the steadily rising sun.

The morning dawned bright and clear and Skharr nudged the boy with his boot.

"Five more minutes," Tryam muttered and dragged the blanket over his shoulders.

He would have liked to pour a bucket of ice-cold water over his head but did not want to waste the little they had. All he could do was resort to another prod, this time a little harder.

"I said five more minutes!"

"I don't give a shit!" he snapped. "If your diamond-studded ass isn't standing in the next five seconds, the next wake-up will be a kick that will break a rib!"

Tryam did as he was told but grumbled as he pushed from the rough bed he'd made. "I thought I was paying you to keep me safe."

"Aye, and if I allowed you your beauty sleep, I would have to keep you safe from those who want you dead in person. That would annoy me and you wouldn't want me to be annoyed."

"This is not you annoyed?"

"Enough with the lip. We'll pack our camp and move on."

Skharr didn't enjoy having to treat the prince like a child, but the yelling did appear to speed him up—although he did note a few whispered curses the boy thought he couldn't hear.

There was no need to take umbrage at the fact that he was unhappy with the situation. He was not his charge's officer nor his mother, and they had to continue whether he was annoyed or not.

Soon, they were on the move and Skharr hurriedly consumed a sparse morning meal of dried beef and a few sips of water, while the prince glowered and partook of much the same as they started their trip in silence.

"Why did you agree to help me?" Tryam asked finally as they pushed on through the growing heat of the day.

He narrowed his eyes. "Why would I not? Your coin is as good as anyone else's."

"So you aren't doing it to curry favor with a man who might become emperor one day?"

"A boy who might be emperor one day," he corrected him.

The contender laughed. "Yes, I suppose so."

"Why do you want to be emperor? What drove you to it?"

The prince paused and focused on the sand for a few moments. "It wasn't the folk who tried to persuade me to do it, I know that much. What convinced me was when my brother invited me to the imperial palace to talk—my half-brother, the current heir. He said it was to congratulate me on my fighting skills in the arena, but I knew it was because he wanted to gauge my measure as whispers had already begun to circulate that I wanted to usurp him."

"Meeting your brother convinced you to try to take his place? How?"

"It's hard to say." Tryam shrugged. "I remembered thinking he would be like my father—a hero in the making—but everything about him simply revealed him to be a pompous ass. He berated servants like he thought it would impress me. From what I could tell, he is a violent fuck who has been raised to have the same tastes as my father, and he is easily manipulated by the viceroy."

"Who is the viceroy?"

"The emperor's oldest and most trusted advisor. If I were to bet on who was behind the attempt on my life, I would place a great deal of coin on him."

Skharr nodded slowly. "Your father is guided by his vices and it makes him easily manipulated. The viceroy would not want that changed despite the succession."

"I knew there would be more of the same decadence in the empire, but my father had only five or so decades to allow things to sink into the mire. My brother would easily have two centuries of it. I…many talked about how the gods willed it, but in the end…well, I knew the empire would not survive another emperor like Rivar."

"Is it truly worth saving?"

Tryam thought about it for a moment and it was laudable that he put some consideration into his answers instead of simply repeating what he had been told to say or what he thought his companion might want to hear.

"Not in its current state," he answered finally. "There might be a few changes and those changes would result in some violence, but I think that in the end, it would prevent the kind of decay and destruction that would result from living under my brother's rule. The violence would be delayed but amplified beyond anything we've seen since the Ancients were deposed."

The barbarian paused to think about that and finally shook his head. "You're an educated little bastard, aren't you?"

"Is that such a terrible thing?"

"No, but I can't help wondering if you aren't a little too young to have the weight of the world on your shoulders."

"For now, all I can do is survive. I'll go into the dungeon on my own."

"On your own?"

"From what I understand, that is the only way for me to complete the path. I've been told that numerous times, at least— that there would be no way for me to find what I am heading in there for if I have a group at my side."

He scowled. "I'm not sure I like that, but if it's the only way... Well, I can get you to the fucking dungeon alive, at least."

"That is all I can ask and at this point, you have already saved my life twice."

The contender was a little too aware of his limitations, and Skharr didn't approve. As a boy, there had been little on his mind that did not involve women and a weapon in his hand. This one, however, acted like he needed to save the world from itself—like there were no others ready to take the work instead.

"Come on, then," he muttered and sucked in a deep breath. "We'll be better off and set a good pace for the day. Let's see if your horse can keep up."

Horse snorted.

"There's no need to be harsh," he retorted.

"What did he say?" Tryam asked.

"Nothing that bears repeating."

"To imagine that a simple fucking prissy-assed noble is capable of causing us this much trouble," one of the Elites muttered.

"It's not the noble who is responsible." Ingold corrected the man quickly and raised his hand to bring the group to a halt. "It's the fucking barbarian spawn of mountain cesspits. I, for one, look forward to leaving him as a hefty meal for the crows. And speaking of a hefty meal for the crows…"

He let his voice trail off. No smell of rotting flesh in the air yet indicated that the deaths were recent, and there was a great number of corpses, enough to indicate that a small skirmish had taken place.

"Dismount and inspect the dead," he commanded and the group complied quickly. They covered their faces and waved their arms to disperse the carrion-eaters that had gathered. Most of the vultures took flight, but a few had eaten to the point of gorging themselves and could only hop clumsily away to a safe distance. They no doubt planned to return to their meal once the Elites moved on.

Fortunately, the inspection did not take long.

"They're not human," one of his men shouted and inspected the bodies more closely. "From what I can tell, the smaller ones are goblins and the larger are orcs—unless our barbarian suddenly grew tusks from his mouth."

"Which is admittedly unlikely." Ingold grunted and studied the corpses quickly with a practiced eye. "Ten orcs, all armed and bested in battle, along with seven goblins. I think our young pretender might have gathered a few more men to help him. He and the barbarian would not have been able to kill all these on their own."

A general sound of assent was heard from his men.

"They found some barbarian raiders and joined with them, most likely," another added. "They infest these parts from what I've heard."

"Then we'll need to prepare for a tougher fight than we thought."

"Captain Ingold, over here."

He moved to where one of his men stood and his attention was directed to tracks on the ground, still visible despite the sand that drifted constantly.

"Three horses," the Elite said quietly. "And no other tracks leading away. Do you think they found a way to obfuscate the rest of their number?"

"It's possible," he muttered and rubbed his chin thoughtfully. "Especially if the others who joined them are familiar with the desert and know how to cover their tracks. But at least now we have a path to follow. Mount up and leave the carrion to their feast."

The group did as instructed and swung into their saddles before they pushed on without a backward glance. Ingold scowled when he passed the tracks. Someone seemed to be moving on foot, which was odd in the desert. Perhaps one of the barbarians had forgotten to cover his tracks or the prince had brought a servant.

"No," he muttered. "He isn't the type."

CHAPTER FIFTEEN

"What else do you know about the dungeon?"

Tryam looked at his companion when he realized that he had simply stared at the horizon, which of course refused to come closer.

"What?"

"You said you were told you would have to go in alone. Did anyone tell you anything else of value or only that you needed to enter it alone?"

He'd had an interesting conversation with the queen while Skharr waited in the outer chamber, but she certainly hadn't provided any jewels of dungeon-wisdom. While she seemed genuinely concerned about his safety, unlike others, he couldn't tell if it was because she wanted to be in favor with him if he happened to succeed—and survive after succeeding—or if she merely wanted to help him with no ulterior motive in mind.

That last thought was easy to reject. She was a queen and everything she did was in the interest of her people.

"Well? Is there anything about the fucking godsbedamned hell-pit you're willing to share, or will you keep it all to yourself?"

"She gave me nothing of real value aside from explaining what the name of the test means. I suppose she's reluctant to be too overtly supportive in case I fail. The captain of the palace guards, however, did mention later that evening what would be waiting for us at the entrance. He deliberately sought me out, although I couldn't determine if he chose to tell me or had been instructed to do so, but perhaps the queen knew and wanted us to be prepared for it."

"And you only mention this now?"

"Well, I did not think you would take it seriously. All told, someone with your experience might—"

"Might what?"

"You cannot deny that you are the kind to mock those things you consider ridiculous."

Skharr regarded him solemnly for a moment and nodded. "That is fair, I suppose. But if monsters are awaiting us, it would be best to know what they are, do you agree? Am I wrong?"

"No, you're not wrong. You are merely a rabid cur."

The barbarian laughed. "Again, that is fair. But enough deflecting. What did the man—or perhaps the queen through the man—tell you to expect?"

"Well, there is also what the few survivors have said. None have been victorious on the Path before, but some didn't manage to enter in the first place. I suppose they were aware that only one could enter it."

"But something is waiting outside?"

Tryam nodded. "Indeed. Or at least that was what the message told me—death awaited us at the door of the dungeon."

"Death?"

"Yes."

His companion sighed and shook his head. "Well then, what form does this version of death take and can I stab it with some type of metal?"

That drew a laugh from the young prince as he nudged his

horse a little closer. "Oh, of course. You have fought a Lich. Death must be a mere inconvenience to you."

"No, death is something to fight or run from. I fought the Lich but I ran from the demon. Both were very impressive representations of death in my view."

"And what kind of representation would a dragon hold? The kind to run from or fight?"

Skharr paused and settled his gaze on the young prince. "That would depend on what kind of dragon I faced. Assuming, of course, that it is not a story peddled to keep folk away from there. We will have to see how large it is."

Tryam nodded and frowned as he tried to remember all the stories he'd heard involving dragons. "The size of a horse?"

"Fight."

"Bigger?"

The barbarian shook his head. "I've never seen any that were bigger than a horse—if you take the wings away, of course. The wingspan does tend to grow to an impressive size."

"Are there no dragons larger than a horse?"

"I didn't say that. There are rumors of a black dragon beyond the mountains to the north of where the DeathEater clan has made its home. It was said that it could devour an entire raiding company in a single swoop."

He narrowed his eyes. "I thought dragons killed by breathing fire."

"They can, I suppose, but like anything else in this world, they need to eat and I doubt it would enjoy the cinders that were left. It would need to leave them alive and use the fire only if it intends to kill without eating."

That made sense to the prince, although the very practical concept had been left out of most of the stories he'd heard about the beasts.

"What happened to it?"

"There are various stories. Some say it was killed. Others

believe that the DeathEater Clan came to an agreement with it to leave the northern mountains for its home. That is the legend The Clan abides by, although the most likely scenario is that they simply fled to avoid being destroyed."

"I couldn't imagine a clan like the DeathEaters running from anything, even a dragon. I always assumed you were the type to stand your ground and fight anything that threatened you, no matter what the consequences."

"We avoid conflict most of the time. In the end, if you manage to navigate the mountains better than others, you find a way to choose your battles, pick the weak off from above, and harrass any who would fight to make the final conflict easier."

"If you are such powerful warriors, why bother with that? Why not simply attack any who come against you?"

"You think like someone who lives in a city, where troops are easy to conscript if lost. In smaller clans, you must remember that if fifteen men die in battle, there will likely not be that many waiting to replace the fallen—or if there were, it would be youths who haven't seen a moment of combat. All tactical decisions must be those taken by your average predator, and all must never allow your quarry to deliver the killing blow."

"But the queen said the clans she was dealing with would always come to try to fight any guards they could see. In some cases, they even abandoned the caravans they were attacking."

Skharr shook his head. "I can't speak for the desert clans, but I doubt it. The most likely scenario is that they tried to run away and when pursued, decided to take a stand and retaliate in as advantageous a position as possible."

Tryam nudged his horse forward. They could see the desert around them starting to change. Instead of the hard earth covered in dry dust, it looked like soil had won through in a few places and a few bushes and dry grasses had begun to grow. It likely meant they were closer to the swamps he had heard tell of, where the dungeon was supposed to be.

"Would you fight a dragon like that?" he asked and reverted to his original topic. "A black dragon?"

"How would I fight against a dragon like that?" the barbarian asked. "You would need some type of magic to even consider dealing with it but in the end, it's best to simply let a creature like that have its piece of land. If it even exists, of course. And then there are the wyrms that have plagued the dwarves over the centuries, burrowing deep into the mountains. Dwarves say they are dragons, even if they can't fly and don't have legs. They breathe fire and are considerably larger than the winged beasts I've seen, likely because they don't need to fly."

"What do you think?"

"About?"

"Whether wyrms are dragons or not?"

Skharr scowled at the youth. "I don't much care what they call them. I'm only happy that I've never run into one of the slime-filled spawn of Janus' hairy ass-crack."

Their conversation ceased when they approached a crest that rose slightly before it dropped away sharply to reveal the landscape ahead of them.

It was almost breathtaking. Three rivers—likely stemming from oases nearby— funneled into the same valley and more water seeped in than what left. The waterways slowed and snaked through the valley as they began to merge, and the water spread farther into the landscape to create a swamp that covered hundreds of miles.

"It's hard to accept that so much water is this close to that much desert," Tryam whispered and brought his horse to a halt while he studied the scene. "Why do you think so many settled in the desert and not here?"

Skharr scowled, and it was clear that he saw the same as his companion had a moment before—there were no signs of houses or civilization anywhere in the valley. It might have been expected that a few farms would have been established in the lush grasslands, but it appeared as though the whole area had been thoroughly—and perhaps deliberately—avoided.

If anyone lived in the swamplands, they did not want it to be visible from a distance.

"It must be because of the dungeon," the barbarian mumbled and turned to pat his horse on the neck to calm the beast, which had begun to stamp his feet and snort. "As I recall, a few of these places have an effect on the world around them. They sometimes drive folk out actively with magic and at other times, do so indirectly."

"Indirectly?"

The warrior's features were difficult to read as he looked into the valley sprawled ahead of them. "Aye. Altering the creatures and the plants to make them act aggressively to humans who come close. I think it was a design to protect those who built the dungeons originally and who tried to keep folk away one way or the other."

"Well, we must advance. There is no way but forward." Tryam tapped his horse's flanks and tugged the pack pony behind him as he began the descent away from the desert and into the valley.

He could feel the change in temperature almost immediately. While he had thought air would start to cool as they left the desert, it somehow grew hotter. Before too long, it was like the heat hung over them to press aggressively into his skin and make him uncomfortable.

The horses sensed it as well, and his mount snorted and neighed softly as he nudged it forward a little more.

"Quiet," Skharr snapped, his hand still on Horse's forehead to calm the beast. "We do not want to attract any attention to ourselves here."

"It's not like I can control what the horse does," the prince retorted waspishly.

"I was not speaking to you."

Orcs, he thought in disgust. Why in all the hells were orcs this close to the cities?

Ingold scowled at his sword as he retrieved a kerchief from his pouch to clean the dark blood that coated his weapon. He had washed the cloth more times than he could count, but the bloodstains never fully came out. A few more wouldn't make much of a difference. He looked up and nodded when he confirmed that his men dealt the final killing strokes to the few survivors.

It was worrying to see the stinky goblin-fuckers so far from their homelands—the deserts across the mountains, where there was nothing but the Dune Sea as far as the eye could see. It was well-known that an agreement with the orc tribes was required to travel across the desert—both because they needed to be held off from attacking as well as the fact that their help was needed to navigate the sea if the caravans wanted to reach the western edge of the continent.

The fact that they had come across the mountains to start attacking those who were in the wasteland on the other side was worrying. It meant something was happening to drive them from their homes.

Not only that, but they were fighting alongside goblins and this was equally worrying, although not the matter he was the most concerned about.

"Captain!"

Ingold looked up from cleaning his sword and bundled the kerchief into his pouch before he turned his attention to what his men were doing.

Those few orcs who had survived the attack were now well and truly dead, but it looked like their weapons had attracted no small degree of interest.

They had not worn any armor, which had made what would have been a difficult battle a little easier. There had been twenty-five of them, all told, with fifteen orcs and ten goblins. The rabid creatures had killed two of his men before they even realized they were under attack. Interestingly enough, however, things had gone rather easily after the two deaths. His men had made short work of the remaining goblins and dismounted to attack the orcs.

The two Elites who had died were wrapped in their cloaks and a few of those who had been closest to them poured handfuls of sand over them and spoke a few words in memory of their past victories.

It was taking precious time away from the chase, which in turn allowed their quarry to advance unhindered, but Ingold knew that interrupting the small ceremony would have a negative effect on the men's morale. He needed them focused on their task.

"Would you like to say a few words over them, Captain?" one of the survivors asked and looked like she was ready to move once he had said his piece.

It was an interesting thought and Ingold moved to the two dead men. The goblins had all but torn their heads off using claws, teeth, and a few improvised weapons, although the beasts didn't quite use weapons in the same way their orc masters did.

"You've fought well in this life," he said softly, his head bowed. "Fight well and bring honor to the emperor in the next, my brothers. Your feats will not be forgotten."

Those around him nodded approval as he collected a handful of sand and poured it over their bodies. He had hoped to go through this effort without any men lost but in the end, he had dealt with worse situations in the past. All he needed to do was survive it and he would likely find a position as commander once Rivar was dead or had abdicated.

To assume that position, however, he needed the support of the Elites. It was inevitable that he would fail if the men believed he didn't have their backs out in the field of battle. He did not intend to allow the success or failure of his venture to be decided by that.

A few more of the men had words to say for the dead, but they did so quickly and were soon mounted again. Ingold was determined to make up the time they had lost. The boy and his group could not be too far ahead now, and he would not let them slip through his fingers.

It was a hard ride, but the climate around them began to change noticeably. The heat clung to the skin, which meant they had progressed beyond the drier reaches of the desert and pushed toward the swamps. It was an unsettling feeling, and he knew their time was running out.

Finally, as they reached the crest of a small incline, they stopped to study their surroundings. The Elite leader took a looking glass from his saddlebags and peered down the road they were following, hoping they could at least see their quarry. The fear that the barbarians were leading the prince through paths that only they knew was worryingly realistic, and if their tracking failed, all they could do was wait outside the dungeon. None of them looked forward to that.

"Finally," he whispered as he leaned forward in the saddle when he noticed movement in the distance.

The three larger shapes of the horses were the easiest to identify, but something else moved with them. It appeared that someone was on foot, walking beside one of the beasts. Oddly enough, the indications were that only one of the three horses was being ridden.

He couldn't make out who was riding the horse, but the sheer size of the man walking was enough to tell him all he needed to know about his identity.

"Is it them?" one of the Elites asked.

Ingold nodded. "Aye, unless you know of anyone else in the world that large, but...I thought there would be more of them."

"More of them, sir?"

He shook his head, stowed the looking glass, and whistled to draw the attention of his Elites. "We have located our quarry. They are moving quickly but we will intercept them. Spare not the horses or yourselves. Ride!"

With that said, he dug his heels into his mount's flanks and grasped the reins tighter as he drove it forward into a canter. The troops surged in behind him in formation, ready for a fight.

And with good reason, he mused. There was no chance that it was only the two of them, which meant the barbarian's friends were likely hidden nearby. They needed to be ready to deal with all of them, and there would be no telling when those still unseen would swarm them.

His hand rested on the saber at his hip, awaiting the sight of anything else that might close in on them as his mount raced forward. The beast's eyesight was better than his, and it would be able to keep its eyes on the prince and his massive bodyguard.

A hint of eagerness filled his body again. It was time to end this arrogant pretender once and for all, and he could finally leave this hellish patch of desert behind him for good.

CHAPTER SIXTEEN

His attempts to remain away from politics and the intrigue folk liked to involve him in for some reason hadn't lasted very long.

Smarter men than him would merely have refused to work the missions he had. The dungeons were less likely to get him killed than working for the nobles who had found in him a convenient solution for their messy business.

The fact that he hadn't died yet had been a matter of sheer luck, thanks mostly to the likes of Sera looking out for him. She had never told him how she had found him when he had been poisoned, although he assumed she discovered there was a contract on his life and had immediately tried to locate him.

Luck—or having good friends in that case—had saved his life. There would be no assurance that he would prove as lucky ever again.

Horse snorted, shook his mane, and stamped his feet, and Skharr turned to look at him. He knew when his long-time friend wanted his attention, and the least he could do was see what the stallion wanted.

"Are you in need of a rest?" he asked and patted the beast's forehead. The only response he received was more pawing at the ground, and the barbarian looked at the persistent action and narrowed his eyes.

"What's the matter?" Tryam asked as he brought his horses to a halt. "Does your horse need rest?"

"No, it's something else." Skharr dropped to a crouch and pressed his hand against the earth. It was still hard like it had been in the desert, and something vibrated it against his fingers. "Something…else."

It was a tremor, but not the kind that told him of an earthquake or an avalanche—not that they would have to worry much about either as they enjoyed the gentle descent into the valley. He turned in a full circle and studied their surroundings intently.

Heat rose from the surface and made it difficult to see anything through the haze of it, but the movement was almost not visible. A dark shadow swallowed the drab grays and yellows that had filled their vision over the past few days.

Someone was following them. He could barely make out horses—at least fifteen of them—that galloped toward them.

"I don't suppose you've asked some of your friends to join you on this?" Skharr asked and still attempted to distinguish helpful details of the group that approached.

"No. Why?"

"Who do you think that might be, then?" He stared at the boy, who took a moment to realize what he meant and shifted his gaze to focus on the shadow that bore down on them.

Tryam peered through the haze, narrowed his eyes, and shielded them with his hand as he tried to make out who their pursuers were. "I would say the Elites who wanted to kill me."

"I'd say they still do." Skharr looked at his saddle and took the unstrung bow and quiver from it, as well as the pieces of armor he assumed he would need.

"What are you doing?"

"Slowing them down. Stay on your horse and ride. Don't stop

until you reach your destination. I will give you the time you need."

"We should fight those murderous fuckers together!" the prince insisted.

The barbarian donned his armor calmly but he scowled at his young companion. "You have your people to fight for. I am telling you as your guard and as your friend, get that horse moving or I'll tie your royal ass to your saddle and do it for you. Go!"

Tryam shook his head, visibly disgusted but knowing this was the right decision. The boy was a fighter, he had to give him that, but he would also have to learn to choose his battles. If there was the possibility that they could enter the dungeon together, he would have found a way for them to fight together.

As things stood, he would not risk the young man's quest for his safety and in the end, they wanted to kill Tryam, not him. They certainly would not expect him to stand his ground and fight them on his own.

"Why?" Skharr asked, talking to Horse. "Because it's fucking insanity. No sane man in his right mind would choose to stand his ground against...what are they? Fifteen men? Maybe more and Elites, some of the best fighters in the empire. Truly madness."

His armor was on and he proceeded to string his new bow quickly.

"Don't bother trying to talk me out of it," he continued, hefted his weapons, and made mental notes of where the best position to fight was. "I'm well known to be a madman and will not be convinced that I cannot survive when so thoroughly outnumbered. I'll always have a chance to kill the scum-swilling bastards instead of them killing me."

Horse offered no response, and the barbarian studied his other weapons and decided he had about as much as he would be able to fight with. A spear and a shield would likely be his best friends against men on horseback, but they would not last for long. Mobility would be his best option when the fighting grew closer.

"You'll need to head off and hide for the moment," he muttered and patted the beast on the neck. "There will be no place for you in this fight. In the end, if I happen to not survive, I don't suppose I could convince you to return to Sera's farm?"

He didn't expect to hear a response and all he could do was smile. Horse would decide what he wanted to do and take himself to wherever he planned to be once he was gone. The barbarian doubted that there would be much mourning.

As expected, the beast moved away and trotted a fair distance to a small patch of greenery, where he began to graze calmly. He wasn't quite hidden but had stationed himself well away from where the fighting would most likely occur.

It would be an interesting battle.

The warrior held an arrow in his bow hand and another in his free hand. With no further distractions, he judged the distance of the horses as he planted three more of the projectiles in front of him. He took care to position them where he could snatch them quickly if he had the time and the angle to shoot as many of the enemy as possible. That done, he returned his focus to those who advanced steadily with an almost palpable sense of purpose.

Skharr took a deep breath and firmed his grasp on the bow as he placed the arrow on the string. Breathing evenly, he counted their distance down in his head and kept his gaze fixed on the Elites, who had neither slowed nor altered their original course. He couldn't tell if they simply hadn't seen him or perhaps didn't believe that he could hit a target that far away, which was why they hadn't raised their shields yet.

"That is your first mistake, you stinking piles of steaming pig turd." He breathed out slowly and released the arrow.

It honestly defied belief. At almost two hundred paces away, the barbarian stood his ground with a massive war bow in his hand. He was undoubtedly determined to buy time for the boy to press on to the dungeon to finish his quest. Ingold simply couldn't allow that.

But despite the impossibility of the situation, the barbarian stood calmly and watched them approach.

The Elite leader looked around again, hoping to find where the rest of the party was waiting. He was sure it was a trap. Dozens of barbarians were surely hidden somewhere, ready to attack them while the giant stood in the open as a distraction.

Something whistled past him, and a choked cry brought his mind back to his men. The one to his right was punched out of his saddle as the arrow slid easily through the chain mail and gambeson he wore and out the other side.

It was an impressive shot—an impossible shot—but there was no time to wonder how they had allowed it to happen.

"Shields!" Ingold bellowed. "Get your shields up, you useless rat-eating goatfuckers!"

Another man fell from his saddle and groaned as he held an arrow that protruded from his chest before the remainder of their troop snatched up the protective barriers carried on their saddles. Another arrow streaked in but this time, it hammered into the shield Ingold held up.

The man was a gifted archer on top of having a right hand that could put the fucking gods on their almighty fucking asses. What else would they discover that he could do?

"We need to put an end to this godsbedammed fucking mountain vermin!" Ingold shouted as the men pulled their horses to a halt. It wouldn't be long before the barbarian decided to shoot at the mounts instead of the riders, and they needed a plan of attack to kill him before they could deal with the prince.

He pointed out a group of five of the remaining fifteen guards. "You ride the barbarian down. The rest, follow me."

Ten of them could kill the pretender with no real difficulty. The boy was a sound fighter, but he had no skill or experience that would enable him to overcome so many who wanted his blood at the same time.

Ingold gestured for those coming with him to move and watched the five others ready a charge at the barbarian.

The warrior still hadn't taken his gaze off the larger group and had already fitted another arrow to his bow and fired it.

Yet another impossible shot drew a headshake from the leader when it slipped between an Elite's helm and shield and sliced through her throat at an almost unnatural angle.

His anger stirred but he reminded himself that the barbarian would soon be dead and it would not matter how he had learned to shoot so accurately.

One arrow remained before he would have to dig into his quiver for more, and there would not be time for that.

He'd selected one of those who tried to circle him to leave with their leader, and the others struggled to avoid the wounded Elite, who slid from her saddle and tried to contain the blood that flowed from her throat.

Skharr had done what he could for Tryam. As of this moment, he needed to fight for his survival.

The arrow was loosed, but the target raised his shield quickly and the projectile embedded deeply into it.

At least they didn't have lances.

The warrior tossed his bow to the side and snatched the spear the dwarves had made for him. It wasn't quite as impressive as the one they had sent him into the tower with, but when facing five men on horseback, he knew it would be as fine a weapon as he could hope for.

He dropped to one knee, felt the vibrations in the earth from the five horsemen charging him, and lowered the spear directly into the horse in front of him.

The beast stared at him for as long as it dared and galloped at full tilt before it suddenly skidded to a halt and whinnied in panic when the spearhead sank into its chest. It wasn't a deep wound and certainly not enough to kill it, but it did manage to stop it.

Skharr dragged the spear back quickly before the head could be broken and lifted his shield as two of the riders who tried to pass him swung their sabers at his head.

The weapon to his left glanced off the shield, but the other slid low and scored a shallow gash across his shoulder between his pauldron and helm.

It was a good blow, and the warrior hissed as he straightened, grasped the spear, and angled it past the head of the horse that was still in front of him.

The maneuver wasn't as easy as he'd thought it would be, but he managed to drive the spear through the chest of the man seated in the saddle, who tried desperately to reach him with his saber.

There was no chance his adversary might be successful, and he used the momentum to lift the Elite off his saddle while the rider tried to hold fast to the reins. The horse reared but stayed on his feet as Skharr dragged the man off and thrust his spear deep into his chest until he could feel no more resistance.

The other four returned quickly and the warrior caught the wounded horse's reins.

"Hey, hey, greatheart," he whispered to calm the beast as he held it in place between himself and the other four men who spurred their mounts into a charge.

It might not have been the nicest thing he'd ever done to a horse, but he would make restitution to Horse later. He watched over the saddle as the four tried to find a way around the animal to strike at him. One finally decided to angle his mount to try to catch his target away from his new shield while another did the same but from the opposite side.

Skharr watched from narrowed eyes as he circled the wounded animal to block the man who attacked from behind him while he lowered his spear to face the one advancing in front.

The Elite hesitated, and the other two appeared to be at a loss as to what they wanted to do. He did not intend to give them the time to find a solution. Instead, he stepped out, tossed the spear up, and caught it in a backhand grasp a second before he launched it forward.

It wasn't his finest throw, but as his target did not expect it, he was unable to bring his shield up in time. The blade caught him in the shoulder with enough force to hurl him off the horse, and the barbarian rushed to where he had landed and now groaned in pain.

Before the man could look up, Skharr had reached him and drove his boot onto the man's neck and applied pressure until he felt bones break under his heel.

When he looked for his weapon, he realized that the fall had snapped the spearhead off and he scowled.

"Fuck!" he cursed, reached to draw his sword clear of its scabbard, and lowered his shield as he recalled everything Sera had taught him.

The blademaster had so much more to teach him, of course, but he had learned a few of the skills she had shown him. He waited as one of the Elites abandoned his horse and now sprinted to where he stood with his saber poised for a strike.

The warrior made a note of where the other two riders circled and tried to find a way to reach him without committing themselves.

He would have the time to deal with the one who had already begun his assault.

The saber flashed toward his neck and he lowered his blade

from the high guard to parry and twisted his wrists quickly to initiate a counter-attack. It thunked into the man's shield.

Before the Elite could make a second attempt, Skharr pushed forward, caught him off balance, and kicked him hard on the knee.

A loud crack and a scream confirmed that the joint was broken, and he swung his sword forward and thrust the blade through the man's chest and out the other side.

His opponent's pain-filled expression faded into blankness and he sagged wordlessly as the barbarian drew the steel out of his chest.

The man's death decreased the number of his opponents to two, but they were still on horseback and the animals that had prevented them from attacking effectively had drifted away to remove themselves from the combat.

It would be up to him how he ended things, but nothing in him would allow him to enter a battle on anything but his terms. He held his sword a little tighter as the two men exchanged a glance. Something about their demeanor suggested that they were looking for a way out of the fray that would allow them to do so with their honor intact.

They soon realized, however, that there was no other way through it but through him. Skharr drew a deep breath, his gaze on the horses that could sense their riders' uncertainty. The animals pranced skittishly to the side but came alongside one another when their reins were yanked firmly.

These, the barbarian thought wryly, were desperate times. He had no horses to shield him and no spear to hold them off with, which meant he would need to find a way to win despite the difficulties.

He planted his blade into the earth and advanced on the two Elites. They retreated instinctively from the man who was, against all the odds, walking toward them with no weapon in hand.

One of them snapped and kicked his horse into a gallop. The other needed a few moments to find his courage before he heeled his horse into motion to join his comrade's charge.

The warrior pushed toward the man who had attacked first and sprinted forward.

The young prince didn't like having to leave Skharr to slow the men on his own. There was nothing honorable about leaving someone to die so he had a better chance at survival. It was like the man thought his life was less important, and that was something he was not comfortable with.

But he also didn't intend to stop and let his companion make that sacrifice in vain. He would need to enter the dungeon and emerge victorious to find the giant of a man grinning and making snide comments when he came out.

His horses moved quickly and kept him ahead of where he could hear the horses approaching from behind. He refused to look back, unable to make himself face what was happening there. Instead, he faced forward resolutely and slipped into a ravine—one most likely caused years before by flooding rains—which might provide a path into the valley ahead.

Almost immediately, he found what he was looking for. The ravine turned into a path that doubled back on itself, circled, and created a passage that was not easily visible from the top. While it had certain advantages, it proved fairly difficult for the horses to navigate as they continued at a slow but steady pace.

Openings had been cut into it that looked like tunnels but let the blazing sunlight in.

"Whoa, there," he whispered, brought his horses to a stop, and narrowed his eyes to inspect his surroundings. The half-tunnel had opened into a larger chamber and sunlight poured in from an aperture above.

The brightness illuminated what was undoubtedly a nest, home to something large that clearly had an appetite for humans as could be seen from the piles of bones discarded all around it.

"Fuck," he whispered and tried to keep his voice low as he dismounted and drew his weapon hastily.

The sound of fighting continued behind them. There was no doubt in Ingold's mind that the barbarian giant had every intention of making his death as costly as possible for those who took his life. Most of his men would be lost in the combat, but in the bigger scheme of things, it was of little import.

He could see the prince riding into the valley below—running away from them, he thought with a smirk, and into the ravines that cut through the earth and into the swamps below. They would find him before he found the dungeon, gut the pretentious little bastard, and leave his corpse to feed the monsters that inhabited the bogs.

As they entered a ravine in pursuit, he motioned for his men to follow in a single file and the group had to slow as they entered the narrow defile. It was not difficult to navigate, and their leader led them forward confidently, his focus on the horses' tracks that were easily visible.

The Elites began to look around and Ingold couldn't help but feel the same curiosity. Something in the pit of his stomach warned him, however, and every instinct in his body screamed that they were walking into a trap. If there was ever a place for the barbarians to attack them, it would be there, and every one of his men hefted steel, ready for a fight.

The ground shuddered, and the horses all stopped of their own accord and rumbled warily deep within their chests.

Gone were the days when he ignored the instincts of his mount. The beast was trained for battle and was utterly fearless, which meant that if something worried it, he knew to be concerned as well.

He peered intently down the passage and tried to determine what his mount was trying to warn him of.

Suddenly, the whole area began to smell of smoke and sulfur, and his heart plummeted into his stomach. It was a chilling feeling and brought memories of the last time he had smelled that particular odor.

His gaze drifted upward and caught a hint of movement as he realized that tunnels were cut all around the path they were following.

Dark scales caught the dim light filtering in from above, and large eyes wreathed in flame stared at him.

Ingold felt like a hand had wrapped around his throat. He wanted to scream but all that came out was a choked whisper.

"Dragon!"

No man in his right mind would do this. The rider's expression revealed both disbelief and the certainty that his target would see the futility of what he attempted.

The horse watched the barbarian warily and it slowed as if in an attempt to draw away from the charging madman. It turned its head sharply as he closed the distance between the two as fast as he could.

They collided with sufficient force to thrust the air from Skharr's lungs. The full power of the warhorse bore down on him and pushed him back, but he stretched his hand around to grasp the bridle, looped his fingers in it, and twisted the animal's head. The struggle demanded every ounce of physical and mental power he possessed, but the beast gradually lost its resistance, turned, and tried to pull away from him.

Finally, the barbarian found his footing again and with

another surge of effort, dragged it to the ground with him and into the path of the horse that charged from the other side.

Both creatures tumbled and landed heavily, and he vaulted over the closest one to where the Elite was still pinned under his mount and fought to free himself.

He had only a short window of opportunity so he grasped the man's head quickly and yanked hard until he heard a crack. The horse struggled to regain its feet, and when he let it go, it kicked a cloud of dust up around them.

Through the haze, he located the last Elite, who had regained his feet and now searched around him for his fallen saber.

He realized where Skharr was and both men studied each other for a moment before they moved. The man scrambled to find his weapon and the barbarian to reach him before he could locate it.

Steel flashed in the dust before he powered into his opponent, however, and he grimaced when a gash opened on his arm. Despite the sudden surge of pain, he allowed his momentum to continue unhindered and the two combatants sprawled in another flurry of dust. The warrior snaked his hand out while still on the sand and caught the man's hand to prevent him from wielding the saber again. His other hand dragged his adversary's helm off before he drove his fist into the Elite's jaw. With a long, gasped breath, he pushed to his feet.

The man was dazed but still tried to fight. Skharr moved toward him and drove his fists into his face. Warm blood spattered his arms, chest, and face, and he did not realize he was screaming until he looked down to see little of the man's skull intact.

Most of it was reduced to pieces of skull, viscera, and blood, which coated his hands as well. He dragged in a deep breath, wiped the blood off his face, and slowly regained his calm as he surveyed the results of the battle. The horses were running now as if to escape the fighting, although the dust around him had begun to settle for the most part.

No, he realized after a moment and narrowed his eyes in sudden concern. They weren't running from the fighting. Something else was driving them away.

A low roar rumbled through the silence and sounded like thunder beneath the ground as it passed him.

"Oh…godsbedammed fucking no. May your cock shrivel and ten thousand carrion lice infest your nether regions, Janus, you goblin-fucking apology for a god. No fucking no." Skharr growled as he gathered his weapons hastily from where they had been discarded. He left the arrows he'd shot and the broken spear but took the rest as Horse trotted toward him and neighed loudly.

The stallion wanted to help. Of course he did.

He waved the beast away. "No! Get out of here!"

Horse snorted but stopped his approach when the barbarian began to run in the same direction in which he'd seen the prince ride.

There was no way he would let the animal get in the middle of a fight with a dragon.

CHAPTER SEVENTEEN

Any kind of victory seemed impossible. The monster had waited for them before they even realized it was there. It uttered no warning with not even a suggestion of noise from a creature that large until it loomed over them and grinned hungrily with fangs the size of daggers. Worse, the beast appeared to be content to wait for a moment or two for them to realize how fucked they were.

It moved impossibly quickly but didn't use the flames that erupted from its mouth for anything more than to prevent them from advancing deeper into the caverns and to panic the horses.

In the end, the irony was that it probably only wanted the horses. Those were the focus of its attack and the massive talons ripped smoothly into them. The deaths of the Elites atop those horses were almost an afterthought and a few were simply left to bleed out as the beast moved on to kill as many as it could in its trap.

A few of the men bellowed battle cries and attacked, possibly thinking only of the honor there would be for those who could kill a dragon. This particular monster could quite easily have been one of the largest Ingold had ever seen. The size was initially deceptive as the long neck made it look a little smaller until it became visible in its entirety.

Covered in dark-green scales, it was almost impossible to see until the flames illuminated the tunnels. Its body was about as large as a horse and it used its hind and forelimbs to cling to the walls. The wings were also tipped with claws that raked viciously to catch those who had attacked it and drive them back.

One of the men pushed close enough to strike and drove his sword into the dragon's back. It was a good blow and the sword was buried in the scales but failed to penetrate to the vulnerable flesh beneath, not even enough to draw blood.

He struggled to pull his blade free to strike again but the effort was futile. The beast's jaws snapped him in half at the waist, and his head and torso fell free while the rest of him remained seated on his panicked horse.

"Get out!" Ingold roared. "Retreat!"

His troop did not need to be told twice and those who still had horses spun to comply and immediately surged into a frantic gallop back the way they had come.

The dragon quickly killed those who had been forced off their horses and its heavy breathing seeming frighteningly loud and close.

One by one, his men and the horses that remained alive screamed as they were overtaken by the carnage unleashed by the monster. The Elite's leader clutched his mount's reins tighter and urged it to greater speed through the narrow pathways carved by the rocky defile. Finally, they raced through the final twists of the ravine and emerged above ground.

Given the heat they'd recently endured, he hadn't thought he would ever be so happy to see the sun again. The heat of it warmed his face as he continued to push his mount to race as far away from the tunnels as he could. He only stopped when he no longer heard the dragon's roars and the screams of his men. One or two of their horses had miraculously escaped and continued to run from the beast's rampage.

His ears rang and his whole body was tighter than a knot when he eventually dragged his horse to a halt and dared to look back the way he'd come.

Only one of his group of Elites had survived with him. The man looked as terrified as he felt, although he had also stopped to look for the group that was supposed to follow them. He was similarly shocked that only he and his leader were left.

All Ingold could think was that they were lucky enough to come face to face with a dragon and live. Very few could claim that kind of good fortune, especially when they had walked into the beast's lair without knowing it was there.

"What do we do next, Captain?" the man asked, removed his helm, and wiped the sweat from his forehead.

Ingold shook his head, unsure of what they should do. Most of the Elites who had been entrusted to him were dead, which left him with only a single man to ensure the death of their quarry.

"We have to return to the city," he decided. "With the raiders patrolling this land, we won't survive out here."

"What about the prince?"

"He's no affirmed prince yet!" he snapped and held his horse firmly to stop it prancing skittishly. "And if the dragon does not kill the pathetic pretender, the dungeon will. If he does not return in a week, we can assume they are dead. Or maybe two. They would not carry enough food and water to sustain them beyond that."

It was an odd feeling to rush toward a dragon's roar. The beasts were difficult to kill even in the best of situations. In tight, confined spaces, Skharr doubted that there would be much of anything Tryam could do against it.

And yet the sounds no longer came from ahead. Echoed roars and shouts issued from all around him and as he followed them, there was no sign of where they might all come from.

He paused to study his surroundings again, his sword still in his hand, and tried to discern what kind of magic could make it all sound like it came from nearby.

Not nearby, he realized a moment later. It was below ground, something he hadn't expected.

The barbarian shook his head in an attempt to clear it as he moved over the open landscape. He noticed holes in the surface, where something had dug beneath and disturbed it—openings, he thought speculatively, that he could drop through to find the prince without having to face the dragon outright.

Or, at least, he could find it on his terms.

"Fucking overgrown hell-spawned lizard," Skharr muttered. "Its kind were no doubt hatched in a godsbedammed fucking fire demon's ass." Sending the prince ahead on his own had been a mistake and he knew that now. He could have held the Elites back and maybe even given the dragon a fight for its life as his young charge snuck through to the dungeon. Now, he'd done only half and was sure that wasn't enough.

Two horses suddenly raced out from a ravine. Neither gave him so much as a glance but galloped frantically away from the dragon.

That was no real surprise. The sounds of fighting had begun to fade, although he could still hear low growls and roars powerful enough to make the earth shake.

Moments later, the shudders grew more intense, accompanied by rumbling from underground. Something began to give beneath his feet, and he looked hastily at a point where the dirt was drawn inexorably into a nearby hole. It seemed larger than the others and it was also one he hadn't seen.

"Oh for—shit! Janus, you hairy-assed troll-fucking almighty turd-brained ass. Your stinking pet will likely be the godsbe-dammed death of me." He hissed in frustration and outrage as the place where he stood shifted toward the hole and took him with it.

The young prince was deeply unsettled by the screams that seemed to come from all the different entrances and all direc-tions. The warped echoes were confusing, and he couldn't tell where the sounds issued from.

For all he knew, dozens of dragons could be attacking. There would be no way of escape for him as he stood in the nest to which they would return with their kills.

The fact that those being killed had tried to take his life was of little comfort. In his rush to evade them, he had walked blindly into a location where he would die anyway. They might as well have driven the dagger into his back. It would certainly have been less painful than death by dragon.

"A foolish plan, Skharr," Tryam muttered and tried to slow his breathing. His horses had galloped away the moment the roars had started, and he hadn't been able to stop them. All he had left was what he had taken from their saddles—his weapons, most of the food and water, as well as a few supplies he thought he would need. Everything else was gone.

The shrieks and the sounds of combat eventually stopped, yet that proved to be of little comfort to him while he waited unwill-ingly for the dragon to return to its nest and his inevitable demise.

Movement above distracted him from his momentary self-pity and he looked upward. Earth and sand were dislodged from the opening above the nest and he realized that someone had dropped into the hole at the top.

The sheer size of the man suggested that it could be only one person, and Tryam couldn't understand how the man had fallen through. The barbarian tried to slow himself, caught the edge, and looked down for a moment before he released his hold.

It was a drop of a little over ten feet, but the fall was softened by the nest itself. Still, it seemed the softened fall was not quite what Skharr had hoped for.

"Bastard son of Janus' poxy whore!" The man growled his annoyance and dragged himself clear of the nest. "I was almost shafted by a godsbedammed rock. Trust a fucking scaley lizard to find a new way to fuck me in my ass. What in all the demon-infested hells is this place?"

"Skharr!" the prince called and waved him to the corner of the room. "Over here, and quickly too!"

The barbarian looked to where the boy gestured frantically and disengaged himself slowly from the debris around the nest. It looked like it had been made mostly of brambles and rocks and was likely used by the beast as a home that not only allowed it to bask in the sun but also to fly clear of the tunnels if they didn't provide enough food.

Tryam wasn't sure if the dragon had made the tunnels itself or if they had been made with it in mind, but he chose not to question it one way or the other. All he could tell was that it would probably return to its nest with the kills it had collected.

An unsettling thought occurred to him as Skharr approached him.

"Are you hurt, boy?" the barbarian asked. "I'll deny ever saying it, but I am damn glad to see you alive."

"Well, you can enjoy all five seconds of it. I think the dragon killed all the Elites and should be on its way here. I assume creatures like that like to bring their meals to their nest to enjoy?"

The warrior did not answer immediately as he was focused on checking what had survived the fall. A few of the arrows in his quiver were broken, but he kept them, possibly hoping to find new shafts for the heads.

"Two escaped alive, as far as I could see," Skharr informed him finally. "Although I doubt they'll wait nearby for us. They won't want to risk being in the area when she gets hungry again."

"She?"

"Only female dragons make nests. The males travel over large territories and hunt more actively."

Tryam nodded. "Well, I don't think they'll have to wait for us to come out. If this is her nest, she will return to it, won't she?"

The barbarian paused and nodded. "A good point. Have you found a way into the dungeon yet?"

"Yes, I have. Can't you see me inside it?"

"Do not try my patience, boy. Have you found a way in or not?"

The prince shrugged and approached the rear wall. "It would appear that this is the door to it. I can see the indentions where it will likely open, and there is writing across the wall in dozens of languages."

"Any that you understand?"

"I understand most of them. My mother wanted to make sure I could understand most languages spoken around the world."

Skharr sighed. "That is certainly impressive. Now, will you tell me what it says on the door or will you give me a language lesson?"

"What was that you were saying about trying your patience?"

"I can try yours, not the other way around. Now, what does it say?"

"It says the doors will open when the queen is on her throne. I suppose it means the doors are connected to the throne in Citar, and we must now wait for her to sit on her throne for the doors to open, yes?"

The barbarian shook his head. "The queen refers to the dragon, and the throne is…well, her nest."

"So, we are waiting for…"

"Yes."

Tryam stared at him, gulped, and glanced at the entrance, where they could hear something moving. In moments, movement was visible in the darkened shadows and a large shape reflected the light that came through the ceiling.

"You have to be very still," Skharr whispered as he drew his bow and an arrow. "And when I tell you to, move as quickly as you can."

"Where?"

"I think it will be fairly obvious. The queen will return to her throne and the doors will open. Be ready to go through with all speed once they do and do not wait for me."

"Do you intend to slow the dragon for me?"

The giant smirked. "That is the idea but I won't linger for it to attack me. I feel I've already earned my pay protecting you as it is."

Tryam could not deny that and his eyes returned to what moved through the aperture.

At first, the creature proved hard to discern, but she snaked her long neck through and scanned the cavern before she entered. She moved slowly and carried what looked like a decapitated horse in her forelimbs while she waddled to the nest on the rear limbs and maintained her balance using her wings.

"She is beautiful," Skharr whispered and again, he could not disagree. An unsettling feeling had come over him as he studied the six-limbed creature, but the way the sunlight glittered on the dark-green scales was sinisterly appealing.

The blood dripped from her maw as she took a bite from the dead horse, but it in no way diminished her beauty. Oddly, that appeal made the creature seem more horrific.

She settled onto the nest and the doors began to draw back slowly along a track. Soon, they clicked into place, as far open as they would get and some twenty paces apart.

Tryam couldn't believe she hadn't seen them already and wondered when she would realize that she wasn't alone in her nest. Perhaps she simply didn't expect to find anyone stupid enough to wait in the heart of her domain.

Skharr gestured to the door with his hand and held three fingers up. The prince nodded at the fairly succinct message, drew a deep breath, and tried against all odds to make it as soundless as possible.

Thankfully, his breathing was not quite as loud as the dragon breaking the dead horse's bones and sucking the marrow out with her long, thin tongue.

The three fingers went to two and then one before the warrior pointed at the door.

Without hesitation, the young contender sprinted as fast as his legs would take him toward the opening.

The sound of his footsteps was enough to catch the beast's attention, and she uttered one of the roars he had heard reverberating through the tunnels. The power of it made his bones shake, but he could not spare even a hasty glance lest he catch his foot on something and stumble or worse, even fall.

It would be nothing short of a tragedy if his quest to become heir to the empire failed because of a tiny branch he hadn't seen until it was too late.

Skharr had already drawn his bow back and loosed an arrow as the dragon heaved herself from her nest. As she moved, the doors automatically began to slide shut but much more rapidly than they had opened.

When the barbarian's arrow buried itself in the dragon's cheek, she backed into the nest again and the barriers stopped and returned to their open position.

"Come on, Skharr!" the prince shouted. His companion was already in motion and raced away from the beast, who now vented her anger in a streak of flame directed toward him.

The heat was overwhelming, and Tryam could feel it scorch the back of his neck even from that far away.

He reached the door and flung himself through as he looked over his shoulder, trying to confirm that the barbarian was behind him.

Thankfully, the huge man was closer than he'd expected. Skharr could move at a frighteningly fast pace when he had a mind to and in this case, he no doubt had every intention to close the gap as quickly as possible.

The dragon clambered out of her nest and advanced on them as Tryam drew a dagger from where it was sheathed on his belt and threw it at her with all the power he could muster.

His weapon flew well and sank into the scales over her eye. The target area was well protected, however, so it failed to cut deeply, but it was enough to distract the monster as his companion dove through the closing doors.

The barbarian was already on his feet when he yanked his shield forward and pressed it up against the doors that were closing behind them seconds before a blast of fire pushed them back. The explosive power of it upended both men, who careened across the rocky floor for a fair distance before they were able to stop themselves.

When Tryam looked up, he realized that the doors had already clicked shut again.

"We'd best keep moving." Skharr shook the shield off his arm. It was still on fire and mostly broken so he tossed it aside with a scowl when he realized how thoroughly ruined it was. "We don't know when it'll return to the nest and open the doors again."

The young prince couldn't help but agree, and they advanced through the darkened passage as far as they dared before they allowed themselves a moment to rest.

Thankfully, the doors remained closed. "I don't think they will open again."

"What?"

"The doors. The sign outside said that they would open when the queen took her throne and would not open again until the hero emerged victorious, or not at all. I assume that means within a certain time frame, although it didn't specify how long."

Skharr sighed and nodded, crouched quickly, and pressed his back against the wall. The prince realized that his arm was hurting and he was tending to it quickly.

"Wonderful." The barbarian sighed as he applied a poultice to the nasty burns. "Another one of those godsbedammed time-controlled fucking hell-pits. What happened to dungeons that allow you to enter or exit whenever you wish to do so?"

"This one is a test, I suppose," Tryam answered and settled beside him to use some flint to light a torch he had brought—the only one he'd kept before the horses fled—to provide more light. "Which is why my people accept the proof—whatever that may be—that the dungeon will give me. But now you are here with me."

"Not by choice," his companion muttered. "And not because you asked. I intended to find another way out until that dragon started breathing fire. It was either hide here or join that headless horse as the dragon's meal. However, I suppose you got your answer."

"Answer? To what?"

"How big a dragon would have to be before one should run instead of fight." He pointed toward the door behind them. "That was the size one runs from."

The prince tilted his head and chuckled after a few moments of consideration.

"Besides," Skharr continued, "I intend to remain with you when you return to your city. This is far from over. Someone owes me for those rabid maggot-brained sheepfuckers, and I intend to take a moment of their time."

"If I had to place a guess, I would say you would want words with the viceroy. He is a mage of some repute, or so the rumor goes. He's almost as old as my father is and has survived that long by being a crafty bastard."

"Can he bleed?"

It was a simple question, yet it still caught him off-guard.

He laughed and shook his head. "Right. I forgot that DeathEaters are not practiced in the art of kissassery."

"We do practice it occasionally," his companion clarified as he bound his arm after he'd poured a little healing potion over the burns. "It would depend on how upset our mates happen to be."

Tryam nodded. "You wouldn't happen to have a DeathEater mate waiting for you somewhere, would you?"

"Hells and fucking thrice godsbedammed no," the barbarian responded vehemently. "If you think I'm crazy, you should see how our women act. Why do you think I never go back?"

"I assumed it was because you didn't want to return to the cold of the mountains."

"No, it's because as insane as you might think I am, our women are much worse. Some might approve of it, of course, but I am far less likely to wake up missing my balls if I anger a woman here."

"Although there is still a chance. Have you considered, however, not angering any of them?"

"I can't make them all happy, which means some will be angered eventually. It's best to avoid those who are capable of inflicting the most damage."

He thought about this with a small frown before he nodded in agreement.

CHAPTER EIGHTEEN

The tunnels gave every indication that they wound on forever, and Skharr wondered who had taken the time to create them. They had even managed to draw a dragon in to guard their treasure.

The Ancients who built these dungeons certainly had an odd obsession with protecting treasure they never intended to spend. What was the point of gathering all their magical power and all their riches in one place?

His memories of what he had seen in the tower reminded him that not all the dungeons had been built to secure riches. As it turned out, some gods truly were asses and simply wanted to watch humans kill each other.

The doors they finally approached brought something similar to mind as he waited while the boy moved closer, narrowed his eyes, and traced his fingers over the inscription.

"What does it say?" he asked. The prince was better-read than he was and waiting for him to translate the writing was preferable to attempting to discover if it was written in a language he could understand.

Tryam did not answer immediately and when he did, it was not quite what Skharr had expected.

"Son of a whore!" he shouted and looked genuinely angry for the first time his large companion could remember. "Spin it, bend it over, and fuck it in the ass like a cheap portside tramp."

Startled by the vehemence of the imprecation, he stared at his young charge. "I don't suppose the inscriptions say that," he said as calmly as he could.

He leaned closer to inspect it. Most of the writing was scribbled and he couldn't understand it, but the drawings were fairly easy to interpret. Three figures wore helms and carried weapons and all stood around another figure on its knees.

"Toss the godsbedammed poxy creature into the water and let the dolphins—"

"Boy!"

Tryam looked at him.

"What in all the demon-filled hells is a dolphin?"

"Oh… A creature of the ocean. It's known to be particularly friendly toward humans—maybe too friendly toward humans."

"Oh. Oh!" Skharr raised his eyebrows. "Why don't you stop trying to think of the many different ways a woman of the night can be fucked and tell me what the godsbedammed fuck this image is? Not that I do not admire the vehemence and creativity in your verbal imagery, but perhaps this is not the time."

"This…carving" —the prince gestured toward it—"is a depiction of the Supplicant and the Three Bodyguards."

"You say that as though you expect me to understand what it means."

"It's a trial, a test of legend. I am allowed three to accompany me for the first three challenges. Only those who would die for the will of the supplicant may come in."

"Three? I thought only you were allowed to enter alone."

"That is what I was led to understand, which is why I am so angry. It would have to be only me in the final chamber, but the initial trials allow for three who would…well, die for me. This is not your fight—not for your land or your people."

"You act as though I have not already put my life at risk to save yours."

Tryam paused and shrugged a little uncomfortably. "Well, you were paid to do it."

"I wouldn't do what I did for simply anyone who threw a coin in my direction. Besides, it might not hurt to know an emperor."

"I could die and all you would be left with is an emperor who is empirically angry with you."

Skharr nodded. "Well, we are barely a few yards from a dragon out there who most certainly is annoyed with me. There would be the Count of Gerstrand as well. As you can imagine, it would not be the first group of people I've annoyed or the second. Not the third either, come to think of it."

The prince chuckled. "Wait, what did you do to the others?"

"I…might have told the count's soldiers to get in line as I shook the sails and left them behind on the docks. It would appear that they misplaced one of their princesses on the ship I stole from them to enable my escape."

"A…princess?"

Skharr raised his hands. "I did not know she was on board. She had no idea that I intended to steal the sloop either. We sailed together for a season or so."

"Oh." Tryam grunted. "What happened then?"

"I wanted to return to land, and she wanted to become a pirate. As it turned out, she had a talent for the work. The last I heard of her, she had four ships in her fleet and harried every trading vessel that happened to sail the deep water around her father's kingdom."

"And I suppose you somehow annoyed her as well?"

"You would think so, but no. I…haven't the sea legs for long voyages on the open water. We took our pleasure together, but in the end, it was best for us to part ways. I do believe I will still find the hangman's noose awaiting me if I return, however. If I'm lucky."

"And if you're unlucky?"

"The king has a man in his army who has a talent for ripping limbs off those his sovereign wishes dead."

"Ah. Very unlucky."

Skharr nodded in agreement. "Now, let us return to the topic of the three supplicants and the bodyguard."

"Three bodyguards and the supplicant."

"Of course."

"If I am reading these writings correctly, it would appear there are three tests, three trials, and three ways to fail."

"Godsbedammed filthy fucking vermin-infested dungeons."

"When we enter the first chamber, we won't need the torches. It seems these strongholds are powered by the gods—which, to be honest, does not give me any real comfort."

"Nor I. The gods—and one hairy-balled ass-fucker in particular—happen to be terrible beings."

Tryam narrowed his eyes. "You speak like you have some personal experience."

The barbarian merely shrugged by way of an answer. "What happens next in this hell-spawned dungeon? Do we have to grapple with a golem made from diamonds?"

"I haven't a fucking clue. All the legends are different when it comes down to it. And wait—did you mean that one of the dungeons you fought in was built by a god?"

"Yes. One who needs to have a hefty sack of troll dicks shoved up his ass very slowly and painfully—and one by one to make it last."

With a laugh, the young prince turned to the door they had inspected and pulled it. He struggled with the weight for a few seconds before Skharr took hold of one of the handles.

It groaned under the combined strength of both men and finally began to swing open.

Cautiously, they peered through the aperture to confirm that they had no more need of the torch Tryam had brought with him. Large sconces hung on the walls and gave off purple illumination, although it soon became clear that they contained crystals rather than flames. These were fueled by some kind of power the barbarian preferred to not think about.

"So...what do you think those tests will be?" he asked as they stepped into the unsettling purple light and the doors closed behind them again.

The young prince sighed and rubbed his temples as he looked around the chamber. "Keep in mind that no one was able to tell me definitively what I would face, as each trial would differ depending on the supplicant. Also, no one could give me details lest it be construed as cheating or favoritism. If I remember correctly, though, the first trial is always one of avarice to test the moral mettle of those who undergo it. A few seem to have involved all the riches any man could ever desire. Others merely offered anything your heart desires—which I suppose could be riches as well."

"I imagine that the kind of man who would want power and the consolidation of it wouldn't search for it in dungeons in the distant reaches of the world," Skharr commented and toyed with a pouch at his hip. "It would make sense that those who come here would only want coin and that which coin can buy."

Tryam nodded. "Well, a riddle will always be mixed with the first test—one that will help us with the second test. If we fail to solve it, we will enter the next level without a hint that would help us."

"And do you know what the riddle is?"

The boy shrugged. "Yes."

"How?" Skharr asked and paused to look at him. "If there are those who know what the riddle is, they wouldn't share it with anyone who would venture in here later. Aside from the necessity that you undertake the quest without an unfair advantage,

MICHAEL ANDERLE

they would either want to honor the spirit of the dungeon or simply wouldn't want to share the riches."

"Yes, that does make sense."

"Then why would you know what the riddle is?"

"Because it's inscribed on the walls."

The barbarian paused to look at where the prince now pointed and narrowed his eyes when he realized that the inscriptions on the walls were legible. Although still written in dozens of languages, he was able to find one in the common tongue.

"I drive men mad," Tryam read aloud. "For love of me, easily beaten, never free. What am I?"

Skharr scowled and tilted his head in thought. He had always hated riddles. There was always a twist to them he could never fathom. He was well aware that he did not necessarily have the brightest mind, and these were always meant to be deciphered by those with a peculiar type of cleverness he lacked.

He turned to his companion. The prince seemed like the kind of lad who would have spent at least a fair portion of his time reading and developing the cleverness required.

"Do you know what it means?" Tryam asked.

"What? I thought you would know. You're the one who reads and discovers things like this."

The boy shrugged. "I've never heard this one."

"Then think hard. We'll need to find the answer if we wish to find our way past the first test."

They paused and considered it in silence. Too many answers sprang to Skharr's mind and he decided regretfully that humans were driven mad too easily. Hints could be found in the second half of the clue, but he could not think of anything that pointed specifically to them and nothing else.

"I can't think of the answer," the prince whispered. "I hate shorter riddles. They're always too vague and are intended to sound clever only if you already know the answer."

Skharr nodded. "Aye. But we could wait here forever for

176

something to happen or to discover the answer, or we can forge on. It was only a hint toward what we needed, yes?"

Tryam studied the inscription a few more times. The barbarian assumed that he was looking for more clues in the other languages he could read, but his sigh of frustration was a clear indicator that they were equally as vague as the one in common.

"I suppose we'll have to keep moving," he whispered and ran his fingers through his long black hair. "Hopefully, the answer will come to us when we need it."

His companion smirked. "That's the way to do it. Hoping we don't need the answer to a riddle is certainly the way to survive a dungeon."

"Do you have a better idea?"

"I do not. I am merely being realistic about our odds for survival."

CHAPTER NINETEEN

Tryam knew the barbarian did not feel comfortable advancing like this. In the end, he did not either. It was unsettling to think that the fate of his quest could depend on whether he could discover the meaning of a riddle and seemed almost unfair. When one entered a dungeon, the expectation was that their fighting skills would be all that was tested.

Perhaps there was more required of him in a quest before he became heir to the throne.

There were too many ways in which it could go wrong. Perhaps this had been what the viceroy had in mind. If the guards didn't kill him first, he would simply die in the dungeon without needing anyone to accomplish it.

Although the fact that the man sent assassins to kill him before he even reached it meant he believed he was somehow capable of making it out alive.

It was odd how the simple feeling of faith from another person—even if it was someone who wanted him killed—made him more confident. The prince held his sword a little tighter as they proceeded down the hallway. Infuriatingly, the riddle repeated itself constantly on the wall, which made it a source of ever-increasing frustration as they continued without pause.

"How do they build these strongholds?" Skharr asked as he studied the fairly wide corridor. "I assume magic is involved, but why would they build it? Why would any of this be created by beings who had all the power in the world?"

"I've long since abandoned looking for logic in the actions of the Ancients. They were never the kind to think their actions through, at least from what I've heard of them. There are innumerable writings about them, but the facts have mostly been lost in myths and legends—stories told by those who killed them to either vilify them or make them appear much more of a destructive force that had to be destroyed."

The barbarian nodded. "All that was told about them among the clans is that they were evil creatures who needed to be destroyed and removed from our lands. We never said much about killing them, although mages are still not allowed within our borders for more than a few days."

"I never heard of the clans killing mages."

"Not necessarily killing them but forcibly escorting them from our territory. Those children born with the gift are sent away as well to the schools of magic in the southern isles."

"That's…horrible."

Skharr nodded. "I've never seen it happen myself, of course, but I can understand their distaste for those with the gift that came from the Ancients. Still, as you say, it is a horrible thing. There is no real explanation for how the rules came into being, and I merely assumed they were established after a long and protracted fight with the Ancients."

"Wars like that tend to bring out the worst in folk, and memories of that type of thing linger forever, although mostly in the form of legends and rumors."

The warrior seemed thoughtful for a moment, but he shrugged

and his long stride didn't falter. Tryam had a feeling that was how he usually dealt with thoughts of this nature. He was an uncomplicated man to his core, and the philosophical considerations of war were never something he allowed himself to be concerned with.

It was perhaps a trifle hypocritical of the man, but the young prince didn't intend to point it out. Skharr was not as simple as he pretended to be, and it was likely that he merely kept his thoughts about the world to himself.

"What can we expect from this level of the dungeon?"

Startled out of his thoughts, he glanced at his companion. "How in the hells would I know?"

"Well, you're the one who has read all about it. You also talked to those perhaps sent by the queen, who has also educated herself on the subject."

He narrowed his eyes. "Yes, well, I have some information on a dungeon that has nothing but legends written about it. That makes me the fucking expert. Why didn't you study dungeons before going into them?"

"Because most of what is written tends to be the work of legend anyway."

The prince grinned. "Precisely. With that in mind, why don't you consider keeping yours open to all the possibilities of what we shall face."

"Keep my what open?"

"What?"

"You said keep mine open. My what?"

Tryam snorted. "Your…your mind!"

"Ah. Never mind, then."

He wanted to laugh, but all he could do was shake his head. It seemed the barbarian was intentionally trying to either annoy him or keep his spirits up. Whichever it was, it was a welcome distraction until they reached the end of the hallway and another door. This was much smaller than the last, and no markings or new information were inscribed to tell them what to expect on the other side.

Skharr slipped past him and stepped through the doorway first, his hand on his weapon as was expected in his role as the prince's defender.

His expression remained unreadable, but suspicion seemed to color his demeanor. It seemed logical that he expected something to happen as they moved into what looked like a circular chamber with mosaics laid across the floor to depict a battle. Men in red armor were drawn up in battle lines against those in white, although there was no indication as to exactly which battle it was. Nothing provided any distinction between either side except for the color of their armor.

"What do you think it is?" Tryam asked after an unbearably long moment of silence.

"A trap."

"What?"

"There's a trap in this room. The mechanisms are exposed on the walls. If we step on something or trip something, the room will try to kill us somehow."

"Oh."

The barbarian turned to look at him. "What were you asking about?"

"Nothing."

"Boy…"

"Fine." He shook his head. "I asked about the mosaic. It's a battle, of course, and a large one so it's probably an important one as well. They don't create mosaics depicting unimportant battles. But I cannot for the life of me determine which it is or who the parties are."

Skharr narrowed his eyes and inspected the tiled image like he hadn't seen it at all when they entered the room. He tilted his head from one side to the other in turn as he studied first the red, then the white combatants.

"It's no battlefield I've ever seen," he muttered finally. "But look at the faces. Not all of them, but some are looking up like the battle is being viewed from above by a god and he is blessing those who look up to him, while the others... Well, they will likely die."

The prince focused on the depiction and frowned when he realized that Skharr was correct. Some of the faces were looking up and seemed at peace, while others were unsettled like those found in the middle of a battle.

It was an unusual juxtaposition of peace and conflict. Now that he looked at it with a different focus, it did seem like they looked down on the battle from above, perhaps from the eye of an eagle or a god who blessed those who looked to them for guidance. It was altogether unsettling, especially as they could see a few of the men already killing each other.

"Truly, it's an impressive piece," Skharr conceded and moved closer to the circular mosaic that took up most of the room. Only a few sections on both sides of the chamber remained unadorned. The young contender followed him, cautious about stepping over it, but there was no other way across other than through and he took his first step into it.

The floor was secure with his first step, but the moment he settled his second foot in place, the mechanisms in the wall began to move slowly and flurried a cloud of dust from the walls.

"What did I do?" Tryam asked and looked around in the first rush of panic. He did not want to remain in the same place for fear that he made an easy target. At the same time, he also didn't want to move in case that triggered something else.

Skharr did not answer and instead, studied the mechanisms intently before he turned to the mosaic. He finally saw something and lunged forward.

"Get off the mosaic!" he shouted.

The warning came too late and the floor gave beneath the

prince. His heart lurched into his throat and his hands flailed for something—anything—to catch hold of.

Something grasped him instead.

A large hand closed in an immediate vice-like hold on his wrist and managed to arrest his fall into blackness. His gaze drifted downward.

"Don't look down!" the barbarian warned.

"Why not?" His question came too late as he had already focused his attention below him.

The inky blackness was broken by something that reflected the light. A large, dark shape moved in the water at the very bottom of the deep cavern.

"Because you're heavy enough to hold as is." Skharr strained and held onto him with both hands as he fought to not be dragged down himself. "And if you continue to wriggle, I won't be able to prevent you from pulling us both through."

Tryam realized that he had begun to struggle almost unconsciously as he fought to try to regain his balance. He forced himself to remain motionless so his companion could pull him high enough that he could gain purchase and help to drag himself onto the floor. His rescuer fell but pushed hastily to his feet and looked for any sign that they would be attacked in another way.

It was an unsettling thought, but Tryam didn't think they would be. They were supposed to find a way across the battle-field despite the fact that the pieces might collapse under them.

"We have to find a way across," he announced and turned to the mosaic.

"The way across has been destroyed," Skharr replied and turned his steely gaze on the prince like a warning. "The mosaic is still intact, but the pieces are barely holding themselves in place. If you step on them, you will fall."

"No, I won't," he insisted. "Not if I find the right places to step. That is how we will find a way across. Something in the mosaic itself will tell me where it will be safe to put our weight."

The barbarian stared at him in silence before he nodded, drew his longsword from its scabbard, and approached the edge to peer through the hole. He had hoped to see where the path was, but nothing provided anything remotely resembling a clue. He dropped to one knee to keep his balance as he pushed the weapon onto the pieces of the mosaic. They fell one by one with each poke until finally, he reached one that didn't.

"That's it," Tryam whispered. "The beginning of the path. The first step."

"All we know is that I cannot push it down with a sword. There's no way to tell if it will take your weight."

The young prince looked more closely at the piece that remained and noticed the eyes of the man who was painted on it, who looked into the sky with a peaceful expression on his face.

"It's faith," he said and nodded firmly as he moved forward. "It's depicting the men who entrust their lives to whatever made it and it shows us that we should do the same."

Skharr scowled and shook his head. "Truly, the almighty fucking gods are giant hairy asses."

"What was that?"

"Nothing. Give me your hand. If you fall, I'll be able to catch you."

Tryam complied and stepped slowly onto the face of the faithful man. Nothing gave beneath him and as he put more of his weight on the depiction, it was clear that he wouldn't fall through.

"That's our path, then?" Skharr asked as he released him. "We step on the faces of fictional soldiers of faith?"

"Whoever made this is piss-arrogant, but it is the path. We'll follow it."

The prince searched for the nearest faithful soldier and jumped across the gap to him.

His whole body tensed, waiting to fall through, but the image supported him without even a faint tremor or groan.

"I should do that, you know," the barbarian muttered and stepped onto the first one. "Test the steps to make sure you know the safe path to follow me. Just in case one is broken, in which case I would be the one to fall through."

"Honestly, you might simply break some of the steps with your weight," Tryam answered as he took another step to follow the path deeper into the mosaic. "I wouldn't want to be the one following you."

"Are you calling me fat, boy?"

"No, merely heavy."

He was not wrong, and Skharr knew it. It was pointless to even try to deny that he was a heavy bastard and in the end, if this dungeon was as old as it looked, others would have put it through its paces.

The faces were close enough that he didn't need to jump much, but Tryam tried to not take any steps unless he had to. Every time he moved to another faithful warrior, he suspected that the floor would drop out from under him, but they held without any issues until he reached the floor on the other side.

Once his feet were on solid footing again, he grimaced at the rapid pounding in his chest that reminded him exactly how close to death he had been.

The barbarian was on his heels and once secure, looked at the mosaic with a scowl. "I'll freely admit that I didn't enjoy having to tiptoe through the magical tiles in the least."

"I think I'd rather face the dragon than use that path again," Tryam whispered.

His companion chuckled and shook his head. "I didn't dislike it that much."

With a rueful laugh, the prince advanced on the door in front of them. He found the environment unsettling but decided to not push himself through it too quickly. The rest of the dungeon would certainly be more difficult and this honestly didn't seem like one of the tests. It felt like a lesson—as if something wanted them to trust in it and have faith in it. Or someone, he thought and wished he'd made more of an effort to learn about the gods.

They stepped into the next room together, both with their hands on their weapons and ready for something to challenge them. Skharr stopped immediately and brought Tryam to a halt as well.

The next chamber was considerably larger and appeared to be more like a throne room even though there was no actual throne visible.

Instead, all that they could see were piles of treasure. Gold and jewels had been flung haphazardly into mounds and mountains across the space, which made it difficult to see where the exit was.

"That's odd," the barbarian muttered. "They don't usually lay the treasure out until you are at the end of the dungeon. I don't suppose this would be the end of it?"

He shook his head. Something about the whole room had made him uneasy when he'd entered beside his companion. The treasures looked like they were carelessly displayed and ready for the taking, and a few of the jewels felt like they would be easy to carry in his pockets if he could simply pick them up without so much as a pause. They could move through the room quickly and come away a great deal richer than when they had started.

"Don't," Skharr warned.

"What?"

"Do not touch any of the treasure here." The warrior placed a hand on his shoulder. "I've been through this before. It will weigh you down and you won't survive to the next test."

"Gold," he whispered.

"Yes," the other man agreed. "A whole steaming shit-pile of it."

"No." Tryam tried to curb his impatience. "The answer to the riddle. 'I drive men mad. For love of me, easily beaten, never free. What am I?' The answer is gold."

The barbarian paused and removed his hand from Tryam's shoulder. "A warning, then?"

"Aye. And I have a feeling there will be dire consequences if we touch anything in this room with the intention to take it for ourselves. Let's move through it as quickly as possible. I feel as though there might be magic in the air that will divert us from our path."

"Agreed."

CHAPTER TWENTY

They moved hastily through the coin-filled room, and Skharr caught himself wondering if he could snatch a few of the gems and coins without Tryam noticing. It was magic, of course. He knew that. There were too many situations in which he had not felt that way in the past. This wasn't a part of him. It was an outside voice telling him he wanted it.

But even so, each step felt like a trial and every time the cool gleam of gold caught his eye, his fingers twitched and his mouth watered. Still, he strengthened his resolve and moved past them and the unnatural fear of what he would face outside the dungeon if he did not take any of the treasure with him.

Tryam stared longingly at the piles of wealth as well, and his expression was a perfect mirror to what the barbarian felt. It helped to solidify the notion that it was the influence of an outside force.

When they reached the door, he felt as though he had been running for days. He closed it behind them, dragged in a deep breath, and ignored a hint of sweat on his skin as he studied the path ahead of them.

Something moved on the other side of the barrier and sealed it behind them. There would be no going back.

"Are you all right?" he asked as the boy leaned shakily against the wall.

"I…I think so."

"You were tempted to take the treasure, yes?"

The prince's face paled and he nodded.

"As was I. It was like a voice in my head tried to tell me how to sneak a handful of coins and gems when you weren't looking. It was…it was exhausting."

His companion's laugh was uneven and shook slightly as he settled into a crouch. "I know I shouldn't but I almost feel better knowing that someone else experienced the same. It's a terrible thing to think, I know, but…"

"Not terrible," Skharr said as his voice trailed off. "It was exhausting. Compose yourself, perhaps have a little to eat and drink, and find strength within. I have a feeling that the next few trials here will be considerably more taxing than simply fighting yourself."

Tryam didn't look at him but rummaged in his pouches and retrieved a few strips of dried meat and his water skin. The barbarian decided to do the same and grimaced when his hands trembled as he took some waybread from his pack and bit cautiously into it. He hadn't felt this winded since he had been poisoned but as he ate, at least some energy was restored to his muscles. It wasn't as much as he had hoped for but it was more or less what he expected.

"Do you feel better?" he asked as he replaced the water skin after a few gulps of the precious liquid.

The young prince studied him with his cold blue eyes before he closed them. "Somewhat, yes. It's not quite what I hoped for but there's some strength in me yet. I'd rather we use this time effectively, though. It doesn't look like we have anything to worry about here. Do you think we should rest? Maybe sleep for a short while?"

The notion was tempting, and Skharr considered it until he remembered what had happened the last time he had paused to rest inside a dungeon like this one.

"It's best not to," he whispered and shook his head firmly. "You never know what can be done to us while we sleep in godsbe-dammed hell-spawned places like these. We'll go through this dungeon, find your prize, and will be out in no time at all."

"So there is no time to rest?"

"We had best not linger when monsters could attack us in our sleep. Already, we know they can enter our minds. It is best for us both to remain awake and conscious of what the other is doing at all times, no?"

"And what exactly do you expect me to do should you be turned rabid or mad and try to kill me?" Tryam asked.

The barbarian shrugged. "Stick a blade in my stomach, twist it, and drag it out—hopefully high enough to let me bleed out quickly. There is a place right here..." He pointed at a spot close to his rib cage. "A wound there will bleed me out quickly."

"You would honestly let me kill you?"

Another shrug followed the question. "I'll try to help you if I have any control in my madness. I might not be able to help myself or you, however. Do you think you would be able to kill me if I were to attack you?"

"I doubt it." He studied the warrior. "But I would have to try. I would know that you were not yourself and since I have your... shall we say permission, I don't think I would hesitate."

Skharr smiled and nodded. "Good. Very good. I like that."

"You like that I would kill you?"

"Ruthlessness appeals to me. There is a finality to it. Those who know what I am capable of would only attempt to attack me if they were willing to put their lives on the line, knowing that I do the same."

The prince nodded. "Mercy is a virtue, you know."

"Ruthlessness does not preclude mercy. If violence is required, you cannot stop short. Hesitation will be the difference between seeing me dead and you on an imperial throne and my killing you and finding myself crippled with guilt for the rest of my life as the empire falls to pieces under your brother's rule. Which is the more merciful?"

Tryam paused and seemed confused as he considered the question.

"Don't answer," Skharr said quickly. "Consider it. Discover what you are willing to do in each position you encounter when you find yourself on a throne and have to make decisions that will impact tens of thousands of lives."

The young prince still had a scowl on his face when the warrior motioned for them to continue through the hallway ahead.

The lighting was the same in every room. They were trailed by the purple glow they had first seen when they entered the dungeon. It was an unnerving uniformity that followed them through every inch of the stronghold.

Something was different in the next hallway, however. The illumination was somehow more intense and seemed to fill the room with greater brightness. After a moment, Skharr realized why.

"Sword," he whispered harshly as he drew his and peered warily into one of the mirrors that lined the walls. His memory of them in previous dungeons was that they never housed anything good and certainly nothing as simple as merely their reflections.

Tryam looked curiously at him but drew his weapon without protest.

"What?" the barbarian demanded.

"I believe that this is the first time I've seen you genuinely terrified."

He realized that his mind had gone back to the last monster he saw in a mirror.

"Fear is important," he retorted and tried to not let the boy hear the hoarseness in his voice. "It reminds you when it is time to run and when it is time to fight. Panic is the real monster that makes you lose your senses so you run like one possessed or freeze in place."

The prince nodded as they continued and watched for any movement in the glittering walls. They walked close together, which made it easier to watch more than one at a time although he wasn't sure why that only made the cold feeling in his stomach a little stronger.

Skharr scowled when the half-expected sound echoed from behind the glass surface. It was more than familiar and one he heard often in his dreams. The heavy tread of plated boots on hard stone soon made it difficult to hear anything else as they clinked closer one step at a time.

"They're here," he whispered, hefted his weapon, and scowled as more footsteps joined the first farther down the hallway.

Twenty paces ahead of them, a black figure stepped out of the mirror. About the size of a man a little smaller than Skharr, he was dressed from head to toe in completely black armor. No reflection of light gleamed where the eyes should be. Everything about the creature was decayed and twisted to create a monster dedicated only to violence.

"What is that?" Tryam asked and took a few instinctive steps back.

"A Black Knight. A creature raised in defense of its master. There will be more."

"More Black Knights?"

"No, more creatures raised in defense of their master."

The barbarian moved forward as more monsters came forth and filled the air with the stench of rotting flesh. He soon stood face to face with the first faceless enemy. The knight held a battle-ax and moved forward quickly to swing it at him.

He took a step back and leaned away to avoid being decapitated by the blow. His adversary stepped forward and swiped with the weapon in an attempt to open his stomach, which forced him to take another step back. He didn't want to engage the knight. It was probably stronger than he was, and there was no point in grappling with someone when there was little chance to gain the victory.

Tryam shouted a battle cry that Skharr did not recognize and charged down the hallway, past the knight, and toward the undead that followed. There was less hesitation in his attack than the barbarian expected, and one of the rotting creatures fell before they even realized they were under attack. They moved slowly as they limped and dragged useless limbs, but they carried weapons and began to assail the young man.

The prince stepped aside, parried a spear aimed at his gut, and arced his sword to decapitate the aggressive creature.

More of them pushed closer and forced him to step back repeatedly in a slow retreat toward where Skharr tried to find a weakness in the Black Knight's armor.

The barbarian's blade clanged against the hardened steel plates with each strike he managed to sneak past the ax, and he wished he had a hammer able to crush the metal and damage what was on the other side.

"Keep yourself at a distance!" he shouted at the prince, who tried to engage too many of the undead on his own. The boy seemed to not hear him and thrust a couple of them back but allowed more to take their place.

"Go fuck yourself, you stinking scum-sucking maggot-brained piece of half-rotted demon turd." Skharr hissed and barely managed to evade another swipe of his adversary's blade that almost severed his head. He immediately leaned forward, locked his blade behind the knight's knee, and used his shoulder to lever it back.

Even a monster like that had to fall and he landed heavily like he made no effort to try to stop himself from falling. He swung the ax again but this time, it had no power behind it and the warrior kicked the weapon away. While he wanted to kill the monster there and then, the boy needed his help.

He rushed forward, sliced the head off one of the undead creatures, and kicked another into one of the mirrors, which shattered on impact.

Something like a low scream issued from the knight as he pushed to his feet, retrieved his weapon, and charged in what could only be described as rage.

Waiting until the last moment took every ounce of willpower Skharr had, but once the monster was close, he stepped neatly to the right and positioned his foot to catch his adversary as he passed. The knight tripped and a shaft of pain arced up the barbarian's leg as it was brushed to the side.

The attacker fell and destroyed two more of the mirrors around them in the process.

More screams followed, and Skharr suddenly realized the significance.

"Break the mirrors when you can!" he ordered, certain that when they broke, it caused the knight pain.

"I'm a little busy here!" Tryam snapped.

He shook his head, not willing to argue with the boy as he drove the pommel of his sword into another mirror. A few more splintered like the power that kept them intact was waning.

The Black Knight surged into another attack and the warrior remembered his training almost subconsciously. He let himself flow through movements that felt unnaturally graceful as he twisted his sword and hammered the pommel into the enemy's head.

The sudden lack of power in the creature was palpable but the knight's distress also fed his rage and he threw himself at the barbarian and swung the ax wildly in a desperate attempt to kill him.

Skharr roared in retaliation as his opponent's fear began to feed into his rage. He dropped his sword and picked the knight up, thrust his weapon aside, and hurled him into a group of the undead that tried to circle the young prince.

"Watch your surroundings, boy!" the warrior snapped. "I won't be here to watch your back every time."

The contender fought well and he was willing to admit that, but it wouldn't end well for him if he fought on his own. He knew how to fight one man, not many, and everything about his technique screamed that he was being held back by instructions and rules taught to him in controlled environments.

He needed to release the beast inside him and he simply was not ready for it yet.

The barbarian growled, picked the ax up, and held the sword in his other hand. He swung both into the mob of undead creatures as he barreled into them to cleave and slice their unarmed, rotting bodies, crush bones, and eliminate them as he closed on his original opponent.

This was simply another knight. He was not on a battlefield or defending a city. His nightmares would not become reality.

The ax buried itself in the man's neck, who did not even try to raise his hands to defend himself.

This was his opening and Skharr attacked with the sword, stabbed forward, and dragged the weapon sideways under the head, which came off cleanly.

Every mirror along the hallway shattered. Those few undead creatures that remained sagged and their corpses turned to dust before the two companion's eyes.

Skharr looked at the prince and tossed the ax to the floor like holding it stung him.

"Thank you," Tryam whispered and wiped the sweat from his

face. He looked sick but showed no sign that he would double over to empty his stomach.

"Progress," the barbarian whispered, cleaned his sword, and sheathed it again. "What...what are you looking at?"

The boy stared at the broken mirrors—or, rather, at the walls the mirrors had previously hidden from sight.

"Another riddle," the prince whispered and moved closer. "The poor have me. The rich need me. I can make you or break you and remain unchanged. Who am I?"

"I feel like this is a one-sided conversation with whatever the answer is," Skharr grumbled. "What do the poor have that the rich need? What breaks us or makes us and remains unchanged?"

"I'm not sure." Tryam shook his head and sheathed his sword, although he needed a couple of attempts. "Would...there is a trick to it."

"There always is with riddles." He motioned for them to continue on their way.

The hallway gave way to an enormous room with a domed ceiling. The space was difficult to look at as if it were oddly distorted enough to conceal the details. Darkness obscured the far end of the chamber that the light that filled the rest of the dungeon could not pierce, although something moved within the intense shadow.

Whatever lurked in the shadowed depths was immense, the barbarian realized after he'd studied it for a few moments. It somehow created the darkness from its being, began to fill the room, and forced the illumination back as it inched forward. All he could see were the eyes that reflected the light and seemed almost luminescent.

He froze and reached instinctively for his sword.

"What...am...I?"

The voice didn't fill the room. It felt more like it was in his head and from the confused look on the boy's face, he could see that Tryam heard it as well.

"The riddle," the prince whispered. "You're the one we answer the riddle to?"

"What...am...I?"

He turned to Skharr.

"There aren't many things poor folk have that the rich need," the barbarian said in a hushed whisper. "What about...an honest tongue?"

"No, something simpler," his companion answered quickly and shook his head. In the next moment, he raised his eyebrows questioningly. "Adversity. Without it, a leader is not taught to continue through difficult times."

"Perhaps, but...I have a feeling that if you're wrong, that gods-bedammed hungry black asshole will have us for its next meal. The idea of being swallowed whole by a bunghole with eyes has no appeal."

"I know I'm right." The prince turned and strode toward the creature. Dozens of eyes that had looked around the room suddenly focused on him. "You are adversity."

The myriad unblinking gazes made no effort to look away but seemed to stare even more intently.

"Explain."

The simple word was enough to send a chill down Skharr's spine.

"All those who struggle have adversity. The poor experience it on a daily basis. The rich who do not have it crumble under the weight of their own needs when they finally face it. A leader needs to understand it to bring those who follow him together and lead them through it. It would break a man if he is not prepared, and it will make him if he succeeds, but the adversity remains the same, unchanged despite the success or failure of those who experience it. It changes others. That is its nature."

The eyes remained fixed on him for a few more moments.

Skharr knew he needed to stand at the boy's side in case his answer proved incorrect, but he almost couldn't stop himself from inching away and he removed his hand from his weapon.

The beast did not respond. It shifted laboriously and the darkness fell back and dissipated slowly. Once it was gone, the creature, whatever it was, had disappeared as well.

The young prince stood alone in the center of the room.

Tryam leaned on his knees and sucked in air like it would save his life. He had held his breath for a long while despite the confidence he'd had in his answer.

"I would have run from that," the barbarian whispered as he stepped beside the boy. "I would have picked you up and dragged you out if I had to, but I would have run if it turned violent."

The prince laughed in response to his admission. "I would too, but...I don't know. Risks must be taken—like charging into the bowels of a dangerous dungeon with nothing but a boy at your side."

Skharr nodded. That was a good point, he had to admit.

CHAPTER TWENTY-ONE

The dungeon's thick atmosphere seemed to hang over him like a weight he had to carry on his back.

Tryam didn't appreciate the feeling. The adversity riddle had made him wonder if the stronghold and his quest was meant to teach him. Perhaps all of it was intended to shape him into the man who was needed to rule an empire.

Especially one he had not conquered himself.

Skharr seemed to suffer a similar kind of exhaustion and now moved a little slower as they continued through the hallways. The prince had lost all sense of time and distance as they pushed forward and he used the time trying to find some sense to it in the hope that it might distract him. They could be miles underground by now and it could have been days since they had entered.

Not more than two, he reasoned. He had never been able to remain on his feet for more than two days at a time.

Neither of them had rested particularly well even before they gained entry, and he sensed the fatigue begin to build in the back of his mind.

"Where are we going?" Skharr asked finally once the silence

between them had dragged on long enough. "We've wandered through this tunnel for at least an hour."

"There will be an end to it," Tryam answered and drew deep, slow breaths. "I don't know why, but I feel like this dungeon is trying to teach me a lesson with every level we reach and with every test. It's like it's preparing me for something."

"What is this teaching you?" The barbarian raised an eyebrow and studied him but let him take the lead. "The boredom you will find when you have to listen to your council debate on the benefits of raising or lowering taxes?"

The prince laughed but his companion didn't laugh with him. "I don't know. It's been a while since we've been able to rest, and I feel we could both benefit from it."

"We cannot stop until we reach the other side, wherever that might be," Skharr answered quickly. "The monsters in here are unlike anything I have ever seen. The creature of darkness that waited for the answer to the riddle was— I don't even know what that godsbedammed bag of turd and trouble is."

"It could have been a beholder," Tryam told him.

"I've never heard of a beholder that could suck the life out of a room. It could be, but it would be unlike any other in the world— or at least those described, seen, or killed. Although that might be because I don't think anything could kill a creature like that. No humanoid, at least."

The young contender nodded and took a moment to lean against the wall. It was cold to the touch, and he immediately felt uncomfortable so he straightened and continued to walk.

Finally, it appeared that they had found the end of the passages and the cold radiated from the walls. He shivered slightly and peered around a room that looked like a cave with ice pillars forming around it.

It became instantly clear that they were not alone. A bulky form with bright white fur hanging from an enormous body lurked within. At least three times taller than Tryam and with a powerful, hulking body, it prowled on all fours.

The monster saw them almost immediately, turned its bright yellow gaze toward them, and bared its huge teeth when it realized they were intruders. The prince knew what it was even before he could see the horns curling around its ears.

"What do you suppose the lesson in this is?" Skharr asked as he took his bow from where it was strung over his shoulder and a couple of arrows from his quiver.

"I suppose that it's never wise to tangle with a fucking yeti," Tryam answered, dropped his pack, and moved to draw his sword. He recalled a few men speaking about the yetis they had fought in the deep north. They were fishermen for the most part and spoke of how the creatures were deathly afraid of fire and that they would never be caught away from their ships without lit torches.

"What are you doing?" the barbarian demanded as the boy suddenly rummaged in his pack instead of drawing his weapon.

"I need you to distract it!" he called and fumbled frantically through his supplies. "And keep it away from me—maybe turn its back away from me if you can."

"Do you need me to sing it a godsbedammed fucking lullaby while I'm at it?" The man was joking, of course, and he fitted one of the arrows to the string as he moved away from where Tryam still scrabbled through his belongings.

The yeti quickly determined him to be the larger threat and began to advance aggressively on all fours. It uttered a roar that made the whole room shudder.

Skharr's first arrow flew quickly before the beast could even react and although it struck hard, there wasn't force enough behind it to pierce the skull.

The projectile only served to enrage it further and it lunged forward and lowered its head to crush him with its horns.

He dove hastily out of the way, rolled over his shoulder, and found his feet with surprising dexterity for a man of his size. Another arrow was already nocked and, after a moment to aim, it streaked toward his adversary.

This one drilled into the beast's body and red blood seeped into the white fur as the arrow embedded itself firmly under its right arm.

"What? Have you had enough, you big hairy butt-faced dungeon-dick?" Skharr roared and drew another arrow. "Or do you think the DeathEater can teach you more? Do you even have a brain hidden somewhere in that gods-awful ugly fucking furry rock you call a head?"

Tryam had managed to locate his torch, but the flint was more difficult to find as his fingers grew colder. His whole body was tense and stiff with the need to help his companion as all the barbarian appeared to be able to do was distract the monster.

A roar of pain erupted, but not from the beast this time. The prince looked up and paled when he realized that Skharr had been caught. He had slipped on the ice and his leg was skewered by one of the yeti's claws. The bow had fallen from his hands and he drew his sword instead, as well as a dagger, and stabbed both into the beast's fingers until he detached the claw from its hand.

"How…how do you like that, you misbegotten hellspawn?" he asked as he pushed slowly to his feet. Despite his belligerent challenge, he put most of his weight on only one leg. "Perhaps you should crawl back into the poxy whore that birthed you or simply smother yourself by sticking your head up your own ass."

The monster's only response was a rumbling growl as it looked at its mangled hand.

Tryam finally located the flint hidden under his food. He yanked it out and struck it against the steel of his sword. Sparks flurried as monster and barbarian prepared to engage each other again.

Skharr was bleeding a great deal from the wound on his leg and would not last much longer.

To the boy's relief, a spark caught on the torch and he jumped up and held it aloft.

He realized immediately that simply brandishing it wouldn't work. The yeti was fully and utterly committed to killing Skharr and the mere presence of the relatively small flames was not enough to even distract it.

"Fuck!" the prince shouted, retrieved his sword, and rushed at the beast as it turned on the barbarian again.

It saw the flames barely in time and stopped short as he approached. Fear gleamed in its yellow eyes as it studied the flames and took a step back.

Suddenly, it leaned forward and uttered a blood-curdling roar, and a cold blast of wind caught Tryam and pushed him back a step.

"It's trying to put the fire out," the warrior called from where he tried to limp into the fight again.

This observation was fairly obvious, and the young contender shook his head as he drew back and, after a moment of consideration, threw the torch at the yeti.

It landed on the beast's shoulder before it could move away, and the flames spread to its fur. Another roar shuddered through the room as icicles plummeted from the ceiling. The creature lumbered in wild circles, unable to stop the fire that had begun to eat into the rest of its fur.

Skharr surged forward at the perfect moment, lurched closer, and buried his sword deep into the yeti's chest while it was otherwise occupied.

The creature continued its attempt to bat the flames away, but it sank slowly to the floor with a pained rumble as the fire burned relentlessly through it.

The barbarian stood his ground and watched with narrowed eyes to make sure it was dead before he removed his weapon and managed to avoid the flames.

"Come on." He hissed and clutched his leg. "We need to move out before this godsbedammed room freezes us alive."

"We need to treat your leg," Tryam replied as the barbarian wound a piece of cloth around the wound.

"We will when we're not in danger of catching our deaths. Now stop yapping and help me."

The prince shook his head and collected his pack and the man's bow before he helped his companion walk clear of the icy cavern.

CHAPTER TWENTY-TWO

The cold of the other room had started to recede, but Skharr continued to shake. His tanned skin was still cold to the touch and a few shades paler than it had been only minutes before. Once they entered a cave that was illuminated in the same way as the others, Tryam located a small pool of water and looked at him.

"We need to rest," the boy insisted, his fatigue exacerbated by helping the hulking beast of a man walk with his injury.

"We can't rest," the warrior stated for what felt like the thousandth time. "We must reach the end of this dungeon and get out."

"We won't reach any end while you're losing so much blood." He brought them forcibly to a halt. "You will only wither and die if we push on. We can stop here, make a rough camp, eat something, and use one of those healing potions we bought. It'll drain your body of energy so you will have to rest until you are fit to continue. I'll keep watch and when I need rest, you will. Does that appear reasonable to you?"

Skharr scowled at him, but either he knew he was right or he lacked the energy to argue and simply groaned as he lowered himself to the floor. The young contender attended to the business of setting up their small camp while his companion worked to seal his wound.

It was an ugly injury but appeared to be clean, with no sign of any infection brewing. He proceeded to clean it even more and checked it carefully before he retrieved the vial of red liquid that had cost them a metaphorical arm and leg to acquire. Tryam remembered its effectiveness from his time fighting in the arena. Harder blows were not allowed but sometimes happened, and healing mages were always in close proximity, ready to treat those who had been accidentally wounded. Or, he thought cynically, perhaps intentionally.

The potion was nothing short of miraculous, and the wound immediately began to close. Skharr gritted his teeth. It was a painful process to force the effect the body would accomplish on its own over a few months—if he survived.

But the injury sealed in minutes and left the barbarian with a light sheen of sweat on his skin. He drew long, deep breaths and traced his finger over a patch of bright red scarring that would need a little while longer to look and feel like the rest of his skin. He covered it quickly with a cloth and leaned back against the cavern wall.

Tryam moved to refill their water skins from the pool but tasted the water first to make sure there was no poison or anything else contaminating the source. If anything, it appeared cleaner than the rest of the stronghold. Perhaps the Yeti had used it as a source for water.

It was an unsettling thought, but he pulled himself away from it quickly and settled beside the larger man to take dried fruits and meat from his pack. He handed some to Skharr.

"I'll take the first watch," the prince repeated. "You need to rest."

The warrior nodded but remained silent for a few seconds as

he took a bite from the food. "That was quick thinking with the fire. I didn't think Yetis had many weaknesses."

He shrugged. "It was a story I heard from some men who hunted for whales in the Northern Sea. I did not expect either of us to survive that."

"You didn't think we would survive this dungeon at all," his companion reminded him. "You had a comfortable life as a lord. Why choose to die in this godsbedammed hell-spawned fucking place?"

The young contender laughed—a mirthless sound—as he sipped from his water skin. "I don't know. I did not ask to be heir to the empire. But when I thought about it, if my brother found himself in a mire that I could have saved us all from and yet did not... Maybe there was a reason, yes?"

"Damned if I know," Skharr muttered and nibbled at a dried apricot. "Sometimes, I will continue to question until a god decides to answer it for me."

"Do you think you can speak to the gods?"

"I think that if the gods don't answer, they don't care what I do. That gives a whole new meaning to freedom, wouldn't you think?"

Another chuckle was the only response from the prince and the two fell silent. The warrior felt spent. It had been one hell of a long day, even before the effects of the healing potion, and his body began to drift into sleep. It felt different than the kind of sleep he was used to. Restless sleep tended to plague him with dreams of the various nightmares he had lived through.

This was pleasant and peaceful. He was in the dark forest near a small river that he had fished in using his bow. He had tried a few times to use the techniques that had been taught to him by a few soldiers he had fought with and who could catch trout with their hands.

Unfortunately, he had never been able to master it. Somehow, he couldn't be fast enough in the water to pounce when the time was right.

The river flowed slowly and minnows darted from one pool created by the rocks to another as they slipped away from their various predators.

Skharr looked up when he heard hooves and footsteps behind him.

He reached instinctively for the sword on his back but was surprised when nothing was there. The bow at his side was the old one he had lost.

The old man's face was familiar, and he narrowed his eyes to watch him as he tugged at his donkey's reins to keep it from being too distracted by a small patch of grass growing in a pool of sunlight that slid through the trees.

"Now here is a surprise," the old man said quietly, approached him, and sat on a rock next to him to let the donkey browse at will. "I did not expect to find you inside one of my creations, DeathEater. What brings you here?"

The barbarian was not surprised that the old man visited him in his dreams. There was little else to do on that farm, although if the claims from his last dream were to be believed, he doubted that the Lord High God Theros would spend his days tilling the earth.

"There is a prince to be," he explained, studied the water, and waited for signs that a fish worth catching had arrived. "Men tried to kill him before he was able to proceed into the Stygian Path. I saved his life and after a time, grew to appreciate his quest to take his place as heir to the empire. I was to escort him only to the dungeon doors but—"

"My beautiful defender chased both of you in, yes?" The old man chuckled, pulled a pipe out, and packed a few dried leaves in before he mumbled a word and whatever was inside began to smolder. "Do you smoke? It would calm your nerves."

"I don't have nerves."

"That isn't what your dreams tell me. You have a great deal that could be assuaged with a few natural remedies."

"Do leaves that were dried and set on fire count as natural?"

The old man exhaled a small smoke ring and smiled. "As close to natural as the dried meat in your belly right now. But enough of that. You were chased into a dungeon and are helping a would-be prince pass the tests. You do realize that this stronghold can be dangerous, yes?"

Skharr shrugged. "So far, I have no complaints."

"Not even regarding that hole in your leg?"

"There is no hole in my leg."

"There was."

He responded with another shrug. "I've survived worse."

"Yes, I suppose you have," his companion muttered around the pipe in his mouth, and sputters of smoke emerged with each word. "I must improve on the challenge, then. You must have a mind to not help him with the final challenge."

"I assumed that would be the case. They have been his tests to pass, after all. He thought they would be his lessons to learn before he took up a position of leadership—like someone is trying to teach him something."

"He is a sharp lad, that one. But did you wonder about his question?"

"What question?"

"You remember."

"Oh, the one about whether he was born for a reason?"

Theros nodded slowly.

Skharr tilted his head. He had been too tired to consider it when he had been awake but in this dream, he found his mind was surprisingly clear. "No, I don't think I would want to know if there were a particular reason for my birth."

"Why not?"

After another moment of thought, he shook his head. "There was a story I heard. I was an adult, of course—it was not the kind

MICHAEL ANDERLE

of story told to children of the DeathEater Clan—but it was about a child. A boy was told from a young age that he was destined for great things. All his life, he pushed toward those great things and left family, friends, and great loves behind until he finally became king. I remember thinking that despite the happy ending, the boy abandoned everything he was to become what he thought he was supposed to be. I would never want that for myself."

"But you would want it for a prince?"

"I'm merely keeping the boy alive. I have no interest in telling him how he should live his life and what he should aspire toward. I leave that to others."

"Others like me? Gods are known to try to drive folk onto what they feel is the correct path."

He narrowed his eyes. "Are you saying that you drove me away from a life of peace and farming?"

The old man chuckled.

Of course, he knew there would be no direct answer from him. "What if there was a reason for your birth but you do not know what it is? Life should bring you your reason for the effort in the first place, as questionable though it may be. The knowledge would only trouble me in my dreams. It is not worth my waking hours."

Theros nodded. "The beginning of wisdom is knowing you need it. Being wise enough to know one shouldn't always seek the answers to life's questions is an altogether different—although no less important—form of wisdom entirely."

The forest vanished and the barbarian hissed, looked around, and reached for his sword again. It was there this time. The cold silver and steel centered his mind and he realized that the prince was shaking him awake.

"I cannot keep my eyes open much longer," the boy admitted. "You need to take the watch."

Skharr nodded. He did not feel fully rested but he doubted he ever would while within the dungeon. For now, he was rested enough.

It felt like he had barely closed his eyes, and when he opened them, there was no clear indicator that any time had passed.

It was an interesting way to wake up and Tryam peered blearily at his surroundings. He half-expected a fight to be ready and waiting for them but there was nothing, only the same kind of silence he had struggled to remain awake under before he finally gave in and had nudged Skharr awake.

"How long…" he started to ask.

"Hells if I know," the barbarian muttered. "At least three hours, by my reckoning, but that may not be right."

"I feel like I just fell asleep."

"Get used to that feeling." Skharr pushed away from the wall he'd been leaning against and stood to his full, towering height, stretched gently, and examined his injured leg. "It's best to not stay in one place for too long, however."

The prince had no argument against that and he scrambled slowly to his feet, stretched his legs, and gave his body a moment to lose its stiffness. Even though he was sure he could sleep for at least a week, he did feel a little better than he had before.

"Would you mind if I ask a question?" he looked at Skharr and waited for the man to retort with a firm reminder that they didn't have the time.

The warrior seemed a little more pensive than he had before, however, and shook his head. "I cannot keep a free man from speech."

"What is it like being considered a barbarian?"

Skharr stared at him, his eyebrows drawn down over his icy green eyes. "How do you mean? Having folk consider you as unintelligent? Perhaps even lacking the graces of civilized folk in their large cities?"

The prince considered it for a moment and shook his head. "No. Perhaps that is what annoys you and is what people have seen and thrown at you and your people because of how they fear you. When you walk among those city folk, they know a killer walks among them. It is easier to feel better about themselves if they can make a joke by degrading those who trigger that fear in them."

"I am a DeathEater," the warrior responded simply as if that would answer the question. When it was clear that it hadn't, he continued. "The Clan goes back generations. When you listen to stories about barbarians, it is always this clan or that which talks about what they have done. There are fights over which has the greatest warriors, the finest healers, the most cunning horse thieves, or who are the most prized as mercenaries.

"They are allowed their disputes because DeathEaters mostly enjoy our own company. When we do choose to join these gatherings, that is when the young of the other clans learn to keep their mouths shut in our company. Those who are older try their best, of course. Every time I went to one or to a festival to trade, it was the same. Those who had learned their lesson instructed the youths to contain their boasts until we were no longer in a position to hear them."

"I doubt the youths listened. Warriors tend to be combative by nature as well as trade."

"The young rarely do." Skharr paused when he thought he heard something scratch nearby and turned to listen, but the sound was not repeated. "There would be one fight, perhaps two if those older and more experienced had forgotten the lessons learned in the heat of the moment. To us, it was a good way to hone our skills. There are what you call barbarians, and then there are DeathEaters."

"Are you saying you are a class above?"

"I mean that we are of a different category altogether. Unfortunately, folk tend to not understand the differences and see all those who are different as a single entity and so judge them the same. In their defense, the other clans fail to disabuse them of that notion. It serves them well and I have learned that with a little thought and consideration, it would also serve me well."

"You mean you play at being a barbarian while you use such sophisticated language."

"Seeing the surprise in their eyes is fairly gratifying." The warrior had collected his bags and now took inventory of what they had. Tryam knew what he would be thinking, of course. They had refilled their water skins with enough to last them a few days but their food would not last them as long. "In all that, I explain so you will understand. In every man, a barbarian is waiting to be released at a time when you must decide what you are willing to accept—death, defeat, or to unleash the rage, the consequences be damned."

"I've heard that before. It is a mental state you have to reach. One of my instructors called it the illusion of peace."

Skharr nodded. "Only then will you taste a little of what makes the difference between you and the man or the monster you are fighting. For those raised among the other clans, it is what they learn as they grow up. For DeathEaters, it is as essential to our survival as the milk provided by our mothers—and even there, a DeathEater mother will force her child to fight for her teat. We grow up knowing to always reach into that area of our minds and to become as familiar with it as breathing."

Tryam nodded as he replaced everything in his pack. "It is a technique that can be taught, yes?"

"Perhaps. It is one thing to be able to slip into that mindset as a learned technique when you desperately need to survive but quite another for it to come to one naturally in any situation, wouldn't you agree? In the end, the line that separates the clans

MICHAEL ANDERLE

from DeathEaters is that they can summon the madness when they need it. We summon sanity when we need it."

The prince looked thoughtful as he shouldered his pack and inspected his weapons. "So, are you saying your sanity and civility is the true act?"

"That I leave for you to discover."

He shuddered. When he thought about it, he wasn't sure he had seen Skharr fully unleash his true nature and he certainly did not want to see it attacking him. The man was an intelligent being but it was taught to him—or perhaps he had taught himself —to hide it.

It was the kind of thing monsters from children's stories were created from and perhaps more terrifying than the dragon he had faced. He could only imagine a group of fighters like him descending in a horde from the mountains.

The thought of that was no less terrifying, but he would have to consider it if he was ever emperor. It would be an interesting addition to have DeathEaters at his side. If one was so capable, perhaps a group of them would be enough to silence even the viceroy.

"Come along." Skharr growled his impatience. "There is no point in chewing the fat all day—or all night."

They followed the tunnel and the barbarian seemed far more pensive and even quiet and subdued. It could be that his leg was not fully healed yet. There was no sign of a limp but he could hide pain as well as any other.

The tunnel opened rather suddenly into a large room when they rounded a corner. The space was large enough that it almost took the breath from his lungs. There was a small outcropping ahead but it cut away quickly to leave only a skinny bridge with no railing that stretched into a darkness that the light around them failed to pierce.

"You know you'll have to face that last trial on your own, boy?" Skharr asked as he studied the bridge. Tryam could see that

214

it took all the effort he had in him to say it. "This last trial is for you and you alone."

He nodded and drew a deep breath that somehow failed to untwist his stomach. "I know."

"Well, at least I'll be there to wish you the best of luck when you head off."

"Do you believe in luck?"

"No, but it is a nice thing to say when you send a friend off to what might well be his doom."

"Loads of comfort, you are," the prince quipped and stepped onto the bridge, relieved to see his companion had not chosen to leave him yet.

"I'm not here to comfort you, only to get you as far as I can."

CHAPTER TWENTY-THREE

Tryam's first few steps onto the bridge felt odd. He would soon face whatever was ahead on his own and moving across the bridge with Skharr close behind him almost felt like cheating. Still, he was happy to have the barbarian with him for as long as possible.

He came to the edge and peered into the blackness. It was a sheer drop of easily hundreds of feet down and a fall would most certainly kill him. Without a thought, he kicked a small rock over the lip and listened as it plummeted into the blackness, waiting for it to hit the bottom.

It did not, at least not as far as he could hear.

"Of course," the prince whispered. "Why make it easy?"

"If there was no need for a bridge, there would not be one," Skharr pointed out waspishly. "What would it matter if you died as soon as you hit the bottom or soon after if every bone in your body was turned to dust?"

The bridge was only two or three paces across, and the lack of any railing on either side along with the looming blackness that stretched ahead of him made the twist in his stomach grow worse. He gritted his teeth and forced himself to place one foot in front of the other while he waited for something to go wrong. It always did. He was in a dungeon and it was inconceivable that something would not be waiting for them.

Only silence greeted him. After a few more steps, he looked over his shoulder and suddenly realized why the darkness hovered around him. A light mist filled the air. While it wasn't dense enough to be visible, it was able to block the light coming from the walls, at least enough to make it seem like he was in the center of something and completely on his own.

If isolation was meant to be the lesson, it had certainly slipped under his skin.

He felt like he might lose his mind if he had to stay on the structure for much longer and almost welcomed the sound of something approaching. At first, he wondered if it had been following them, but he soon realized that it came from the front.

Tryam drew his sword and held it firmly with both hands.

"Are you feeling a little on edge there, boy?" Skharr asked.

"Aren't you? This fog makes it difficult to see more than a few paces ahead of us at a time."

The barbarian nodded and his hand was already on his sword. The unsettling scrape of something hard and the patter of bare feet continued to approach.

Movement in the fog was the last warning, and the warrior drew his blade quickly.

The prince had seen pictures of the monsters they now saw but he had never expected to see any in person. Troglodytes had been thought of as extinct for centuries. The pests lived deep underground and proved annoying to not only dwarves but also goblins and other creatures that felt comfortable in their subterranean homes.

All he had read appeared to be true. They were monsters of limited intelligence whose existence away from the sun had led them to live without eyes or with eyes small enough to make no difference. They were completely bare with pale green skin and a thick, lumbering body with short, crooked legs and long arms that hung to the ground. The thick, sharp claws scraped over the bridge as they walked.

"A small tribe," Tryam whispered and nodded firmly. "I would guess that they are not a part of the dungeon itself but snuck in after being driven out from their previous home. Wouldn't you say?"

"It makes sense." Skharr looked curiously at him. "You know what they are?"

"Troglodytes. Haven't you seen them before?"

"Not in the putrid godsbedammed flesh. I assumed they were extinct."

"It seems not." Although the man was right about the putrid flesh. He likely had a better sense of smell than most since he'd discerned it a few full seconds before Tryam had, and it was an overwhelming stench. "They are always dependent on their hearing and smell to track their prey."

"So, we should—"

"Stop talking, yes."

The barbarian stepped around him, careful not to bump him over the edge before he advanced on the group. It seemed he had nothing against using the position to their advantage and pushed forward as he lowered his shoulder to catch a couple of them before they realized they were under attack and were pushed over the edge. The creatures uttered no sound as they fell, and a few more tried to return the favor with no signs of distress like the loss of a few of their own was not a problem worth contemplating.

As his companion recovered his balance, Tryam stepped in to cover him and drove his sword directly into the closest of the creatures. The skin felt leathery but the blade cut through it easily.

The stench was even worse when it issued from an open wound and it appeared to drive the others into madness. A few pushed their comrades off the edge in their rush to attack, and the prince retreated a couple of steps and swiped his sword in a sideways arc to sever the head from another one. It rolled off the bridge and the creatures behind thrust the body after it.

Skharr was ready again, and the mountain of a barbarian roared as he rushed forward into the group and swung his sword like it was a club to carve into the creatures around him. It was an interesting tactic and surprisingly effective, but those that were left tried to attack him when he slowed.

The prince stepped out in front, cut the limbs from under one of them, and used his momentum to push his shoulder forward to thrust the remaining two over the edge of the bridge.

Tryam glanced at the warrior, who looked around to make sure no others remained on the bridge.

"Are you all right?" the younger man asked and pushed a few errant strands of hair out of his face.

Skharr looked at his arms, where a few scratches were visible. His gambeson also showed gouges but nothing had cut in deep enough to seriously wound him.

"I'll be fine. We won't stop."

There was nothing to do but agree and they pressed forward with their weapons still drawn and remained alert for a sign of more attackers that might come.

It was an unsettling position to be in and he knew his companion felt it too. They could not remain there for long.

Nothing appeared to harass them again and they finally saw the end of the bridge through the mist. Tryam relaxed as he stepped away from the structure and onto a small piece of flat ground that led directly to another bridge, this one considerably smaller and made of rope with wooden planks.

A totem stood in front of it, not large enough to block it but enough to prevent them from seeing whatever was beyond.

He approached cautiously and studied the writing chiseled

into the stone facing him. This time, it was written only in the common tongue.

"Here you fight your greatest enemy," he read aloud. "Take nothing with you that life did not provide. If you fail this test, do not expect to ever be. And never more in this world will you reside."

"It rhymes," Skharr muttered. "Why do they always rhyme?"

The prince scratched his cheek. "Well, that's about as fair as a warning that you will die can be."

"True." The barbarian shrugged and turned his attention to the bridge. "It does seem that way. I cannot help you here. This is for you and you alone. I also cannot see any other way out, so I will wait as long as I can. If you do not return in two days, I will try to leave as much food and water as I can spare for you."

It was about as much as he could ask of the man, and he nodded. "Skharr, it has been an honor. I came with civilized men who lacked honor, and I found an honorable man who might be considered less civilized by most. Even so, I would not have any other at my side."

He extended his hand, and Skharr gripped him by the forearm in a warrior's hold. "I'd rather not wait here too long. Make haste, retrieve whatever you need, and make it out as quickly as you can."

Tryam nodded again and turned to the totem before he removed his armor piece by piece. Once those were gone, his clothes followed.

"What are you doing?" the barbarian asked and looked away.

"Take nothing that life did not provide," the young prince answered and hesitated before he removed his undergarments as well. "Life provided me only this body. Everything else was provided by others. I suspect I am also taking my enemy with me. The enemy inside me is my greatest."

"That is one way to look at it." Skharr fixed his attention on the bridge. "I hope your understanding is correct or you will find that your…ahem, fishing gear will be the first thing any monster waiting for you will snap off."

He shuddered and looked longingly at his sword. "That might make me wish to give up right here."

His companion laughed and shook his head, and he couldn't help but join in.

"Those handprints…" The barbarian pointed at the marks on the prince's back and chest. "They are magical, I assume?"

Tryam nodded. "Aye. I'll know I've passed my tests when they disappear."

Their laughter helped, but it failed to take away the unnerving feeling of being bared to the elements.

"Can I ask you one last favor, Skharr?"

"Of course."

"Don't ever tell anyone how white my ass is."

The warrior laughed again. "It is a memory I will drink away on many a night."

He moved around the totem and stepped onto the bridge. Thinking of it as that was almost a little too generous, he decided as he balanced carefully on the wooden planks beneath his feet and grasped the ropes on both sides for balance.

The structure shook with every step and he was afraid that a cord would snap, but none did. Resolute, he ignored the desire to look back and simply put one foot in front of another. Heading out alone was an interesting feeling. Through his entire quest, he'd had help in some form or another and of some quality or another, but there he was, well and truly alone.

It was invigorating and terrifying at the same time and only made worse by the fact that he could feel a distinct draft in his nether regions.

Finally, he reached the end and stepped off the shaky structure. He increased his pace and approached another flat area located against the wall of the cavernous room.

His elation at reaching the end of the bridge faded quickly

when he realized there was no other way off the flat area. A cursory examination of his surroundings revealed a small pond of clear water on the far side. Any hope that he would be able to swim into the next section was dashed, however, when he moved closer. It was about as deep as his hips and the clearness of the water showed no way out. The water filtered in through a crack in the wall but it wasn't large enough for him to swim through.

"I won't be fishing with my...uh, gear, that much is for certain," Tryam whispered and glanced across the bridge. The mist remained thick and thoroughly blocked any sight he might have of Skharr.

He shook his head and the pool made him realize that his mouth was dry. A quick inspection led him to see that there was nothing wrong with the water. He tested it and decided it tasted of nothing. This was odd, given that clean water deep underground tended to have a sharp, mineral tang.

This one had no particular taste but as he swallowed his first mouthful, something seemed to change in his body. The exhaustion he felt suddenly increased to the point where he was unable to stop it from overtaking him. He fell to his knees and his head nodded forward. Panicked, he scrabbled wildly for something to hold onto before his whole body sagged and he was unable to stop his eyes from closing.

The dream was already odd. He knew it was a dream immediately, and when he looked around, he realized he stood in an instruction room that he was familiar with. Weapons were hung all along the walls and the floor was padded with bamboo made to improve the quality of a fighter's balance.

He was still naked. Dreams tended to give him clothes if he wanted them to, but there was no reaction when he looked at himself. It was like he was in someone else's dream. The strangeness was difficult to fathom but before he could focus on it, weighty footsteps drew his attention.

"Pick your sword up, boy!" a familiar voice shouted.

Tryam looked to the side at a powerful man with a barrel chest and thick arms, despite being almost a full foot shorter than he was.

"You want to be someone, boy?" the man demanded. "You show up without your clothes to my instruction and you think I'll let you shift away like a witless worm? Pick your sword up or I'll kill you like the mindless pig you are!"

He remembered the man's voice. His first instructor only spoke that way when there was no one around to stop him. He recalled the blows from the man's staff battering him relentlessly, even when he asked him to stop.

And when he woke the next day, the man had left from the villa and been replaced by a much kinder instructor—and one who had much more skill to teach.

Tryam grimaced and reached for his sword. It was a dream, but all the old feelings pushed to the surface. He relived the fear, hot tears running down his cheek, his breaths coming in pants, and words that required five or six attempts before he managed to speak them.

"Speak clearly, you useless maggot!" The instructor picked up a wooden sword from the racks and stepped into the fighting room. "I won't waste my time on a worthless creature unable to speak his own name!"

It was unsettling to think he was back in this room. He had mostly forgotten about it, and his hands found no sword as the instructor moved closer.

His ears rang and his cheek ached with the strike. He fell heavily and tears trickled over the growing bruise where he had been struck across the face with the full force of the man's training weapon.

"Get your lazy ass up!"

His heart pounded. Training came to his rescue and he looked at his sword on the rack in front of him. He could finally kill the bastard, cut his sword in half, and sink the blade into his gut, then watch him bleed and beg for mercy.

The anger rose too quickly and almost before he knew it, the blade was in his hand and pointed at the instructor, who didn't appear to see it.

Nothing life did not provide. His emotions were overruling him. He looked at the sword.

"Will you simply stand there like a whining goatfucker or will you do something?"

Nothing life did not provide. His sword was not provided by life. He shook his head, resisted the rage that roiled inside him, and dropped the blade on the floor.

"I always knew you were a useless pile of dogshit." The instructor raised his weapon and swung it. A calm filled Tryam as he extended his hand and caught the weapon.

"I am not weak," he whispered and held the sword firmly as the man tried to yank the practice blade away. "I was never weak. You were the one who needed to instill fear in a small boy. But my emotions no longer rule my heart. I rule over them. I rule over you."

He squeezed the sword in his hand and the wood splintered between his fingers.

It suddenly felt like a test. The instructor fell back.

"You always were a useless boy," the man snapped. "No one will remember your name. The only thing special about you is the drunken seed spurted into the womb of your whore of a mother. Nothing else. You will never be anything but the shadow of your father."

The words were familiar. He recalled the man saying them as the blows fell relentlessly. He could hear them ringing in his ears as his half-brother paraded himself about.

"I am not ruled by you." Tryam still felt the rage but it filled him now, empowered him, and elevated him as he walked toward the man. "I rule over you. Now bow."

Fear filled the man's eyes as he dropped to one knee with a hint of surprise. This, then, was the power of words. They were given to him by life—words that only he knew how to use properly.

The room fell away and the rage in his body suddenly dissipated. The test was complete, but he feared it was far from the last.

CHAPTER TWENTY-FOUR

The darkness remained, yet when Tryam looked down, he could see himself again. It was a strange realization but he had difficulty putting it into words.

Something moved in the blackness and drew his attention. A monster shifted and rumbled as it looked for its chance to strike.

The prince reached for his sword but he was naked again with no weapon and nothing to fight the monster with but his bare hands.

Even in the blackness, he could not see anything that might provide some indication of what he faced. Cautiously, he looked around for anything that would help him—perhaps an advantageous position or a rock he could throw.

Nothing presented itself as a viable option. It was only him, the darkness, and whatever panted ominously in the pitch-black shadows. He could feel its hot breath on his skin and an old story came to mind, one that had kept him awake at night. It felt as if his fear was feeding the form of the beast to give it a shape in the darkness.

In his imagination, the creature stood over ten feet tall and was covered with ragged brown-and-gray fur. It had an elongated jaw and large yellow eyes, and drool dripped from its maw.

The story of the Golden-Haired Princess and the Werewolf persisted in his mind. He recalled feeling fear of any woman with golden hair as the story had revealed in the end that she was the monster.

Now, it stood in front of him and its long tongue licked its fangs as it stared unblinkingly at him.

There was nothing to fight it with. The creature had nothing to fight him with either, but the fangs and the claws appeared to be more than sufficient to gut him.

Fear was not a terrible thing, he reminded himself. Skharr's words returned to him. Panic was the killer. All fear did was remind him that he was alive and that he wanted to remain that way.

The werewolf growled and took a step forward as he inched back.

Skharr's voice whispered in his head again. In every man, a barbarian waited to be released when he had to decide what he was willing to accept—death, defeat, or to unleash the rage and fuck the consequences.

Failure was death and defeat. It meant that all this was for nothing. Those were the consequences. If he ran, the wolf would kill him. If he gave himself up to the inevitable, he would die and he would not be a prince, merely another bastard son of a mindless old man with a taste for young women with curly black hair.

He sucked in a deep breath as the hot breath of the beast in front of him raised goosebumps across his body.

Accepting the inevitable was liberating, somehow. There was no other choice. All he could do was attack. The monster was the obstacle in his path and the fear coursed through his body like fire. He threw his head back and laughed.

Tryam recognized that it was an utterly mad sound and

completely unhinged. He was an animal backed against the wall with no way to go but forward.

The prince screamed—not at anything in particular but because his lungs needed to for some reason. Or no reason. His whole body felt alive with it as he rushed forward and his adversary lowered itself into a reciprocal attack.

It was strong. The claws slashed across his chest and he laughed again with that maddening, powerful, unwavering feeling of no other options available. He released all the repressed emotions against his former instructor and all the shame of the times when he needed to parade himself for those who thought of him as nothing more than a beast for them to ride to greater heights.

The cowardice in his life fell aside, together with the fear that he would fail and amount to nothing. There would be no one here to see him fail. It was impossible, but the laughter continued as the beast barreled into him and drove him to the floor.

The fangs dug into his arm and he thrust his arm in deeper to the place the jaw clamped down where the teeth no longer protruded.

He sucked in a deep breath despite the foul stench that emanated from the werewolf's maw. It only made him laugh more as he reached into the open jaw and grasped its tongue.

It was slick and writhed against his hold but he did not release it. His fingers clamped around it. Part of him registered the insanity of thrusting his hand into the mouth of a ravenous monster, but madness would be the only thing that saved him.

Laughter…madness…there was no more meaning to the concepts as he gripped the tongue and pulled with all the power in his body. Warm blood rushed over his bare chest and shoulders. The creature roared in pain and tried to drag itself away from the madman who had pulled its tongue out.

Tryam tossed the organ aside, pushed from the ground, and drove the werewolf onto its back. The lethal claws raked across his shoulder, chest, and back, but the pain only served to add fuel to the fire. He screamed now as he battered his fists into any part of the beast he was able to reach. While he was wearing it down, it would last longer than he would.

He moved in closer and extended his hand toward the monster's eyes. They were closed but he pushed against them and thrust his fingers inside. The soft flesh gave way and he ripped through it as more warm blood spurted over his fingers and his arms. He continued the pressure and the monster thrashed and fought to buck him off. The prince refused to relinquish his grasp despite the fact that his entire body was jerked and wrested by the creature's struggles. His fingers dug deeper into the eye sockets and burrowed even further.

Finally, the monster no longer writhed against him and the claws ceased their wild raking at his flesh. He leaned over it and waited for it to change into its original form but after a while, he realized that would probably not happen.

It required arduous effort but he managed to scramble to his feet. He stared at the werewolf while a part of him still expected it to somehow attack again, but the beast sprawled motionless in a pool of blood that spread gradually across the floor. He wasn't even sure if it was a real monster or if werewolves truly existed.

At that point, Tryam realized that a great deal of the blood was his own. His knees buckled beneath him, and he dropped beside his kill. Still, he had accomplished something extraordinary. Killing a werewolf with his bare hands was surely something he would be remembered for, right?

He laughed again. It was a weaker sound and one of amusement now instead of madness, and he coughed at the end of it.

"Nice try, you big bastard, but it seems I'm far crazier than you," he whispered and patted the matted fur of the monster as his eyes closed of their own accord. Breathing felt almost impossible and he slipped into blackness.

"That which dies first is truly dead." A voice spoke in the

blackness or perhaps it was in his head, and Tryam opened his eyes and tried to focus.

The darkness was gone, which meant the voice had not come from there. He frowned slightly at the familiar feeling of sand beneath his feet and the scent of rosemarine flowers from the petals that were cast out before every fight. The sound of the crowd was oddly unsettling and was complemented by the low bellow of the horns.

He remembered it all with particular vividness and realized that he was in the arena again. The sun glared relentlessly on high and he squinted his eyes which were shielded only by the helm he wore.

"Well, I'm not naked anymore," he whispered after a hasty glance. "I suppose that is an improvement."

The comfortable weight of armor surrounded him, although he needed a few seconds to make some sense of it. His death—or at least the possibility of it—still hung over him, and the prince was not sure if he was in some kind of afterlife or if this was truly happening to him.

It was a full suit of armor, the kind he remembered being fitted with during his fights in the arena, and included a shirt of mail and a sword he held tightly lest it vanish.

While a very nice sword, it was unfamiliar. Although, he decided, it was perfectly balanced as if it had been made to fit in his hand.

A man stood across from him in armor that glinted silver in the sunlight and he brandished a sword in a way that suggested skill with the blade. It was difficult to see who it was, but he was about the same age as him. The young contender reached the conclusion that this was an odd afterlife if that was indeed what it was.

The other man shouted at the crowd, who cheered in response. Those who looked at Tryam booed vociferously to show that he was clearly not the favorite.

"Why should we consider you?" the other man asked and now addressed the prince. "What is special about you aside from your father? Any man can fight as you do, and all we can see is a child playing at being a prince."

Tryam looked around. They were words that had hounded him since his brother had spoken them, and he realized who he now confronted. It was the prince and heir, carrying the emperor's weapon.

"A brat!" Cathos continued and marched around the arena while his every word was echoed by the crowd. "With no place in the world but a footnote. Merely another bastard, sired on nothing to be nothing."

The prince hesitated when the madness began to flood him again. This time, it felt wrong. He was not in control and did not unleash the monster himself. Blood rushed in his ears and insisted that all he wanted to do was gut the useless prick.

He surged across the sand and tightened his hold on his blade as the heir turned, realized he was under attack, and parried while he tried to escape the swinging blade.

Tryam pushed forward to corner him close to the side. All his strikes with the sword were blocked, but he leaned closer and hammered a kick into his half-brother's midsection with sufficient force to catapult him into the wall of the arena.

The man fell from the impact but rolled in an attempt to protect himself from the raging prince.

"No...no matter what you do to me," Cathos challenged as he pushed to his feet, "no matter what you make of yourself, know that when you spill my blood, it will be the blood of an emperor, while yours will be nothing more than that of a common dog."

The anger that surged through his body suddenly dissipated and Skharr's words returned to him. It was like the barbarian stood there with him. The young and belligerent needed to be taught a lesson, but not at the cost of their lives.

"You were never meant to be emperor," Tryam whispered and

fought to contain the heat rising from the pit of his stomach. "You were raised to be a pawn, a great lord of nothing, something for your betters to blame when the empire falls."

The heir narrowed his eyes, unsure of what to say next as his adversary approached him again. This time, the contender attempted a calmer and more methodical approach that kept the other fighter on his back foot. He sliced and slashed and gradually forced him to retreat step by step until he was backed against the wall. Tryam ducked under a wild slash at his head, hooked the guard on his sword behind his opponent's knee, and dragged his leg out from under him.

Cathos fell with a loud groan and glared at him as he pressed his blade to his neck.

"It is not what you are that defines you," Tryam whispered, sheathed his sword, and extended his hand to help the other man to his feet, "but what you do. That way, you will be remembered for more than merely who your father was."

Something seemed to shift in the world around him. Suddenly, there was no hand in his and he held no weapon in his grasp. He no longer wore any armor.

The arena was gone and he stared at a ceiling far over him. It was illuminated by what looked like flowers and moss that filled the room with an odd, purple light.

Was he in the dungeon again?

Tryam forced himself to stand slowly and looked around before his gaze settled briefly on the rickety bridge he had crossed to the small flat area. From there, his scrutiny moved to the corner where the pool had been. It had vanished and in place of the water, a sword stood propped against the stone wall.

It looked much like the one he carried—a bastard sword with an embossed hilt carved from burnished bronze, ivory, and what might be oak that came together in a lion's head pommel.

The weapon was exceptionally beautiful, and he drew it to inspect the blade.

He could see his reflection in the gleaming steel. Blood caked his chest and arms and all but covered his bare skin. It was almost black and certainly didn't look like blood. Quickly, he glanced over his shoulder and realized there were tracks in the pooled blood on the stone floor, as well as a space where the werewolf's body had lain.

It was chilling to think that the beast had somehow walked away as he was very sure he had killed the monster. Part of him protested that it had been nothing more than a dream, but the evidence that it had been real was visible all around him.

Bemused, he returned his attention to his reflection. Beneath the blood, he could see that the handprints on his chest were gone and assumed that those on his back had vanished as well.

He turned away, reluctant to remain in that small and lonely flat area, slung the sword over his shoulder, and began to cross the bridge. The mist enveloped him as he continued to where Skharr was hopefully still waiting for him.

There was no way to tell how long he had been asleep—if he had been asleep. He wasn't sure of anything but it seemed as if he had somehow been dreaming and yet not dreaming.

Oddly enough, the exhaustion he'd felt before was gone, and so was the fear he'd experienced when he'd crossed for the first time.

Thankfully, as he approached the other side, the barbarian's voice carried to him.

"I can smell you from here, boy."

Tryam chuckled. The insulting remark seemed almost endearing from the man's mouth.

With a small smirk on his face, he proceeded slowly until he reached the other end. "Are you sure you didn't simply hear my footsteps on the bridge?"

Skharr was seated on the ground with his armor off while he worked to repair where his gambeson had been damaged by the troglodytes. It was extremely odd to see the man with a needle and thread in hand.

The warrior noticed the young prince staring. "I'd say you'll have to learn how to fix your armor, but as emperor, you most likely won't."

He realized that the man saw him completely in the nude and covered in blood while he held a sword against his shoulder.

"Are you curious enough to ask?"

After a moment, the barbarian shook his head. "Not particularly. The fact that you survived and appear to have collected the proof that you completed the dungeon trial is enough. But you might want to wash that blood off before you put your clothes and armor on."

Tryam looked down at himself and nodded. His companion had made a sound point indeed.

CHAPTER TWENTY-FIVE

A t least they had the good sense to refill their water skins before the prince began washing the blood from his skin.

Skharr was fairly curious about how he had come to be covered in it but not enough to ask. Whatever he had gone through, it was for him and him alone to consider. Asking any questions about it felt like he would step beyond his bounds. This whole adventure was Tryam's quest, after all.

All he had to do was get the boy in and out alive and preferably without resorting to certain magical items he had been given. He carried a knife given to him by an elf that purportedly granted him a wish if he stabbed himself in the heart with it. Although he wasn't sure if he would have used it to save the young contender, it was an option and was ready to be used if he was willing.

There was an impressive amount of blood and it soon fouled the pool of water they had found before. He had heard some movement from beyond in the chamber where they had left the yeti's burnt corpse. When he'd investigated, it had only been a handful of scavengers that dispersed quickly the moment they saw something larger approaching, too quickly for him to see what they were.

Tryam somehow looked different. The warrior had tried not to stare, given that the boy had lacked his clothes for most of the return walk and there was no point in making him feel uncomfortable.

But still, a change had most certainly occurred. He was a little more pensive, calmer, and far more settled. It also felt like he was better grounded. The jittery youth was still present, but he appeared to have a little more control over himself.

It did beg the question of exactly what had happened to the boy. Skharr did not want to assume that he needed to kill a dragon or some other monster and bathe in its blood, but it did seem like it was more or less what a hairy-assed self-serving god would ask of a prince who wanted to be emperor.

He had questions about the sword as well but assumed it was something the boy would talk about when he was ready to do so.

His curiosity notwithstanding, he abided by his decision to not ask questions. There would be enough time for that later.

"Well, then," Tryam said as he pulled his clothes and armor on and strapped his new sword to his shoulder while he wore the other at his hip. "I suppose we should attempt to find a way out. Unless you think we should retrace our steps and hope the dragon isn't on its nest anymore—although that does beg the question as to whether we would be able to open it from this side without her being there."

"We can assume the doors will be closed if she is not, and I feel we will not be able to open it from the inside even if she were." Skharr hesitated when a vague sensation touched him and he peered around the room. It felt like something or someone had tapped him lightly on the shoulder to draw his attention to one of the far walls.

The thought of how the yeti hunted from deep inside a

dungeon occurred to him, and he realized there was a heavy wooden door on the far side of the room.

"Am I seeing things?" he asked. "Was that door here when we came through the first time?"

The prince narrowed his eyes as he swung his pack over his shoulder. "What—the door? No, it was not there when we came through here. I swear I inspected every inch of this room while you were sleeping."

It was large enough for the yeti to move through and seemed easy to open, even for larger hands. Perhaps the beast hunted outside and returned to enjoy the cold the other room provided.

"Fucking godsbedammed slime-pit magic," Skharr muttered as he approached the door warily. "You'd think they would find an easier way to do all this, but no, they have to be all...mind-fucking mystical about this shit."

He stepped forward and pulled it open slowly while he remained alert and waited for something to come through to kill them.

The door swung wider on creaking hinges and he stepped out with his hand on his sword as he moved through it. A small tunnel led from there toward what appeared to be sunlight.

"Skharr?" Tryam asked as he stopped behind him. "What do you think will come next? We cannot walk to Citar. Well...I suppose you could, probably, but I would find it a little more difficult."

"We will face that problem when we reach it," he replied and advanced cautiously toward the light that gleamed from beyond the tunnel.

Inching toward it did not change anything so he moved faster. It was easy to determine that they would not emerge in the desert. The heat remained, of course, but there was a dampness to it that had been absent in the wide sands.

He stepped out and shielded his eyes from the glaring

sunlight above them. A horse whinnied and he frowned, not quite believing what he saw.

Horse grazed peacefully like he had expected Skharr to step out at this precise location. The other two horses that Tryam had brought with him for the journey were there as well, and it seemed their possessions were all still strapped in place.

"How...how did they know where to find us?" the prince asked in confusion. "Even we had no idea where we would emerge."

The barbarian didn't want to attribute it all to Horse. He was an intelligent beast—even more so than him—but something else was at work in this place beyond the stallion's canniness.

"Do you believe in the gods, Tryam?" he asked as Horse turned and nuzzled his shoulder.

"I...might. Why do you ask?"

"Because I have a feeling they believe in you."

"What does that mean? How does that answer my question?"

"It does not." He shrugged, removed his helm, and slid it into its usual saddlebag. "And it matters not either. There is an old saying to not look a gift horse in the mouth and I feel we should abide by it."

The young prince stared at him for a moment before he shrugged. "Very well. Should we return to Citar? We can rest there before we continue to the Imperial City."

"Is that what it's called?"

"I am sure it had another name in the past, but my father has changed it to represent the crown jewel of his empire. So, to Citar?"

Skharr shook his head. "If your assassins were to wait somewhere to intercept you before you return to your father, where would they lie in wait?"

Tryam checked the packs and seemed surprised to see them still full of what they had left behind. "Citar, I suppose. What do you propose, then? Return directly to the Imperial City on our own? It would take us weeks."

"Not on our own. We could probably find a small caravan and use them to hide our movements."

"Very well." The prince mounted his horse once he had returned his possessions to their proper places.

"How do you feel?" the warrior asked.

"Like my troubles are far from over."

"You have good instincts."

The desert would never be Skharr's preferred environment, but there were certain elements that made it an advantageous place to be.

For instance, they could see a caravan moving from the city of Citar from miles away. Their campfires had been the easiest to locate at night and from there, it was not difficult to trace their path through the dusty landscape.

"They have increased their pace," he told the prince, who shielded his eyes to try to see them. "They are being pursued."

"What makes you say that?"

"They have strayed from the course they've been following for days." He retrieved his bow and quiver without moving his gaze from the distance. "Either they are lost or they have realized that they are about to be attacked from those hills there."

He did not wait for his companion to reply but had already pressed forward as he spoke. By now, they were close enough to the caravan for the travelers to know they were there. They had not slowed to allow them to approach but had not left any guards behind to engage them either.

Sure enough, as the string of wagons veered away from the hills, horses suddenly appeared and thundered down the slope while their riders whooped war cries and raised their weapons to attack.

The barbarian knew the prince was in position behind him and grinned when the boy urged his horse into a gallop.

There was something to be said about the stamina of DeathEaters, but he was well aware that he could not outrun a galloping horse. The only thing to worry about, of course, was the fact that the caravan most likely thought they were part of the raiders and would join the attack.

Skharr skidded to a halt and narrowed his eyes on the enemy horsemen who continued their headlong charge toward the caravan. Calmly, he lifted his bow and nocked an arrow to the string.

His practiced eye estimated that it was less than a hundred paces. While not the longest shot he had ever made, it was still a challenge. He drew the arrow back to his cheek, took a moment to gauge the distance the horses would travel while the arrow flew, and loosed it.

He immediately drew another arrow from the quiver without waiting to see whether his first would find its target. His quiet certainty that it would was confirmed moments later by a scream of pain and surprise.

With another arrow fitted to the string, he walked forward again. The raiders looked around for those who had attacked them when one of the horses stopped and danced restlessly without its rider.

Drawing back felt as natural as breathing, and the arrow streaked away to fell the man who had turned to look in his direction first. It was another fine shot, he had to admit, and he hefted his weapon in readiness while a handful of the riders turned to see where the arrows had come from.

Their charge had been interrupted, and this gave the caravan guards time to establish a few defenses. Working quickly, they circled a few wagons into position to prevent the horses from trampling them. Those with bows began to shoot and killed one of the raiders and wounded another.

The enemy group displayed a hint of confusion and looked around as if unsure what to do next, although they maintained their charge. Skharr wondered if he had accidentally eliminated one of their leaders and quickly nocked another arrow and continued his advance. After a few steps, he raised the bow and released his shot.

The projectile knocked one of the riders off their horse and the group turned their attention to what they thought was their largest threat at this point.

He froze in the process of drawing another arrow and considered how much time he still had left. At least one more, he decided, before he needed to think about how he could avoid being trampled.

Suddenly, another horse raced into view. This one was much larger and taller than the ponies the raiders used, and the rider held a sword in his hand. Tryam intercepted the marauders as Skharr fired another arrow that hurled another of the raiders from her mount, and the prince swung his blade in lethal arcs at the enemy around him. A head was severed and spattered blood on the others as the raiders' charge was dragged to a sudden halt. The caravan guards surged out from behind their protection to try to help.

Their assistance was appreciated, but the barbarian dropped his bow, unslung his quiver, and left them both on the ground as he advanced on the stalled group. If there was ever a time for him to attack, it would be when their horses were not moving.

The young prince kept them constantly on the defensive and his armor made it difficult for their cavalry sabers to injure him.

One managed to circle and aimed a strike at the boy's unprotected back.

"Not likely, you scum-sucking goat-fucking hill vermin!" the warrior roared and lunged behind the man, hoisted him off his saddle, and hurled him to the sand. Before he could stand, he stamped his boot on the man's neck until the raider spat blood.

He drew his sword next and nodded approvingly as Tryam drove the raiders directly into the group of caravan guards who were on their way to help them.

Twelve of them were left now and for the moment, it was only the two of them. Skharr stepped around Tryam's swinging weapon and drove his sword into the stomach of another raider who attempted to sneak onto the prince's flank. The force of the blow thrust the raider off the saddle and flung him aside as the barbarian stepped around the boy's mount.

He was a warhorse, one used to being in these types of situations, but he tried to avoid trampling the warrior and twisted to plow through a handful of ponies. They stumbled and some fell, and Skharr jumped away and narrowly missed being bowled over as well.

The caravan fighters arrived, dragged those who were still mounted off their horses, and left them alive for the moment. The barbarian knew for a fact that if the attack had lasted longer, the fighters—enraged by watching their friends die—would have killed or mutilated the raiders until nothing but blood, viscera, and mangled flesh remained.

The shorter time of the fight meant they had coin on their mind, and he knew they would take their prisoners back and would likely earn themselves a little extra if they managed to keep them alive.

The captain was still on horseback and rode to where Skharr looked around to make sure Tryam was unharmed.

"I know you," the man stated by way of greeting as he slid from his saddle and studied him warily. "Well, I think I know of you. Not many fit your description. You are the Barbarian of Theros, are you not? From Verenvan?"

"Not from—" He shook his head. "Never mind. Yes, that would be me."

"I thought we had met our end the moment those raiders came out of hiding." The man glanced at Tryam, who sheathed his weapon. "We thank you both for your intervention. Are you escorting this one?"

Skharr looked at the prince and wondered what could have made the man think he was escorting the boy. He wore nothing that identified him as anything other than another warrior. Except perhaps the sword, he decided after a moment. That did stand out more than a little and was the type of weapon someone with means might wield.

"No," he said quickly before his companion could answer for him. "We have both been called in for work by the Theros guild at the Imperial City. I don't suppose you would be able to get us that far?"

"Not as far as the Imperial City, but we should be able to push you to Geron. You'd be able to join a convoy from there, I'm sure."

He nodded in agreement and the guards returned to the caravan, where they were all preparing to continue their journey. Tryam cleaned his sword while Skharr took the time to collect his bow and arrows—including those he had fired—before they joined the group.

They did not travel too far before they set up camp, and a handful of the men invited the two newcomers to feast with them on what they had collected from the raiders.

"Why didn't you tell them you were escorting me?" the prince asked as they settled in for the first warm evening meal they'd had in days.

The barbarian looked around to make sure no one was listening to them before he shrugged. "Already, too many want to kill you. It is best to not tell all who would listen of your location or true identity, yes?"

"Well...yes, but if it is known that you are escorting me, would that not already be well-known?"

Skharr nodded slowly. "Yes, but still. Anything we can do to slow your pursuers should be done."

"Then you should stop advertising who you are."

"I cannot exactly hide it."

"You can try."

"And lie to our new friends here? They would know it in an instant. I am not…trained in court politics as you are."

The boy opened his mouth to continue the discussion but after a moment, shook his head and rolled his eyes when he chose to not pursue it. The boy was right, of course. Anyone who knew they were traveling together would know who he was, but not all would know it. This hopefully meant that hiding the prince's identity was about as good a chance as they had to reach the Imperial City unhindered and unharmed.

And from there, once again, it was all up to the young contender.

CHAPTER TWENTY-SIX

Fortunately, a convoy in Geron—a smaller town at the fringes of the desert—was willing to take them to the Imperial City.

Skharr told them they were two guards who needed to reach the city as quickly as possible and the prince decided he was right to do so once he'd considered the situation. It had the added advantage that they did not need to pay any coin for their trip as long as they joined the guards who escorted the small convoy.

As much as he feared they would be attacked along the way, Tryam was happy with the peaceful nature of their trip. It felt like years since he hadn't been in a situation where he needed to fight for his life, but his instinct told him that would change when they reached their destination.

Sleep was more restful than he'd expected, although he was strangely comforted when he slept with his new sword in his arms. The two companions woke early in the morning to train, but the further they progressed with it, the more he realized that the barbarian still struggled with that weapon type.

His basics and foundations were sound. While his footwork was impeccable, there was too little movement in the hips and too much reliance on the power and speed provided by his arms and shoulders. He was still the superior warrior, and he reminded himself often that the Skharr he faced in training was considerably different than the man he would face on a battlefield.

But the sword was a subtler weapon, and the subtleties were what he had difficulties adjusting to.

The trip to the city required a few weeks of travel, and the warrior paused to study the expanse of the land and narrowed his eyes as his gaze swept the entirety of it.

Three rivers ran through the center of it, all leading to the ocean and capable of bearing ships. They were spanned by massive bridges that were easily visible as their arches were taller than the walls that surrounded them.

From where they stood, the city seemed to spill beyond the walls. It sprawled for miles and merged almost seamlessly with the farms that took advantage of the rich flatlands that stretched as far as the eye could see.

"Have you never seen the Imperial City?" Tryam asked, interested in his companion's reaction.

"Never." Skharr shook his head. "I've only ever heard of it. Folk told me there was a great deal of coin to be earned by a man of my skills in the arena, although I never liked the rules that surrounded blood sports."

The prince narrowed his eyes and pointed to another huge, round structure that rose above the walls. "There it is. The place where folk considered for the first time that I might be their emperor. Thousands cheer your name with every victory. It's easy to become addicted to the feeling. So many believe in you and urge you to win."

The barbarian shook his head. "Bloodsports. I have never understood them."

"They are forbidden in most other civilizations, but ambassadors from every one of those come to watch and cheer as loudly as the crowds—in private, of course, but they do."

Skharr had no answer to that and jerked his head to the side like he was forcing himself to think of something else as he moved to join the caravan that continued into the city.

It was impressive in its own right. The walls stood almost a hundred feet high with towers at regular intervals. All buildings surrounding the walls had been cleared for about a hundred paces to prevent an attacking army from finding any cover from arrows raining from above.

A wide moat was fed by the rivers, although the bridges crossing it looked like they had been in place for more than a few decades.

The Imperial City had not been attacked since it had been renamed, and while Tryam knew it was only a matter of time before that changed, he hoped things would be different once it happened.

He did not want to get ahead of himself with how things would go, of course, but with them approaching the gates, it was difficult to not consider the possibility that he might survive this against all the odds.

Skharr paused as they stepped through and narrowed his eyes.

"It is a little…too much the first time," the prince said reassuringly and patted him on the shoulder. "But you will find your way through it. So many cultures are mixed in with one another, but in the end, it becomes a tapestry."

The larger man paused and inclined his head in agreement. "That is not what gave me pause, however." He gestured unobtrusively to the side with a small movement of his head.

Tryam shifted his attention to where the city guards watched those who were entering.

One did not wear the same armor as the others or carry similar weapons. Two, he realized when he looked more closely, and he recognized them immediately. Both had tried to kill him not long before.

And yet it somehow felt like it had been ages past.

"Captain Ingold," he whispered and scowled when the man noticed him and instantly revealed his recognition when he stiffened.

He wondered if the Elite would have seen him if Skharr had not pointed him out, but it didn't matter. Tryam did not want a man still aching to slip a dagger in his back to be free to act whenever he chose to, and he wanted to end the matter quickly.

Ingold tapped the other guard on the shoulder and moved out into the crowds to follow the two new arrivals. Only one of his group had been a member of his party of assassins and was most likely the only one who had survived.

"Follow me," the prince said and gestured decisively. "I know this city well enough and we'll find a location in which to deal with them."

The warrior had questions, that much was obvious, but he gave them no voice and simply clicked his tongue for Horse to follow him. The other two beasts plodded behind them. Tryam didn't know what had happened to the animals while out on their own, but the two had come to follow Horse around like he was some kind of leader.

They veered away from the caravan, which made sense as their business was more or less concluded and they had other business to attend to.

It was a short walk to a small square, where folk were in the middle of conducting their business in stalls for the day. A small fountain had been built in the center, into which children tossed coppers, hoping for wishes. It was a simple structure with no ornamentation, and the prince sat on the edge and rested his sword across his lap.

Skharr immediately realized what was happening and stepped aside. The two men approached hurriedly from behind them and advanced on the boy, who sat calmly and comfortably with a small smile on his face.

"Hello again, Captain Ingold," Tryam said. He spoke loudly and instantly drew the attention of the crowd around them.

The captain paused and squinted at him, thinking there was some kind of trap, but he couldn't see anything that might suggest how it would play out.

"Prince Tryam," Ingold replied and folded his arms in front of his chest as a few hushed whispers rippled through the crowd when they learned the youth's identity. "You should not have returned to the city."

"If I had not, I would have been a coward." He looked at his sword and stroked the pommel. "Instead, it is you who remains the coward. You're alive only because you ran away while a dragon consumed your men. With thought only for yourself, you left them to die. I happen to know that cowardice is vehemently punished among the Emperor's Elites and the penalty is death. Will you accept your penance or will I have to enforce it myself?"

The captain looked at the silent crowd and laughed. "I always hated you—a sniveling, weak-spined excuse for royalty. If I let you return to the palace, you would not survive the day. I am doing you a favor, truly. A quick death is more than you deserve. Niemar, send word to the heir's counselor that Prince Tryam survived the dungeon but not the return journey."

"Sir." Niemar snapped a quick salute but hesitated until Ingold drew his sword before he turned to execute his orders.

Tryam smiled and remained seated as Skharr caught the young Elite by the collar and thunked his head into a nearby wall.

It was quickly and quietly done. The prince doubted that any of those present had seen it, as engrossed as they were with the drama unfolding between him and the captain.

"You call me a coward but you used my men as bait," Ingold replied, his sword still poised to attack. "You showed no hesitation in sneaking past the beast that killed them. Such a cowardly prince would not have entered a dungeon, much less completed it. It is my duty to keep a piece of gutter-swill shit from the throne."

"So much so that you would stab him in the back?" he asked as he stood but didn't ready his weapon yet. "No, wait. My memory failed me for a moment. You paid another to stab me in the back instead because you lacked the stomach to do the deed yourself. Enough hiding behind your cowardice, Ingold. Make your last action an honorable death."

The captain had waited for an opening and he lurched forward and arced his blade at the prince's head.

Steel scraped on leather and Tryam swung his weapon to block the attack before it could strike home.

Ingold's surprise was short-lived. He was an experienced warrior and he drew his blade back quickly and slashed at his adversary's gut.

It missed and the prince moved to the side with his blade in a firm low guard and a hint of a smile on his face as the crowd retreated to give the two combatants the space they required. A few of the locals rushed away to alert the guards, but it seemed unlikely that any would come.

The Elite leader had no doubt seen to it that they wouldn't.

He met another slash with a parry and continued to move in a slow circle around the man, although he took care to not give him an easy target like Skharr had taught him to do.

The captain advanced in a rush of cut-and-stab motions as he tried to overcome the prince with a rapid flurry of strikes. By the time he was forced back, a hint of surprise and frustration colored his features.

Tryam left him with a small gash in his arm as a parting gift.

As tempting as it was—especially knowing he could drive the man to greater anger if he wanted to—he resisted taunts and goads that sprang to mind. The captain's humiliation would not come in the form of verbal sparring.

"Fuck!" Ingold snapped and surged into a new onslaught with a wild stab at the boy's stomach. He drove forward and the prince sidestepped the strike and let the man's momentum carry him past.

The Elite slashed viciously in passing but the fountain was closer than he'd anticipated and instead of being able to twist to enter the fray again, he struggled to regain his balance before he tumbled into the water.

His breath rasped when the cold steel of Tryam's sword pressed against his neck and he turned slowly.

He waited for the killing stroke, his gaze watchful, and when it didn't come, he pushed the sword aside with his own and clambered out of the fountain.

The crowd was silent as all present watched while the prince toyed with the captain.

"I'm disappointed, Ingold," he whispered, almost sure that the man contemplated his odds of survival if he ran. "When I take the throne, I'll have to find better men to guard me."

That made the man snap and he screamed and rushed at the prince, who waited for him with the certainty that revealed how fully in control of the situation he was.

The young contender intercepted a wild slash, pushed his opponent's weapon aside, and closed the distance between them. He slid his blade in behind the captain's knee and jerked it up to almost sever the man's leg and force him off his feet. His adversary grunted as his back met the rough cobbles.

Tryam stabbed his weapon toward the Elite's chest but Ingold caught the blade with his hand.

The captain's gaze flickered to where Skharr stood over his unconscious man and he shook his head.

"No," he whispered.

"My days of giving two shits about what useless maggot-brained ass-licking lackeys like you think are over, Ingold," Tryam said. His voice was low and calm, meant for only the two of them to hear. "I will be emperor, and I will destroy those who try to use my people for their personal gain. You have my word on that. Unlike yours, it does mean something."

He drove the sword down and it passed through the man's fingers and into his chest. The captain had no chance to reply and simply gasped and looked down before his eyes lost focus and his body went limp.

The young prince was only vaguely aware that heavy footsteps approached as if from a great distance. Suddenly, one of the crowd shouted.

"Tryam! Prince Tryam!"

Others took up the call and soon, they all chanted his name.

"Prince Tryam! Prince Tryam!"

Skharr laughed and extended his hand to steady him.

"I think they like you, boy," he quipped as the prince cleaned his sword of the blood. "I'd like to think I had a part to play in that."

"More than a part," Tryam answered and patted the giant of a man on the shoulder. "Come. I think it's time I had a word with my brother."

CHAPTER TWENTY-SEVEN

All was not well in the world.

Reyvan looked out on the city below his window and scowled at the clamor he could hear. It sounded very much like chanting or people shouting something, and his men had been sent to find out what was happening.

Things had not devolved to the point of civil violence yet, it appeared. From what he had been told, the indications were that the citizens of the city were celebrating.

What had stirred them to jubilation appeared to be a matter of some mystery, but one of the rumors was more distressing than the others.

The viceroy narrowed his eyes as the Elites at his door stopped a man from entering. The weasel-like informer had a long nose—broken more than once—and greasy brown hair that clung to his head.

His clothes were common and his stench that of the city sewers, but the ruler gestured for the guards to allow him to approach. As he did so, the official placed a perfumed kerchief to his nose as a barrier against the smell.

The man dropped to a knee and lowered his head. "Apologies for my delay, Viceroy, but I return with news."

"Definitive?"

"De...what?"

Reyvan sighed. "What is your news?"

"I saw it with me own eyes, Viceroy. Prince Tryam has returned to the city. He was followed by Captain Ingold, who... Well, he picked a fight with the young'un."

"Am I to assume that the streets are rife with the celebrations of the death of the prince?"

"No. Oh no, milord. Quite the opposite. Tryam stuck the captain but good and left him to bleed out on the streets. Folk learned he'd come back. They's happy about it, I think."

"Are they, now?" he asked, retrieved a gold coin for the man, and tossed it on the floor. The weasel scooped his prize up, scrambled to his feet, and rushed to the door.

Reyvan's reputation certainly appeared to precede him.

"What are your thoughts, Viceroy?" a man behind him asked, and he turned to the commander of the Emperor's Elites.

"I think it is time for the emperor to meet a very tragic end," he whispered. "The man is known to have a weak heart in his old age. It would be most unfortunate for it to give out while he was rutting some young woman or another, wouldn't you agree? We will need Cathos to be crowned emperor quickly to put all questions of succession—and thoughts of civil strife—to rest immediately."

Espin bowed his head. "Long live the emperor."

The viceroy nodded and flicked his wrist, and the lord commander strode out of the room to fulfill his commands.

More worrying than word of the prince returning was who he had returned with. The talk of a giant of a man—a barbarian dark of hair and light of eyes—reminded him of one such warrior from his long distant past.

It seemed almost like another life, one he'd lived before he fought for the empire or served the emperor.

Reyvan shook his head to dislodge the unsettling memories, took a deep breath, and stood briskly to address his guards.

"Bring the crown prince to the throne room. It is time for him to fulfill his destiny."

"Yes, Viceroy."

It had seemed like an exceptionally good idea to use the crowds for his benefit. There were still those who wanted him dead and in the end, it would be better to use the shield provided by the popularity of a prince just returned from his successfully completed quest.

The people would keep him safe and hopefully, no more attempts on his life would be made.

Unfortunately, it meant that word would spread quickly, and he had not moved more than a hundred paces from where he had left Ingold's body before folk began to hang out their windows.

Soon, they wanted more and surged out onto the streets to form up around him while they shouted, chanted, and celebrated.

A few children approached him and thrust flowers in his hands.

"Is this what it means to be emperor?" Tryam asked Skharr a little dubiously. If the truth be told, he felt rather overwhelmed but hid it well.

The barbarian had insisted that he mount his horse to put a little distance between him and any who might use the crowd to enable them to creep close enough to stab him in the back.

"That depends entirely on the kind of emperor you are," Skharr replied. "But yes. They'll throw flowers at your feet and cheer as you walk past, and mutter curses and drink to your demise when you're not among them."

That was something he would have to get used to, the contender acknowledged ruefully, and it was also something to consider as they approached the imperial palace.

A group of guards was already positioned in front of the gates to block the entrance and form a line to contain the people who pushed forward.

A handful had already begun to yell at the guards to move out of the way, but Tryam raised his hand to stop them as he rode forward with Skharr beside him.

"Move out of the way," the barbarian warned, "or I'll move you."

The defenders began to ready their spears, but the prince dismounted hastily and stepped in front of his companion before any violence could ensue between him and the men. He had a feeling the warrior could easily force a path through the guards, and the crowd would join him as they would not want to simply stand by.

It would turn into a battle—or, more likely, a massacre—and he could not allow that to happen.

"Stop!" he snapped and nodded when Skharr immediately relaxed and glanced at him to see what he had in mind.

The people fell silent but the guards remained tense as if they expected a fight. All of them stood with their weapons poised to attack while he approached, but he deliberately left his sword sheathed.

"I am Prince Tryam Voldana," he announced in a voice that carried well through the courtyard where they were all gathered. "And I have come to claim what I have earned. I have completed the Test of O'Kruleth Demari and have earned the right to be named heir to the emperor."

The guards exchanged a few uncertain glances before their captain stepped forward.

"I cannot allow all present to advance into the palace," the man announced and gestured to his men to lower their guard.

The command was only obeyed by a few of them.

"I will stand before my father." Tryam took another step forward until he was less than a full pace away from the captain. "Skharr DeathEater will be my escort."

The guards exchanged a look and had already begun to shift to the side before their captain motioned for them to do so. He guessed that none of them wanted to fight Skharr either.

The prince couldn't shake the feeling that someone would stab him in the back as he walked through the group, but nothing of the kind happened and they entered the palace with a small group of guards to escort them as they approached the throne room. Once again, a tingle prickled the back of his neck and he expected someone to try to slip a dagger in.

Thankfully, none came, not even when the doors were pulled open and he moved into the room.

Tryam had expected it to be empty, but his assumption was wrong. Someone was seated on the comfortable throne and wore the uncomfortable crown, but it was not his father. A familiar face—one that looked a great deal like his own—stared at him from the pinnacle, while a group of armed Elites waited at the base, as ready for a fight as those standing guard outside.

"Welcome back, Tryam," Cathos called from the royal seat. "I am pleased that you survived your time in the dungeon. Assuming, of course, that you entered it at all. I am glad to have such a brother to stand at my side."

The prince focused on his half-brother, narrowed his eyes, and drew a deep breath. Violence was not always the solution, but the assumption of events was difficult to ignore.

"Where is the emperor?" he asked, looking around the throne room.

"Your emperor is before you," said a deep, booming voice near the throne, and Tryam realized he'd overlooked the viceroy standing there. "Unfortunately, while you were away, your father fell ill and did not recover. Your brother was crowned emperor in his stead. Long live the emperor."

"Long live the emperor!" the guards around him roared as one.

The prince looked around the room and his gaze settled on Skharr beside him. He liked to think he knew the barbarian well enough to know when something bothered the man.

And there was no doubt that his companion was agitated. His green eyes were focused on the viceroy and something akin to horror and pure rage flicked across his face.

Tryam wanted to ask what had Skharr so fixated, but now was not the time.

"I have completed the Test of O'Kruleth Demari." He pulled his shirt off to show all present where the hand marks had been at the beginning of his quest. "Unlike some, I have earned my place as heir to the empire. Failing that, I have earned the right to contest my brother's crowning."

"I am more than willing to prove my right to the throne," Cathos retorted and stood slowly. "I would choose a second to prove my rightful place."

One of the Elites stepped forward with his hand on his sword.

"No," Tryam whispered and shook his head. "If I am to prove my right to the throne with my hands, Cathos must abide by the same rule."

The would-be emperor looked at the viceroy, who smirked and shrugged.

"Does his majesty think to allow his brother to contest the throne against any hands but his own?" Reyvan asked and folded his arms in front of his chest.

The rest of the guards looked at Cathos. They would fight if ordered, but he had to know that the men who would die for him expected the same from the man they were fighting for. If he was unwilling to fight for his throne, it would be a severe blow to the image he needed to maintain.

"In either case," Tryam noted as he pulled his shirt on. "I would have Skharr DeathEater as my second in this fight."

The viceroy appeared to not notice the warrior's presence until it was pointed out, and his eyes widened and his mouth gaped slightly before he composed himself.

"Skharr," the man whispered and took a step forward. "It is… good to see you again."

"I doubt that," the barbarian snapped in response. "Otherwise, you would not have poisoned your brothers and sisters in arms or opened the gates for our enemies to slaughter all those who stood inside the walls of Vernosh, looking for safety."

"It was for the greater good," Reyvan replied softly. "I do have to admit that the years have been kinder on you than they have me. I knew there had to be some magic in your blood to let you live longer than life usually grants humans. Once you are dead, I will finally have the opportunity to study it more closely."

"Kind?" Skharr hissed in barely suppressed fury. "I'll show you how kind the years have been to me!"

He took a step forward, and two of the guards moved to intercept him. One already had his sword out, ready to fight, before the prince intervened.

"Skharr!"

Tryam barely registered that he'd drawn his sword from its scabbard before he surged forward to intercept the two. He darted behind Skharr and drove between the giant and his attackers.

It was a light, deft move to deflect both their attacks and push them to the side.

"Kill them!" the viceroy shouted to the guards. "Kill them both!"

"Don't think that will stop me, sorcerer!" the warrior roared and drew his sword with a whisper of steel.

"Sorcerer?" Cathos asked, more than a little confused that the fighting appeared to have started without him.

CHAPTER TWENTY-EIGHT

He had not imagined that it would happen this way, although he had realized there would be some resistance from those who wanted to keep him from the throne.

Skharr's past acquaintance with the viceroy was an unexpected development, however. Tryam had never seen the man like that before. In fairness, they had not known each other long, but seeing the rage sweep over the barbarian was a terrifying sight.

Now, however, he had his own fight to consider.

The two guards had no qualms about attacking their prince who might also become their emperor. Once they turned aside from their attacks on Skharr, they were all too happy to focus their efforts on the contender.

Tryam studied their attack, used his wrists in quick movements to deflect their blows, and pushed them away when they intended to strike at his neck, his head, or his chest.

He took a hasty step back to avoid disembowelment and immediately reversed his attack.

A couple of guards pulled away and moved to engage the

barbarian before he could cover the distance between him and the viceroy.

They were fine fighters and indeed some of the best, but they were unprepared for the kind of battle they faced and the first man was felled with a single stroke. The blow sliced the man from the shoulder almost to the hip and carved through the armor he wore with ease.

Skharr fell back to evade a blade that swept perilously close to his neck. He yanked his sword out of the dead man, slashed the second guard's arm, and severed his hand at the wrist.

The Elite screamed and clutched his bleeding stump before his attacker swung the silver pommel of his sword to crush his skull.

His screaming stopped, and the Elite slumped to the floor.

"It's for the best, I suppose," Reyvan mumbled as he unclipped the rich red cloak from his shoulders and let it fall. "For so many years, I've worked from the shadows and let others do my work, but there is an oddly perverse pleasure that comes from doing it myself. I have missed it."

Skharr's sneer was chilling as he flicked his sword to clean the blood from it and homed in on the viceroy.

Reyvan was in his later years but he nevertheless conveyed the appearance of a warrior as he muttered something in a foreign language. The ruby on his ring, worn on the middle finger of his right hand, suddenly began to glow and he pointed it at his enemy.

Tryam jumped back, distracted by what was happening to his friend. The blast of fire from the ring succeeded in drawing the attention of the two guards as well.

He realized that the other Elites had moved away from the throne and seemed content to allow things to happen without their interference.

The flash faded abruptly, and the young prince was surprised that Skharr remained in the same position with his sword held in front of him like a shield.

The barbarian chuckled and glanced at the weapon. "These enchanted weapons are indeed useful, wouldn't you say?" It amused him to let the man think the blade was responsible rather than the amulet he had strung around his neck. "Although I think you're far weaker than I remember. I suppose poisoning your brothers and sisters in arms would take something out of a man. What did they pay you to betray us, Reyvan? Thirty pieces of gold? Some magical bauble?"

"Peace," the viceroy snapped. "A witless toad like you would not understand that, but peace was all they had to offer me. There were other benefits, as you can see, but in the end, I did what I did to stop the fighting."

"And all you had to do was sacrifice a city." He hissed in open disgust and shook his head.

"I saved lives!"

Skharr laughed. "I wonder how many I'll save by taking yours."

Another blast from the ring was deflected as easily as the first, and the viceroy scowled at the ring and muttered a curse as Skharr continued his relentless advance.

The official began to retreat and waved his hands in a commanding gesture at the ceiling.

Once again, light erupted from the ring and this time, it arced upward and streaked into the support structure. The resulting crack was thunderous and pieces began to plummet toward the barbarian.

"Damn it!" Tryam raced to assist his companion. The two guards who had attacked him were distracted enough that they made no attempt to stop him as he rushed away.

The warrior was not standing still, by any means, but he was distracted by the marble debris that continued to fall. His enemy took advantage of his lack of focus and launched repeated attacks at the man in the hopes that he could catch him off guard.

While the giant managed to evade most of them, one struck powerfully as he spun to avoid a large, rough-edged projectile and two other magical blasts.

Skharr gasped in pain as the force hurled him to the marble floor and as he slid across it, Tryam realized that his armor had been scorched at the point of impact to leave an angry red burn on his skin.

The same rage the young prince had felt before suddenly bubbled to the surface and he gritted his teeth. Heat rose within him like the breath of a dragon as he charged the sorcerer.

The warrior was injured but not incapacitated and pushed to his feet, his sword still in hand. Tryam now attacked the viceroy, which left his companion to deal with the two Elites who were ready to kill their prince.

Even wounded, the hulking mass of barbarian was difficult to stop, and both men were bowled over when he simply barreled into them. The force of impact thrust the breath out of them as he rolled onto his feet.

He was able to kill one of the guards quickly, but the other was already standing and now turned his attention to the prince.

The young contender scowled as the viceroy pushed him back. Whatever was in Skharr's sword was absent in his and the heat from each blast was frightening. The older man took another step forward, his courage almost fully returned.

"Foolish child!" Reyvan spat on the floor and turned to the side. This time, an unseen force struck the prince in the stomach, forced the air from his lungs, and powered him onto the floor.

Tryam had rushed into a fight with a sorcerer. It had not been his most intelligent decision, but he pushed to his feet and sucked deep breaths in as the viceroy drew a dagger from inside his sleeve.

"You had the chance to stand alongside your brother and

perhaps take his place one day." The man punctuated every word with a blast of power to force the prince back step by step. "But you chose to fight instead. We'll simply have to find another to replace you."

He gasped when the wall pressed into his back, and the sorcerer grasped his neck.

"Tryam, no!"

His companion's booming voice was enough to distract the viceroy for a moment. The prince took a step forward and swung his sword expertly to slice the man's hand off.

Reyvan screamed as he staggered back but he looked at his other hand, which still held the dagger. He was too close and moved too quickly for his target to stop, block, or even evade.

The contender felt the point of the dagger dig into his side, but only the point. A massive hand had intercepted the weapon and stopped it from driving home.

"Now, you rabid soul-sucking magical fucking ass-crawler, let me show you the same kindness you showed me." Skharr growled and twisted the viceroy's arm savagely until it snapped. The man screamed but the sound cut off abruptly when he drove his sword deep into his back.

Tryam took a step around the barbarian and focused on the guard who continued to approach behind the giant. He raised his sword to deflect the blow that was aimed at the warrior's back and continued his motion in a practiced arc.

The guard stopped, fell back a few steps, and clutched his throat as blood began to pour from the wound. It streamed over his chest and even pushed through his mouth and nose before the Elite dropped to his knees and his eyes closed quickly.

Skharr looked at the prince, who shrugged and cleaned the blood from his sword.

It seemed unfair that the warrior's weapon appeared to clean itself, but that was not a matter for the moment. He wondered if there was a trick to it he might learn.

"That was well done," the man noted and kept his weapon drawn as he looked at the other guards.

"Well, I am a quick study," Tryam replied and frowned at a diamond-shaped wound in his hip. "I would have improved faster had I a better teacher, however."

His companion opened his mouth to protest but shrugged and conceded that he had a point.

The prince turned his attention to the throne, where his brother still stood and seemed uncertain as to what to do next. He had stopped his descent halfway and now hesitated as Tryam advanced up the steps toward him.

Cathos stared at his sword as he came closer, gritted his teeth, and tried to summon his courage as he tripped and fell to land heavily and scramble back a few steps closer to the throne.

"I won't kill you, brother," the contender said softly and sheathed his weapon. "You are not a bad man. I suppose you never were but you are not the right man to lead this land. Step down and become someone worthy of respect and trust—not for who your father was but for who you are. He"—the boy pointed at the dead viceroy—"most likely killed our father and would have ruled with you as his puppet."

He offered his hand in silence, and after a brief moment of consideration, the other young man took it and stood slowly. He moved down the steps to where Skharr remained beside Reyvan's corpse.

Cathos studied it for a moment before he spat on it with surprising vehemence.

"Fool that I was," he whispered and shook his head. "I'll not be a fool twice."

His brother nodded and turned his focus to the throne above him. It felt unreal to be this close to it. He drew a deep breath, climbed the last few steps, and stood in front of the ornate seat.

A second of hesitation was all he could spare before he turned with a resolute expression, settled on the throne, and finally looked at the room below.

"Allow me, brother," Cathos said as he hurried up the steps. He removed the crown from his head and gently, with reverence and a pause or two to determine how it would work, settled it on Tryam's head.

"Long live the emperor," he said.

"Long live the emperor!" the guards roared in echo.

Skharr smirked and shook his head as dozens of servants streamed in. They had watched and waited for the violence to end and quickly went about the work of cleaning the room and removing the mess that had resulted from the combat.

Others entered to take up the call and cheer and celebrate a relatively peaceful succession.

He turned his attention to the dead sorcerer and drew the dagger the elf had given him before he entered the tower.

"I told you," he stated coldly as he dropped to his haunches and rolled the sorcerer's left sleeve up to his elbow to expose a tattoo of a rearing horse that was still present on his skin. "Only those who were worthy would be allowed an honorable burial. They trusted you, and I swore on their graves that they would see vengeance."

He slipped the knife under Reyvan's skin. It cut surprisingly well, and it was quick work to remove the tattoo. Once the skin was free, he hurled it as far as he could.

"My promise is kept." He patted the dead man on the cheek. "Enjoy your torment in the afterlife. None has earned it more than you."

CHAPTER TWENTY-NINE

Feasts were uncomfortable affairs, although most folk seemed to enjoy them. The Imperial City was celebrating the ascension of a new emperor. All the different houses and notables had come together to pledge their allegiance to Tryam, and it was only right that they were allowed to celebrate too.

As more people and groups entered, it became apparent that the feasting would last for a few days at least. Ambassadors from the various kingdoms and states inside and outside the empire had arrived to acknowledge the new emperor.

All those who would not have looked at the boy twice were there to declare that they were in full support of his rule over them. A couple of them spoke of prophecies from their mages and prophets that announced his ascendance. One even mentioned a dragon's fire, and Skharr assumed that he, at least, was not lying about it.

But in the end, as the third day of revelry came to a close, the barbarian exited the palace with no small relief. He had become something of a known figure in the city, as Tryam had asked him to stand at his side during the formalities that were required for an official transfer of power. Now, however, the new emperor had a full contingent of Elite guards ready to die for him if it was needed.

It would soon be time for the barbarian to move along again. Others in the world were looking for him as well.

"It is odd to find you here."

Skharr had heard footsteps ascending to the rampart he had climbed to, but he'd assumed it was another guard making his or her rounds.

Instead, a man in full plate armor with his helm tucked under his arm stepped into view.

"I needed fresh air," he replied and stared at the night view over the city. It was beautiful with a clear sky and a full moon, and thousands of stars reflected on the three rivers that wound through the city.

He decided he could probably traverse the landscape as though it were in the middle of the day.

"Too many sycophants pawing over the emperor," the man agreed, stopped beside him, and placed his helm on one of the parapets. "You'd think they knew all along that he would be emperor and had cheered him on from the beginning."

Skharr shrugged. "Maybe they did. He was popular in the arena, I'm told. Who…are you?"

"My name is Elric. Emperor Tryam named me Lord Commander of his Elites. I was in the throne room during the… test of succession, and he said he will learn to trust me and the rest of his guard."

"You'll have to forgive him for not trusting you immediately. His previous experience with the Elites was when they paid a man to stab him in the back."

Elric laughed and nodded. "I cannot fault the man for wanting to keep you around him as a last line of defense. Of course, that was under the previous Lord Commander Espin."

"What happened to him?"

"He was found in his quarters, hanging from a crossbeam. The assumption is that he killed himself, of course, but given that Viceroy Reyvan was pulling his strings... Well, anything is possible."

The barbarian smirked and returned his gaze to the moonlit city.

"It is not often that one sees a DeathEater so far from home," the other man commented as the silence hung between them.

With a small smile, the warrior answered. "It is not often that we need to travel so far into civilization. You'll find my kin where the wars are waged and in the past few decades, that has been many, many miles from this city."

"And yet, even here, I have heard rumors of a DeathEater who carved through many lands far from this place. The rumors are... conflicted, as they always tend to be. They said this DeathEater was a warrior, a brigand, an assassin, a thief, and a prince, all rolled into one."

"That sleeping mat is well-stuffed."

"Indeed it is." Elric chuckled again, although it was a nervous sound.

"Perhaps all the conflicting rumors are true. Perhaps some or all those titles might apply to this rumored DeathEater. We are well-traveled, after all."

The Elite commander nodded. "The strangest story I heard is perhaps the most menial and yet speaks more to the man than the myth. As legend would have it, this DeathEater, a veteran of a thousand battles, spoke to his horse as if it was intelligent enough to understand it and he never rode the beast."

"Do you not consider horses to be intelligent creatures?"

"Not particularly. And yet I have asked and it has come to my attention that you have a horse and yet you go everywhere on foot. The kitchen staff have even told me that you ask them for apples to take to him in his stall in the stables."

"It is considered the mark of an intelligent man, among

DeathEaters," Skharr replied, took a deep breath, and exhaled in a soft sigh, "to have a horse and never ride him."

"Who can tell?" the lord commander asked and fidgeted with the sword at his hip. "I've never met a real DeathEater before. Bringing myth and reality together is often a troublesome affair."

"Do I live up to the legends?"

Elric tilted his head to look speculatively at him. "You did kill a sorcerer, after all. I believe that does set a high standard on its own. How did you find a sword that would stop a magic-user's blast?"

That brought a laugh from the barbarian as he shook his head. "I thought it was a neat trick. My sword is about as magical as my boots and I simply let Reyvan and everyone else think otherwise. It was a charm or snippet of spellcraft I had worn around my neck in case I needed it later in the fight and I was disarmed for some reason." He slid his hand into his shirt and pulled a magical amulet out from beneath the cloth. "A mage friend of mine sold me this. It is said to dampen the magical abilities of those who come within its sphere of influence."

"A crafty warrior is one who lives the longest, I am told. Even so, it's an impressive feat to kill a sorcerer, no matter how."

"The fucking rabid demon-birthed whelp received the justice he deserved. Of course, I would have liked to prolong it a little—perhaps shove a nest of hungry roaches up his ass and let them devour him slowly." He sighed. "Sadly, emperors take precedence and I had to be satisfied with consigning him to whatever hell hairy-assed Janus might decide was appropriate."

Elric turned to look at him again with genuine curiosity. "And what have you decided? What will you do now that you've added kingmaker to your list of accolades?"

Skharr nodded when he realized why the man was present. Tryam had sent him to gauge how long they could rely on the barbarian's services.

"I'll leave," he answered honestly. "Horse has a home I expect he wishes to return to. He's getting old."

"What is his name?"

"Horse."

"You named your horse…Horse."

"Aye." He gestured impatiently to move them on from that particular discussion. "You would not happen to know of a leatherworker in this city who would be able to take this"—he took another amulet out from under his shirt—"and fashion it in such a way that it rested on Horse's chest protected, unseen, and unable to fall off no matter how hard he runs?"

Elric leaned closer to inspect the item. "It is magical, I assume?"

"Will you ever speak of this discussion?"

"Not a word—at least nothing that is not already known to others. You have my assurance on my honor."

Skharr had a question or two about how much that honor was worth, but he decided not to bring that into question now. "Perhaps my brother Horse might yet join me in a few more adventures before we retire."

"Would you retire, DeathEater?" Elric asked and narrowed his eyes as he leaned on the battlement to stare at the same stars the warrior was watching. "I don't think I've ever heard of a hero in a ballad retiring. They always find a tragic last stand in which to make their death as honorable as possible."

He sniffed. "Honorable my stinking ass. It seems the kind of perverted turd-coated end to a good life that mush-brained god Janus might scratch out of his slimy ballsack and wave around for simpletons to see as a prize. But a barbarian who doesn't quit fighting may have a chance at that."

"I know it's new and you'll simply have to get used to it."

Horse snorted and shook his head as Skharr held the new bridle up for him.

"It's perfectly comfortable." He was interrupted by another whinny. "No, I have not worn it myself but it was made by the best leatherworker in this godsbedammed city."

The stallion took a step back, although he had little room to fully escape.

"Fine, if you want me to wear it, I will." Skharr hung the bridle over his head and shoulders and glowered at the horse, who whinnied again. "I know it doesn't fit, you dumb shit. It was made for you. Now bring your lazy ass here so I can put it on you."

The beast finally acquiesced, walked closer to him, and let him slide it over his head. It was a little more involved than the last one, but Horse ceased his complaining when it was pulled on.

"See? And you were worried that it would be stiff and unyielding. Do you think I would fit you with something you didn't like?"

Although the stallion tossed his mane, he voiced no further complaints.

"And if it works for you like it did for me then we, my brother, will be together until you finally tire of me."

A damp nose nudged him in the chest.

"Fine, or when a fine mare turns your head."

Horse snorted loudly and Skharr smirked.

"Yes, I thought you'd like that one. Now come along. We have places to be. I grow tired of this fucking blood-bought capital."

The beast could only agree and the warrior strode out of the stable and let Horse follow him through the doors and into the courtyard.

A few of the hands were working there, although they were quickly interrupted by the sounds of booted feet on the cobbles.

Skharr paused as he watched the prince—the emperor now—approach him, followed by a small troop of armed and armored guards.

"Did you think you could leave without proper farewells, barbarian?" Tryam asked and folded his arms in front of his chest.

"I hoped. In truth, I have never been one for formalities."

"Well, formalities or no, I owe you a great deal. Not least of which is my life, but I can fulfill the contract I made with you."

He nodded to one of the guards who carried a small chest filled with coins that was quickly attached to Horse's saddlebags.

"It is a little more than what was written in the contract, of course, but given the time you spent guarding me, additional danger payment, and because I know I couldn't talk you into remaining, I thought I'd like to extend my gratitude in common currency. I do hope that with enough gold, you will at least listen to my requests in the future."

Skharr peeked inside the chest and raised an eyebrow before he closed it again. "I think you bought my attention, Prince…er, Emperor Tryam."

"I'm not the emperor yet. I have yet to face the official coronation. You couldn't remain for that?"

"Did the coronation not already happen?"

"Not the official one. You know us civilized folk like our… formalities. Could I not convince you to stay?"

The barbarian shook his head. "I've spent a little too long in the light. Your country needs to move forward with you at the helm and without any distractions."

"You think you'd be distracting?"

"A giant bastard standing next to the emperor and making him look tiny by comparison would be a distraction, yes."

Tryam laughed and shook his head. "Well, you're not wrong. And it is a very wise observation from someone most would deem uncivilized."

"Yes, well…" He chuckled. "Should you need me, put the word out into the wind or perhaps among the priests of Theros. I have a feeling it will find me."

"The priests of Theros?"

"A messenger would suit you equally as well."

The young man took a step forward and extended his hand. He took it and grasped Tryam firmly by the forearm.

"I look forward to that day, you big bastard."

Skharr winked and grinned before he clicked his tongue, turned away from the young emperor and his entourage, and broke into a light run while Horse trotted beside him.

Thank you for not only reading this story, but coming back here and reading our author notes, too!

Fan Moment of the week: A fan reached out to commiserate with me that an 8" statue of Red Sonja is about the legal height before one might suffer one's spouse annoyance. I have to agree. Neither of us are willing to test that theory, yet. Although I do have a signed Boris print in my office.

So, I wanted to push Skharr away from the city and take him out and about. Not focusing on his existing relationships in book 03. Plus, I needed to get him ready for GodKiller in book 04.

Skharr's back-history is a bit of an enigma, even for me. All I knew when creating the character is he has a pretty amazing story back there, but he wasn't terribly proud of a lot of it. So, he chose to start fresh with his life.

On a farm.

We have learned that didn't get him too far when a God sought him out. And for the record, Theros DID know what he was doing when he was traveling to Skharr's little ranch. He gave the bandits in the woods a fair chance to do the right thing before he killed them.

Theros didn't think they would do the right thing, *but he tried.*

So, we are about to go into editing on Skharr's latest adventure and I just have to say you MUST read it. I promise you will at least chuckle a few times, if not outright laugh about the dragon talk in THAT story.

I'll leave you with that idea. Just…read it. It is every bit as humorous as I had hoped when writing up the beats ;-)

Ad Aeternitatem,

Michael Anderle

P.S. *High Lord God Janus is an Ass.*

CONNECT WITH THE AUTHOR

Connect with Michael Anderle

Website: http://lmbpn.com

Email List: http://lmbpn.com/email/

Social Media:

https://www.facebook.com/LMBPNPublishing

https://twitter.com/MichaelAnderle

https://www.instagram.com/lmbpn_publishing/

https://www.bookbub.com/authors/michael-anderle

BOOKS BY MICHAEL ANDERLE

Sign up for the LMBPN email list to be notified of new releases and special deals!

https://lmbpn.com/email/

For a complete list of books by Michael Anderle, please visit:

www.lmbpn.com/ma-books/

Made in United States
North Haven, CT
31 May 2022

19690703R00159